BETTER TO SEE YOU

ARROW TACTICAL SECURITY

ISABEL JOLIE

Editor: Lori Whitwam

Proofreading: Jessica Meigs

Cover Design: Damonza

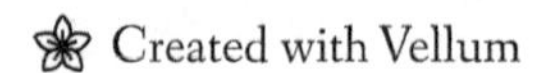

BETTER TO SEE YOU

"There are various kinds of wolves...those who are charming, quiet, polite, unassuming, complacent, and sweet, who pursue young women at home and in the streets. And unfortunately, it is these gentle wolves who are the most dangerous ones of all."

—Charles Perrault, *Little Red Riding Hood*

CHAPTER 1

Ryan

The black ball comes out of nowhere, a blur in my peripheral vision. In one fluid, subconscious motion, my hand rises, and it smacks my palm. Beyond my monitor, Trevor grins.

"Solid reaction time." Trevor, my business partner, former SEAL team member, and closest friend, plops down in my office chair.

"Can you cover an interview for me this morning?"

"What time?"

"Nine thirty. Rusty Callaway. Stella has his file. If I can meet with him once my meeting wraps, I will."

Stella is Arrow's HR director, and Trevor's soon-to-be wife. They aren't yet engaged, but I've never seen Trevor so serious about a woman. Mentally, he's committed for life. They say when a man loves a woman, he'll do anything for her. Well, Trevor killed to protect her. In my book, that's as committed as it gets.

On my monitor, a small window in the upper right corner

shows a view of the entrance to Arrow's reception area. A couple enters and approaches the desk.

"Who's that?" Trevor asks.

"My nine o'clock. Jack Sullivan. An old Naval Academy classmate. Flew up from San Diego."

"Who's the woman?"

The dark-haired woman standing beside him is tall, nearly as tall as Jack, and he's a little over six feet. Her long hair falls midway down her back. There's a briefcase hanging off her shoulder, and the strap sinks into her shoulder pad, something that is noticeable from the bird's-eye of view of our security camera.

"I assume his wife. He invited me to his wedding ages ago, but I couldn't get leave. Never met her." She's wearing a shapeless black pants suit. "Could also be his colleague."

"What's the meeting about?"

"He needs our services." I tap my fingers as Tabitha Patel, our receptionist and highly skilled gatekeeper, verifies their licenses. "Needed to meet as soon as possible."

In my office closet, I store extra suits, ties, and workout clothes. I thumb through my options and select a navy suit coat. Jack's wearing a tie, but I don't bother with one.

Trevor studies the screen. "What's he do?"

"He's CEO for Sullivan Arms, the gun manufacturer."

"I own one of their handguns. What's he need?"

"Didn't say. Said Arrow Security came highly recommended. Checked out our site and recognized me. Said he needs complete discretion."

"Rich guy. Guns. Interesting. If he didn't have his wife with him, I'd bet on a ransom hanging over his head Ashley Madison style." Ashley Madison is a site that married individuals seeking a discreet relationship use. We had a high-profile client a couple of years ago reach out to us to identify someone hacking the system and threatening select wealthy users.

"That's not Sullivan's style. He's good people." Trevor questions my judgment with one lift of his eyebrow and a cocky smirk.

Rumors swirled around Jack Sullivan back in the day. Because of his wealth, cadets observed his every move. He qualified as a celebrity in our ranks. But I never saw any sign he let it go to his head. If anything, he worked harder than the rest of us.

Everyone believed once he finished his time with the Navy, he'd leave the military to run his family's company. One quick internet search after his call showed me he'd done just that. According to the latest *Forbes* list, his net worth looms near the billion threshold.

The woman glances up and looks directly into the camera. Dark eyebrows arch over observant eyes.

"His wife's hot." While I agree with Trevor's assessment, I am much more intrigued by the reason for an urgent visit.

"You want to stay for the meeting? Until nine thirty?"

"Nah. I'll head down and get Callaway's file from Stella. Shout if you need me." Trevor pauses and taps the doorframe. "Maybe he just needs a security detail?"

"We shall see." There's no point in guessing. He's in the elevator.

Arrow Security conducts most of our work off-site, and, as such, most of our office cubicles remain empty. We offer both physical and IT security services, surveillance, protection detail, and we work with government entities on international projects. Unbeknownst to the public, the National Security Agency, or NSA, the Central Intelligence Agency, or CIA, and the Federal Bureau of Investigation, or FBI, are all clients.

Typically, Arrow handles projects when the government wants to be able to deny culpability should something go wrong.

And we handle private citizens' requests when standard law enforcement doesn't offer a solution.

On my way to the elevator bank, I nod at a few individuals in the cubicles along the way. They wear headsets for the job or to listen to music. The employees in the open cubicles typically work on surveillance, watching videos or monitoring reams of electronic communications. Sometimes we have coders in-house, but it's rare. We have two partners who manage tech security, and they both reside farther north in Napa.

The elevator dings, and the doors open.

Jack Sullivan flaunts his wealth, from the well-fitted three-piece custom suit to his shiny dress shoes to the gleaming gold Rolex on his wrist. The dark-haired stunner at his side is a natural beauty, but her inexpensive interview suit doesn't match his aesthetic.

Since opening Arrow, I've interviewed hundreds of candidates, most of whom don't wear suits daily and own one suit for interviews and funerals. The sleeves on her ill-fitting jacket hang loosely. Her pants ride too high above her ankle. Scuff marks mar the tips of her sensible, low, black heels. The thin gold choker around her neck contrasts with a larger chunky sea-glass necklace. Brown eyeshadow and dark eyeliner accentuate large, dark eyes that dart past me, taking in the room, possibly scanning for entrances and exits. In person, her hair is closer to dark chocolate than black, with long bangs that frame smooth skin and an angular jaw. Her pale pink lips are bare, her nails short and trimmed.

The last time I saw Jack, he'd told me he'd found the one. That was over fifteen years ago. The woman at his side might be in her late twenties, but she could also be in her early twenties. There's no way she's his wife. Would Jack hire a young lawyer?

As I approach, Jack faces me head on, shoulders back, with no trace of a smile. The woman at his side angles her body toward

Jack and clasps her hands nervously in front of her. I extend my hand to my old friend.

"Jack Sullivan. It's been a long time."

"Ryan Wolfgang." He grips my hand in a firm handshake. "Do you still go by Wolf?"

I force a cordial, professional smile. Wolf is the name I went by at the Naval Academy, and it stuck throughout my military career. With a foo-foo last name like Wolfgang, I gladly embraced the shortened moniker my friends gave me. But, in the business world, I prefer Ryan. Within Arrow, my closest friends still call me Wolf.

"Sometimes." I let his hand go. "You can call me Ryan. Or Wolf if you prefer." I turn to the woman at his side and offer her my hand. "And you are?"

"This is Dr. Rolfe," Jack answers for her. Her handshake is unexpectedly firm, and she maintains eye contact.

"You can call me Alex." Her hand remains in mine a beat too long as my gaze begins to drift over a borderline too-skinny figure swallowed by ill-fitting clothes. She swallows nervously. I release her hand and redirect.

"Shall we meet in the conference room?"

Jack and Dr. Rolfe pause at the end of the hallway, taking in the cavern of desks and monitors. Offices line the perimeter of the open cubicle area. Open doors offer views of office desks and windows with bright blue Santa Barbara sky. The far glass wall opens into a conference room with a long table and a window with a view over buildings. Off to the horizon, between buildings, glimpses of the Pacific Ocean hint at the proximity of the beach.

"Just this way," I direct. "Can I get you any coffee or something to drink?" They both decline, and I close the door. "Tell me, how can I help you?"

Dr. Rolfe pulls out a notebook and a pen. She rolls her chair and situates it a foot away from Jack's chair, angled so she can observe us both. Chew marks mar the end of her plastic pen. Her long, thin fingers are bare. *Definitely not the wife.*

Sullivan smooths his tie and leans forward, resting both forearms on the table. Under the fluorescent lighting and in this proximity, deep wrinkles around the corner of his eyes show, as does a hint of red around the whites.

"Can anyone hear us?" he asks me.

"No. This room is soundproof." Dr. Rolfe scans the corners of the room. There are visible camera lenses in the corners beneath black glass globes. "No cameras are running. Nothing is being recorded."

Jack gazes down at his clasped hands. He raises his gaze, and I am met with a mask of professionalism.

"My daughter, Sophia, is missing. She's only fifteen. Will you help me find her?"

"Have you been to the police?"

"Last night. The officer on duty said most missing persons are found within twenty-four hours. They suspect it's a misunderstanding or a runaway case." Jack's pasty skin, tired eyes, and the fact he flew to me say he's not placing any weight on a simple misunderstanding.

"How long has she been missing?"

"Since yesterday evening."

"Do you think she ran away?"

"Maybe." His shoulders hunch inward. The youthful pride I remember is absent. Sadness and desperation are taking root. "When I asked around, Arrow Security came up multiple times."

"That's good to hear. But missing persons isn't our specialty." Alex's pen pauses against the paper.

"But kidnapping and ransom are." Jack stares me down. Direct, open, forthright. Qualities I remember from our Naval

Academy days. Back then, he seemed older than his age. And that holds true today.

"You think she's been kidnapped?"

"I honestly don't know." He shakes his head. "She could have run away. But I still need to find her. And I need discretion. I only want to work with people I trust."

"Has anyone contacted you?" Jack Sullivan is a wealthy man. It's reasonable he would suspect a kidnapping.

"No. Nothing." He drops his head. "But she's been gone less than twenty-four hours." His chest lifts and his gaze zeroes in on the far right corner of the room. "Look. The police may be correct. She may be off with friends. I am strict. Maybe she tired of it. This could be rebellion. And if that's the case, I don't want this played out in the media. I want to find her and bring her home. But if it's kidnapping, and they want a ransom, I want you locked and loaded, ready to go."

Dr. Rolfe's pen flies over the notebook as he speaks. *Why is this woman here? And what the hell is she writing down?*

"When did you last see Sophia?"

"Yesterday morning before school. I had a business dinner and got home around ten. A friend dropped her off after school at around four thirty. That's the last time anyone has seen her." I glance at my wrist. Sixteen hours since she'd last been seen. "Last night, when she wasn't home, I tracked her location."

"Using what?"

"An app I have on her phone."

"And where was she?"

"The phone was in her bedroom."

"Did you find any sign of struggle?"

"No."

"And why do the cops believe it's a runaway case?"

"Her age." He stretches out his hands. "She's fifteen. We live in a safe, gated community. The officer on duty last night said they see these cases all the time."

Dr. Rolfe's pen stills. She looks in my direction but not directly at me. "There's no sign of struggle. Leaving the phone at home is the action of someone not wanting to be found. If someone had taken her against her will, you'd expect the phone to either be with her or tossed and destroyed."

"Dr. Rolfe, what is your role here?"

Jack's fingers tap the table, and his gaze remains locked off to the side. It's as if he's not entirely present.

"Oh, ah, I'm a family friend. Or, well, I was a friend of Sophia's mother. Cassandra." She looks to Jack. He slowly turns his head and glances between the two of us.

"I asked Dr. Rolfe to join us because she is a preeminent profiler. She is an expert in the criminal justice field. And, as she said, she's a family friend. I trust her." He rubs his hand through his hair and then pinches the bridge of his nose. "If the media gets wind of this, it has the potential to blow up. I have a nephew who lives in Houston. They've painted him to be a playboy. If she ran away, I don't want it to be hitting gossip columns. It could impact her college chances. Or, like my nephew, she could play into the spotlight." His jaw flexes. "I don't want any of that. I just want to find her. And I want people I trust working with me."

"I'm an associate professor at UCSB." Dr. Rolfe points out the window in what she most likely presumes is the direction of the campus. "I also consult on criminal cases."

At the elevator, I had registered her eyes as dark brown, yet I misjudged. Her dark green eyes remind me of a forest, a soothing, earthy shade easily mistaken for ordinary brown. The pale skin around those green eyes is noticeably smooth, her lips full, her cheekbones pronounced.

"And exactly how many cases have you consulted on?"

"Two cases for the Santa Barbara Police Department. I moved here last summer. Most of my experience stems from cases in Great Britain." *Stems from?*

"Her father is Dr. Henry Rolfe." Sullivan says it as if the name should mean something to me. It doesn't, but I mentally store it for a background check.

A missing persons case. "And her mother hasn't seen her?"

Alex's gaze falls to her lap. Sullivan's chest rises several inches. He swallows.

"Cassandra died almost three years ago. Sophia came to live with me after her mom's death. Sophia and I…we've gone through a lot together. That's why I don't believe she would run away. But…" He stretches out his hands again, palms flat on the table. His chest rises on his inhale. "I don't know. I've been told I can be hard to live with."

"Why?"

He answers with a loaded look that seems to ask *seriously*?

"I mean, what kinds of things happened that might have caused Sophia to leave?"

"Normal stuff." He rests back against the chair. "At least, I think it's normal. She didn't like her curfew. Said it was earlier than anyone she knew. She had plans to go to a concert with friends, and I said she couldn't go without a parent. I was apparently the only parent who required an adult chaperone." He gazes out the window. "I didn't allow her to date." His fist raps the desk. "I'm strict. But I've observed my nephew. I don't want Sophia to be some Paris Hilton."

I glance at Alex. Her expression is sympathetic. Soft.

"What about the FBI? Don't they handle missing persons cases?"

"Twelve and under, they would automatically become

involved. They are less likely to take on a case like this," Alex answers.

"Have you tried?" I direct my question to Sullivan.

"No. If the police aren't taking it seriously, why would the FBI?" His professional mask slips, exposing hints of the emotional father within.

"I have contacts within the FBI. None in missing persons, but I can inquire."

Sullivan clasps the knot on his tie and wiggles it loose. "Do whatever you need. Just be discreet."

"You've contacted all of her friends? Anyone you can think of that she might be with?"

"All of them. It's pretty efficient to do that these days, thanks to texting." He places his head in his hands and roughly massages his forehead. "I don't know what to do. Please. I'll pay you whatever you want. Tell me your fee, and I'll double it."

I can understand why he is offering money, but from my perspective, it's not about the money. The much bigger question is if Arrow is the best solution. Unfortunately, I do have some personal experience with teen troubles. But I don't believe Jack could possibly know. The records are sealed, but I, of all people, understand that doesn't mean the records can't be discovered.

"Does she drink? Could she be involved in drugs?"

Jack closes his eyelids. His nostrils flare. "I don't know." When he opens his eyes and looks at me, I see a sad shell of a man full of self-doubt. "If you had asked me yesterday, I would have said absolutely not. But now, I don't know. I don't know anything. Not for certain."

Arrow's specialty isn't missing persons, but we can track people. We've found plenty of people who didn't want to be found.

"Does she have credit cards? Cash?"

"Probably both. She doesn't have a spending limit on her credit cards. I'm not strict with her on spending. I've never needed to be." Jack looks between Dr. Rolfe and me. "Come back with me. I'll fly you down in my helicopter. Maybe there's something in my house I missed."

We should search the house for anything he overlooked. Her bedroom. I'd like to check out his security cameras, walk the grounds. If he's right and this is a kidnapping, they'll be calling soon, but if we can get a jump on learning who these people are, we'll be in a better place as we negotiate ransom. And if she shows up randomly today, then all I've lost is one business day and one more trip to San Diego. If she did indeed run away, she probably did some degree of planning or research.

"I have a helicopter. I can fly down," he responds with a slow blink and a tight nod. Reflexively, I check my wrist and mentally scan my schedule. "I can leave in a few hours."

"Alexandria?"

"You didn't say..." Her pen lowers. "I met you here because you asked. I can't just head off to San Diego. I have responsibilities. I have a class to teach." Jack spins his chair to address her.

"Alex. Sophia is missing. Sophia. Cassandra's daughter." Jack's voice rises several decibels, breaking all professional bounds. "She calls you Aunt Alex."

The woman closes her eyes and bows her head, remorseful. The pressure is unwarranted. We don't need her. She's inexperienced.

"I can go down. She doesn't need to come." But Jack doesn't seem to hear me.

"Cassandra thought the world of you and your father. She'd want you to help find her daughter. And I trust you. You know her."

I stand, backing away from the table to give them a moment.

It's possible he's dating her. Ample emotion undulates between them. If they need space, I'll give it to them.

"I can't just leave. I have a dog," Alex pleads.

"Get someone to take care of it." Jack's tone is determined and insistent.

"I have to prep my TA." Color rises in those pale cheeks, and I suspect she's panicking.

"Maybe I can drive down. Or when are you leaving?" The young professor looks to me like I'm a lifeline. "Can I ride with you?"

CHAPTER 2

18 Hours Missing

Alex

The framed photograph sitting on my dresser slows my packing efforts. A slight layer of dust lines the curved wooden top. Sophia must have been ten. Our heads are bent together, and we're lying on the bright white comforter at the Savoy. Cassandra snapped the photo just before room service delivered hot chocolate and cookies as a bedtime snack. I'd expected to watch a Disney princess movie, but Sophia's tastes had changed. She'd been into the magical world of superheroes, and she pleaded to watch *Deadpool.* Cassandra laughed at her and said no way. Mother and daughter settled on *Thor*. The big, muscular, beefy hero worked for me. I remember questioning the violence level for a ten-year-old, but it's not like I would have ever said anything.

I give up on packing, lift the photo, and use the corner of my comforter to clear the dust. Sophia's loose blonde curls shine bright in the photo, perfectly off-setting her gorgeous dark blue eyes, exact replicas of her mother's. One year later, she got braces. A year after that, Cassandra died. When she got those braces off, no traces of the giggly girl in my photo remained. She'd grown up, in too many ways.

Oh, Sophia, where are you?

Trace, my elderly cockapoo, lies on his back, tail wagging, in a position that begs for his belly to be rubbed. Sunlight streams in through my bedroom windows, and he's basking on the carpet, clueless the suitcase means his mum is about to depart.

"What am I going to do with you?"

He watches with old man eyes as I wrangle clothes into my smallest suitcase. Every day, more white hairs sprout along his nose. At fourteen years of age, he's healthy, but he can suffer from separation anxiety. My little buddy likes his pack near. I crouch on the floor beside him. His eyelids close in appreciation as I rub his soft underside, and his little tail wags back and forth.

My next-door neighbor mentioned Santa Barbara has a great doggie daycare. More than one person has recommended Dioji, and I've seen their ads. But I worry about my old fella. The idea of dropping him off at a strange place doesn't sit well. And he hasn't yet attended the required orientation to see how well he plays with others, so it's not even an option. *Shat.*

My next-door neighbor's daughter always asks to pet Trace. The young girl reminds me of the Sophia in my photograph. Sweet, initially shy, but quick to warm to a person. A few minutes of conversation, and the shyness melts.

"You like her, don't you, buddy?" He licks the back of my hand. "Our neighbor and Sophia. You like anyone who gives you love." My old man is an egalitarian lover. "Maybe our neighbor would like to make a little extra money?" *Doesn't hurt to ask.*

All the houses on Haley Street are packed together like sardines, and as such, it takes me a nanosecond to cross into my neighbor's yard. As my knuckle raps the door, it occurs to me she might think me quite mad. We've never popped over to one another's home. We've only crossed paths on the sidewalk.

The door cracks open, and I paste on my friendliest smile, hoping she'll open the door further. The wide, friendly smile works. The door swings wide. She's wearing a headset, her hair is up in a ponytail, and she's got her phone in one hand, but her expression and posture are welcoming.

"Hi. I'm so sorry to bother you. I live next door. I have the stout cockapoo. Trace?"

"Oh, right. I recognize you. I'm Jenny."

"Nice to meet you. I'm Alex. Look, I know this might be forward, but I've been called out of town. Is there any chance Jocelyn might be interested in making some extra money? I need someone to walk Trace and feed him, and she always likes to love on him. I'm short on options, otherwise I'd never bang on your door."

"Of course. No problem. She'll be happy to do it. She'll probably beg to let him sleep here, if you're okay with that."

"Oh my god. Of course. If she wants to. Anything. I owe you guys so big."

After giving Jenny my spare key and promising to text instructions for care, I turn my attention to the other matter in my life. My job as an associate professor at UCSB in the psychology and brain sciences department. The one thing worse than being a part of a department termed brain science had been my father's derision.

"You are taking a position at a location without a criminal justice division? Have you gone mad?"

No, Daddy dearest. Not mad. Desperate. The two are different.

I dial my TA. As a first-year associate professor, I teach my classes. This request for my TA to fill in won't reflect well on me, especially if any of the students complain in the end-of-year satisfaction surveys. But this is Sophia. Cassandra's daughter. And really, even if it wasn't a personal matter, if I want to build out my CV as a police consultant, I need to be flexible.

"Timothy?" I check the screen to confirm the call is connected. "Timothy, are you there? Timothy?"

"Alex? Hello?"

"Timothy?"

"Yeah. Hey. Damn earbuds didn't connect."

"Hey. I have a huge favor to ask. Can you cover my three o'clock psych class today and my nine a.m. criminal minds class tomorrow?"

"Are you serious?"

"I know it's a huge ask. I'll send you all my notes. And I have video you can show for tomorrow's class."

"Is everything okay?"

"Yeah. I've been pulled in on a case, and I have to go to San Diego."

"A case? Like for the police?"

"Missing person. We could find her this evening and I'll be back for the nine o'clock class."

"That's awesome. I mean, not about the person. You're working a case. Cool."

"I'm flying down in a helicopter." That bit's exciting.

"No fucking way. Like for the police or the FBI?"

Mr. Wolfgang's ice-blue eyes and grim countenance come to mind. My heartbeat slows as if he is fixing me with his steely gaze, sucking the oxygen from the room with his commanding presence. Those broad shoulders and height demand respect from those he towers over, but it's more than his physical presence. He's the type of man who doesn't do small talk. He had been serious, attentive, and aware. He'd also seen right through me and discerned I had little to no experience to offer. But Jack had been correct. I do know Sophia. I love her, and I loved her mother. Therefore, he can trust me. No matter what we discover Sophia has gotten herself involved in, he can trust me. I'll be there for them both. My discretion is assured.

Still, I'll need to be at the top of my game or Mr. Wolfgang will dismiss me as useless. The man epitomizes no bullshit. He's the founder of the best security firm in the state and one that takes on a variety of work. I would never want to consider Sophia's hardship a blessing for me, but there's no denying this situation opens a door.

"Arrow Security? You've probably never heard of them." With my phone propped between my shoulder and ear, I maneuver my clothes so my hairdryer will fit in the suitcase.

"They did the security for that big vineyard event last month."

"I don't remember that." I get my news from the BBC and online sources. If I pick up a local newspaper, it is for weekend events.

"When the NSA caught members of Spectre in Santa Barbara? You don't remember that? One of those cybercrime organizations being right here?"

"Of course I remember that. I just didn't connect the wine festival. Rumors were he was here for that event, right?"

"Yep. That's great that you get to work with them. Go. I've got it covered. Send me your notes. I'll text with any questions."

"Timothy?"

"Yeah?"

"Thank you." I hope my gratitude flows through the line, because he doesn't have to do this for me. He could make a big stink of it if he wanted, and our department head would probably sit me down for a reprimand.

"Hey, don't mention it. Oh, before I forget, your dad called."

"He called you?" I suppose he picks up on my disbelief, because he chuckles.

"No. He called the office. Caller ID didn't show, and I thought it was pizza delivery. Said to call him."

"It's his weekly check-in," I mumble. I should call him, but I won't.

"Hey, so, am I going to see your case on the news?"

"Let's hope not."

"Why? Won't pictures of the missing person everywhere help you find him?"

"It's a high-profile person. Discretion has been requested."

"Ah, now I want to know. Inquiring minds want to know, Alex."

"And that's precisely why discretion has been requested. I'll send everything for class over in a bit. And thank you! You're the bees knees, love!"

I hang up and rush to finish packing. I shouldn't be staying more than one night, but I thumb through my clothes, double-checking I've brought everything, then move on to setting out Trace's food and snacks.

Timothy's question about publicity nags at me. He's right. In a missing persons case, time is of the essence. Circulating photos can bring lost ones home quickly. Even if she willfully ran away, seeing her photo everywhere might make her think twice about staying gone. It might dawn on her that her father loves her, even if he's an overbearing mongrel. Prohibiting dating feels positively prehistoric.

"He loves you. And he's never been a parent before. Not really. He's figuring it out. Be patient." That's what I'd told

Sophia more than once. How bad did things get? Why didn't she call?

As I turn out of my drive, my phone rings. A close-up of Sloane's smiling face covers the screen. She's a fellow assistant professor at UCSB and my closest friend Stateside. I set the phone down in the passenger seat, camera pointed up, and answer.

"Hey, can't talk long. I need to use my phone for directions. What's up?"

"Timothy just told me you got a consulting gig. That's awesome! And it's with Arrow Security?"

"Is Timothy telling everyone?"

"Probably. This is so cool. And you probably want it getting out, don't you? You become a high-profile police consultant and it's a surefire way to get you a professorship. Whereas I've got to research and get published."

"I still need to get published." But her glee has me smiling and gets my excitement kernels popping. Sloane's right. Consulting on real-world cases will be a huge boon.

"Did you get to meet any of the military guys?"

"I met the owner, Ryan Wolfgang." His name rolls off my tongue. It's a lovely name.

"He's one of the former SEALs working there." Sloane squeals, and I roll my eyes. "Is he as hot in person as on the news?"

"I didn't see him on the news." I refrain from admitting that he's right fit. Truly gobsmackingly gorgeous.

"You're never in the psych faculty break room. Sherman insists on keeping the TV on the local station. But fuck, he's hot. He's got, like, a Superman vibe. Not the original, but one of the more recent ones." Given I have seen none of the Superman films, I can't contribute to that line of conversation. I could offer that he's built like Thor, but there's no need to feed Sloane's madness.

"He's taller than I am."

At six foot one, it's noteworthy when I meet someone who dwarfs me. Growing up, I'd been the tallest of all my friends. My ancestry includes both Swedes and Russians...and somewhere back there, some mighty tall people. In a feat of genetics, I stand taller than my father by one inch. Nicknames growing up included gazelle, heron, and giraffe. Here in the States, everyone assumes I play basketball.

"Is he hot?"

His intimidating, icy gaze floats before me in my mind's eye joined by his ultra-serious countenance. All business. The broad, massive shoulders, slick dark hair, and powerful jawline.

"He's attractive, but he's older."

"How old?"

"I did not ask."

"Is he single?"

"I definitely did not ask *that*." I'll be working with the man. I do not need to think of him in a sexy way. Asking his dating status would be a professional blunder. "Sloane, do you need anything? Because right now I'm lost. And I'm in danger of being late."

"Oh, I wanted to see if you need me to dog sit."

"Seriously?" The notion tugs at my heart. "That's so thoughtful."

"Well, Timothy said it was last minute."

"It is. I banged on my neighbor's door and begged her. But—"

"Next time, call me."

"You are such a love. Let me go... I don't want to be late."

"Late for a date."

"It's not a date. This is work." I love the girl, but she's about to take the biscuit. "I'll call you later."

One wrong turn leads to multiple wrong turns. Maps continually tells me to turn after I've passed a turn, then she re-routes. My palmy hands grip the wheel as I tear down the narrow street. This place is off the beaten path. There's no shoulder. Just dirt and a distressing absence of road signs.

Maps announces, "At the next intersection, make a U-turn."

I follow the directions.

Maps announces, "At the next intersection, make a U-turn."

"What the frick is wrong with you?"

I turn off into a private dirt drive. Pull up a different map source. I study the road names, find my turnoff, and slam on the accelerator. The back wheel lurches downward, and the whole car bounces up. But it's okay. I regroup, evening out on the asphalt. I smash the accelerator. The horizon angles from left down to right. No, that's my blessed vehicle angling.

A flat tire.

My British grandmother would say something mild, like, "Fiddlesticks." But, no, a flat tire when I'm running late warrants a full-out guttural, "Fuck!"

CHAPTER 3

18 Hours Missing

Ryan

"Did you get the update on Syria?"

Trevor enters my office as my laptop powers down.

"I read it. What's your take?" We have a security detail in Syria watching a CIA officer's wife and daughter. It's an unusual situation, as the man hired us privately. If his identity has been compromised, the CIA will remove him and his family. He clearly fears this is the case, but he won't be the first man to prioritize career. Life in the field differs from a life at Langley.

Trevor rests his hands on the back of my office guest chair, leaning forward, his expression thoughtful.

"You think we need to increase security?" I prompt.

"Karsyn said someone is tailing the wife. And he saw their gardener talking to the kid's tutor."

Staff talking to each other might seem benign, but in countries plagued with the kidnapping industry, it's something we watch out for. A general rule of thumb is to not let people who work with you interact. They can piece together your schedule. It's the advice we give our clients in such countries, and it's something we monitor to ensure safety. Of course, the vast majority of our clients work for corporations and are targets because their company has an insurance policy to pay the ransom.

The CIA officer presents a more perilous situation. We don't know what he's working on, and we would never ask. But if his identity is compromised, then the list of potential reasons for tracking his family expands. Of course, security isn't cheap. Increasing his security level means additional salaries.

Trevor remains silent, watching me.

"Karsyn is on the ground. What does he say? Does he want additional resources?"

"Says he's good for now." Trevor's lips twist. I know that look. He disagrees.

"What?" I prompt.

"Karsyn doesn't think our client can afford to increase security."

I shove my laptop into my bag. Frustrated. Our client isn't our only concern. If we were better funded, we could throw money at a case like this and not worry about profitability.

"What do you want to do?" I ask again.

"He checks back in two days. Let's see how things are going. If he's truly compromised, the CIA may pull him and his family out before we could get additional staff out there."

Two days will give me time to review the financials for that project. Arrow is doing well. Our original funding came from our Napa-based partner. We've been profitable since opening our doors, which is virtually unheard of. But it's conceivable that we are at one of those growth junctures where additional investment would be advisable.

"How'd your meeting go this morning?"

I let Trevor know I had business in San Diego this afternoon, but I didn't share details.

"Sullivan's daughter wasn't home when he got home last night."

"He can't locate her?"

"Police think she ran away and will show up. But he's a wealthy guy." That's all I need to say to Trevor.

"He hired Arrow?" The unstated question in his skepticism is *why*.

"If she's a runaway, he wants discretion. And he wants to find her as quickly as possible."

I pull my backpack over my shoulder and head to the door. Trevor follows, talking to my back.

"If she's a runaway, is this the case for us?"

Trevor's insightful question weighs like a stone.

Trevor and I both came from less-than-ideal home lives. I headed straight to the Naval Academy. He signed up for the Navy on the day he turned seventeen. We both understand wanting to get out of a bad situation. We are under no delusion that home is the best place for all teenagers.

His question underlines the questions that have been running through my mind since Jack Sullivan left our offices. Was Jack dating someone Sophia didn't like? Did he bring women home regularly? Was he a crap dad? Abusive? What, exactly, would she be running away from? Or was she running to something, something like perceived freedom, maybe drugs, alcohol, or a lover?

Trevor doesn't want us expending resources if Arrow isn't the best solution. Typically, we protect people. Our fledgling security company has never taken on a case like this. But we know how to locate people. We have a successful track record locating adults with much more skill than a teen.

"If it was your daughter, or son, I'd help you."

Trevor doesn't have any biological kids of his own, but his heart adopted Stella's son. He gives a slow nod. "Roger that. I've got your six. Let me know what you need."

Trevor doesn't need to tell me he's got my six. He'll always have my back, and I'll always have his.

My steps echo through the concrete stairwell, and my thoughts return to Syria. It would be nice to be able to send additional resources without thinking twice. With a solid investment base, we could do that. Someone like Jack Sullivan is the kind of man who would gladly invest in a company like ours. We hire veterans, and we do good work. It's something I might talk to him about—after we locate his daughter. That's assuming he's still the good guy I remember and not some twisted fuck who gave his daughter a reason to run.

Traffic is light, and twenty minutes later, I pace the sidewalk in front of my helicopter. It's a clear day with winds out of the southwest. The flight path to San Diego is one I fly frequently. The helicopter is prepped and ready to go. So am I.

This trip could be a waste of time. But I keep thinking about our meeting. Sullivan entered the room as a consummate professional, a leader of a multinational corporation. In under twenty minutes, his guarded veneer cracked. He's scared. Potentially desperate. Given the local PD offered little support, I can't blame Sullivan for seeking alternative options. It's an instinct honed by the Navy. If one option fails, you find another. You find a way.

I flick my wrist, checking the time. I scan the parking lot and the road leading up to the helipad. I exhale. Dr. Rolfe said she would be here. Jack doesn't need her. The woman is a criminal profiler.

A family friend. Right. A likely story for a young woman who could grace a runway. He pleaded with her, but I still am not sure I understand why. If it hadn't been important to him, I would have never agreed to cart her to San Diego.

She knows Sophia. Does she know Sophia better than her own father? Jack's wife died. Sophia's mother. Is Dr. Rolfe a mother figure? She's young. Is she more of an older sister? I remember Jack telling me about the woman he was going to marry.

It had been right before the Naval Academy graduation. Some of our classmates were headed out, and I waved them off, planning to get some extra time on the weights. Sullivan's class was graduating, but I still had a couple of years ahead of me. He fell into step beside me.

"You not going out tonight?" I asked. We didn't leave the premises often, so most of the cadets high-tailed it out when allowed.

"Nah. My girl can't make it up. I'm headed back to call her."

"Phone date?"

"Yep. I'll take whatever I can get. You got someone?"

It wasn't a particularly surprising question, given I stayed behind. There were websites dedicated to how hard it was to have a relationship at the Naval Academy. To not go out when given the chance meant I wasn't even trying.

"No. No point." And I'd meant it. My plans aimed high. I wanted missions. Relationships weren't on my radar.

"You say that. But when you meet the one, you'll feel differently. Trust me. Cassie changed my world." He smiled. I had the sense he'd say more, but the path split. "Hang tight, Wolfman. You ever need me, call."

I never called. Also never found someone to change my world. But I sure as hell planned to be there for Sullivan when he called me.

His daughter could have run for any number of reasons. The reason didn't matter. He wants to find her. He wants her safe at home.

I check the time. Jack's family friend apparently holds no appreciation for timeliness. I'd expect more from a professor. Ten minutes late. That's ten minutes I could have used in the office or we could use to find Sophia.

Trevor called her hot. Hot is a subjective term. Her tardiness shifts my skepticism in her qualifications to a suspicion she will be a vexing operational component.

Objectively speaking, the tall woman is attractive. If I met her randomly at a bar, she might catch my eye. My type, if I have one, is typically curvier. Not quite as tall and rail thin as Dr. Rolfe. But some men go for the waif, supermodel type. She could be Sullivan's type.

In our meeting, she had been serious and focused. Admittedly, her notetaking bordered on obsessiveness, and the activity struck me as typical of a novice. I did some light online research after the meeting. She holds a degree from Oxford and a university in Ireland.

I didn't do additional research, as I don't need to know more about her. I don't need to give her any thought. As long as she doesn't hinder us, like she is doing at this exact moment, then she can hold Sullivan's hand while we locate his daughter.

The hum of a combustion engine catches my attention. A shiny, light blue Volkswagen Bug tears into the gated entrance. The car whips haphazardly around one hangar, tires spinning loose gravel in its wake.

The driver drives like a bat out of hell, dangerous and out of control. I cross my arms, suspecting I know the driver. The blue Bug spins onto the narrow runway, and my blood pressure spikes.

No one should be so obtuse as to drive on a runway.

I raise one arm in the air to flag the asshole down.

The driver wears sunglasses, but her dark mane and height in the car confirm my suspicions.

The vehicle halts mere feet in front of me, and the engine stops. The door opens, and before one foot hits the ground, I grit out, "No."

She freezes.

"You can't park here."

Unbelievable.

The woman is late, drives like a banshee, obstructs a runway, then attempts to park next to the helipad. I point to the row of cars thirty feet away.

Alex huffs loud enough for me to hear it, as if huffing is an acceptable form of communication, and slams the door closed. A ridiculous white daisy bounces in her cup holder as her ancient vehicle backs up, then rolls forward. Her back right wheel is about half the size of her other wheels. I force my gaze away from the unsafe tire, the one that should be used to drive to acquire a replacement.

It's conceivable she had a flat tire, but given she just drove down the runway, it's more likely she's using her spare as a permanent tire. Unreal. Sullivan's family friend is unreal.

One man and a flight instructor are two hangars down inspecting a Cessna. The man waves before heading back into the small office building with metal siding. Overall, a slow afternoon for the facility.

Twenty feet away, on the other side of the hangar, sits my helicopter. All I need is my cargo.

Cargo I apparently shouldn't have agreed to fly.

Dr. Rolfe's long legs cover ground at a rapid pace. Her wheeled suitcase bounces along behind her. A tan leather tote bag hangs from her shoulder. She traded her black interview suit for slim dark jeans and a blazer, but her jewelry and cream V-neck top remain the same. She wears ankle boots with a couple of inches on the heel, which raises her nose to my chin. I reach out for her bag, and she shuns me with a shake of her head.

"I've got it."

No need to argue with a woman who knows her mind. "Let's go."

In the helicopter, I hand her a headset. She fumbles with the harness.

"I'll do it," I command.

Her chin juts out and lips flex. I can't see those green eyes behind her shades, but I recognize defiance. *Not on my plane.*

I jerk the end of the strap, tightening the harness. I don't miss her quick inhale. Her V-neck blouse slips, dipping to curve around the swell of her breast. Color flushes her pale skin. I check the strap over her waist. I grit my teeth and execute laser focus on the harness, not her gaping blouse, so we can get out of here.

The safety rating on my helicopter ranks as top of the line. I don't expect to fall out of the sky on this trip. But if she plans to fly with me, her harness will be buckled correctly.

Her chest stills, as if she can't breathe in my presence. Tough. With one last check on the buckles, I move back into my seat. I slip my headphones on and speak into the mouthpiece as I buckle my harness.

"You comfortable?" In my irritation, it is conceivable I buckled the harness too tightly.

She doesn't speak, only nods.

"Speak."

I still can't see those eyes, but the way she presses her lips together, it's pretty clear she's pissed. I exhale some frustration so I don't bark like a drill sergeant.

"Speak so we know your mouthpiece is working."

"Are you the one flying this?"

If I had any doubt, her tone confirms she's pissed. *Tough shit.*

"I am. If you're going to change your mind, now's the time to do it." *Be my guest, princess.*

"How many years have you been a pilot?"

"I've flown choppers on missions. And I've flown for years as a civilian. Bought my first helicopter two years ago. I fly at least once a week on average."

She looks straight ahead with her hands resting on her lap. The pad of one thumb slides back and forth over the edge of one short nail. Her lips aren't quite as scrunched up, but there are no other tells. I can't get a read on her.

"If that's not good enough, you can drive." It's not that long of a drive. She'll be there before nightfall.

The woman nods. Unless she speaks up, I won't know what she's thinking. I am not a mind reader. I am on the verge of suggesting she get out and drive herself after she buys a new damn tire when a soft "still in," comes through the headset. I swallow. Refocus.

All right. Let's do this.

Slowly, I open the throttle. The helicopter jerks and lifts. The concrete pad below us falls out of view as we rise higher, above the buildings, above the treetops, and up and over the ocean. She leans closer to the glass, peering out over her view of the coastline.

"I'm sorry I was late. I had a flat tire."

My muscles relax, and a degree of exasperation dissipates. "Did you change the tire yourself?"

"I had a little help from a YouTuber named Stan the Auto Guy."

Changing a tire isn't for the helpless or weak. She had enough gumption to figure out how to do it on her own.

We fly for a few minutes in silence. The headphones block all noise, and the resulting void of noise invites meditation.

"Do you agree with Jack's decision to keep this out of the media?" Her question rings with uncertainty. But it's a good question.

"If it were my daughter, or someone I loved, I'm not sure it's the path I would choose. But I've never had to deal with being in the limelight. And, while I like Jack Sullivan, he's a trust-fund kid."

"What does that mean?" A sharp accent comes out in her question, and it spins like a stiff reprimand.

"Where's your accent from?"

"Scotland. My mother was American. I have dual citizenship." Interesting. I detected an accent, but it's more noticeable on select words.

"What I meant by trust fund is that Jack hasn't had to deal with things not going his way. He probably assumes she'll return home unscathed, and to him, the worst-case scenario is if she has to deal with the media casting her as a runaway or a troubled teen. How well do you know Jack?"

I watch her carefully as she answers. She's looking out the window. Her hands rest on her lap, still, her fingers in constant flux. "Not well."

"But you know Sophia, right?" Sullivan described this woman as a family friend.

"I do. But the last time I saw her was at Cassandra's funeral. She was twelve."

She's still staring off to the side, which allows me to observe her undetected. Her dark hair is cut in layers and falls in waves around her. This woman has legs for days. Those long legs extend up to the front of the helicopter.

Silence resumes. Her fingers tap her thigh, and one ankle

bounces. If she hasn't seen Sophia in three years, they can't be close. *Why would Jack reach out to her?*

"Do you have a feel for how realistic it is that she ran away?"

If she didn't run away, if this is a kidnapping, then the trajectory of our investigation will change fast.

"No. There's a world of difference between twelve and fifteen. And she lost her mum. That one event will change a person. But..." Her words trail. Her fingers trace the outline of the harness. "The girl I knew wouldn't have run away. She had a good head on her shoulders. Sweet. We keep in touch via WhatsApp. When I got home after our meeting, I read through all of our prior messages. She seemed happy."

That's what I feared. That we would not be dealing with a missing persons case for long. That soon we would call it an abduction case. Given Sullivan's net worth, the scenario is reasonable. A ransom carries with it some good news. For one, they'll keep her alive. And two, while Arrow doesn't have expertise in runaways, that's not the case with kidnappings. We handle K&R, or kidnappings and ransom, all over the globe.

"How long before we get there?" she asks.

"Little over an hour. We'll head down along the coastline, then cut in. Sullivan has his own helipad, so that's where we'll land."

"He has a helipad at his house?"

"From what I understand, estate is the correct nomenclature." My attention splits between the controls, the view of the Pacific coastline, and my passenger's long legs. The jeans are tight on her ass and thighs but loosen below the knee, and, due to the way she's sitting, they end several inches above her ankle boot, revealing smooth, pale skin. She's either a sunblock adherent or she doesn't spend a great deal of time outdoors.

She leans to the glass, checking out the panoramic view. To our left lies a seemingly endless stretch of sandy beach lined with rows of houses packed together, the black line of the 101, and the hills and valleys that rise into the San Rafael Mountains. To our right, as far as the eye can see, the wide-open sea sparkles with the occasional white of crashing waves.

"You were friends with his wife. But you've never been to their house?"

"No. She visited me. I say she was my friend, but…she was over ten years older than me. She stayed with us when she did a study-abroad as a college student. My dad is a professor. Over the years, we had a lot of exchange students. But Cassandra and I bonded. Kept in touch. She brought Sophia to London once, and I met up with them."

"When was the last time you saw Cassandra?"

"Probably four years ago. It was after their divorce."

"They divorced?"

"Yeah."

A lot of military guys divorced. But Sullivan clenched his hand when I asked about Sophia's mother. My interpretation of his reaction was that the topic was emotional or difficult for him.

"Was it a bad divorce?"

Static crosses the line, but I can hear her exhale. I glance sideways. *Is she emotional?*

"Is there a good kind?"

"I suppose not. I just mean, did they fight? Or was it public?"

"I think as far as divorces go, it ranked as proper. Cassandra said she'd always expected they'd divorce before the ten-year mark."

"Why?" Ten is a random number.

"In California, after ten years, you split the estate if there's a divorce."

"That's right. He said something about that." His father had been livid about the marriage.

"Yep." She smiles. Dr. Rolfe is a moderately attractive woman, but when she smiles, the needle moves considerably higher. "They eloped. I got the sense his family did not approve. I mean, they liked Cassandra. But his father believed in prenuptial agreements."

Based on my research, Sullivan's estimated net worth is approximately $950,000,000. I'd expect his father did believe in prenups.

"So, they divorced before the ten-year mark. Did she get a good settlement?"

"If the hotel suite she booked at Savoy is any indication, she wasn't wanting for anything. But she never said. And I would never ask." She sounds affronted. "How would you even ask someone that? How much money did you get?"

"Without a doubt, there are articles out there with mentions of the divorce settlement."

"I'm sure, but that doesn't mean I need to ask." She kicks her long legs in front of her, stretching them out. If she were wearing a mini-skirt, I would have an incredible view of long, endless legs.

The thought comes out of nowhere. She's potentially Sullivan's love interest. I redirect my attention to the control panel. We lapse back into silence. I begin a mental lap of the information we need.

"How did Cassandra die?"

"A car hit her at an intersection. Thirty-four years old." She clucks her tongue. "It was by chance Sophia wasn't with her. And, yes, they were divorced, but her death hit Jack hard. He cried at the funeral. At the reception afterward, he excused himself. You could see the tears welling up. They may have divorced, but he cared." Her assessment matches what I picked up earlier.

"How did Sophia handle it?"

"How would any twelve-year-old girl handle the loss of her mother?"

I exhale. "I am only asking to better understand the situation."

She shifts in her seat. "Sorry. Sophia was quiet and reserved. But well-mannered. She shook hands with any adult who offered. They had this fancy reception at the Ritz Carlton after the funeral. Waiters passed around tea food, you know, small sandwiches and fruit punch. I remember thinking that she must have wanted to be anywhere but in that room. All these adults she didn't know kept coming up and offering condolences. Portraits of Cassandra were on easels everywhere you looked."

"Who planned the service?"

"I'm not sure. They cremated Cassandra, so in lieu of a graveside service, they did a luncheon reception. I remember feeling badly for both Jack and Sophia. They were both in so much pain, and yet they were shaking hands with all these businessmen and acquaintances."

"Did Jack and Sophia seem close?"

"Not at the funeral. But I think they were each in their own world of hurt. From what Cassandra said, even when they were married, Jack traveled frequently. Business trips." She runs her index fingernail along her upper lip. "At the reception, I had time to speak with Jack. In private. A little room away from all the people paying respects. And he told me he hadn't been involved in Sophia's life. But he would be. He promised he would be there for her. He choked up. I believed him."

"So, you don't think he stepped up? He stayed away, and that's why he's now suspecting she ran away?"

"I don't have enough information. Is it possible that she and her father didn't grow well together? Did he not live up to his word, and he remained distant? Continued to travel and be more absent than present? Of course. Is it also possible something nefarious happened? Yes. I don't have any data. With luck, when we go through the house, we will find evidence that leads us to her."

Dr. Rolfe might be young and inexperienced, but her instincts are good. Her thought process is logical. The reason I agreed to fly down is that I needed to investigate. We can hypothesize all day, but we need evidence.

"And what kind of evidence will you be looking for?" I ask as a test. She asked about my flight experience earlier. Digging into her knowledge is fair.

"Ideally, we'll find evidence of a struggle. A crime scene."

"You want a crime scene?" Her eagerness reminds me of a young recruit eager for battle with no realistic concept of the devastation war delivers.

"The crime scene is a silent witness. Without one, we're short important information." To me, that statement sounds like the voice of a professor. And it doesn't apply much to someone willingly running away.

"Got it." In my experience, we don't worry too much about the crime scene. On missions, we leave cleanup to others. "What else?"

"All of her electronics. I'd like to piece together her online life for the last year. See if there are any clear behavioral changes."

"I've got a team locked and loaded, ready to go through it all for us."

"So you're trying to say I'm not needed?"

I remain focused on the control panel, but I give her the courtesy of an answer. "Arrow doesn't need you. Jack does."

"Got it."

Minutes tick by. I pissed her off, but it's just as well. When we land, she can serve her purpose and be there for Jack.

"My observational skills are strong. When we meet with her friends, I might pick up on something."

Whatever you say, princess.

"Do you think Jack will give you access to his electronic communications?"

"It depends on how confidential some of his business matters are." I expect Jack will volunteer any relevant information. But the British princess isn't wrong to ask about access to everything. There might be something there Sullivan doesn't consider relevant that could help us. Especially if this ends up being a kidnapping.

CHAPTER 4

22 Hours Missing

Ryan

The San Diego skyline graces the horizon, maybe twenty miles away. Two hangars with tile roofs border one side of our destination. A Sullivan Arms branded sign angled skyward atop a brick platform clarifies ownership for those flying over. There is a small runway stretching along the field and three helipads. Per the instructions Sullivan's assistant emailed, I land in the helipad numbered three.

This is not Sullivan's house, as I had assumed. The land sits on the top of a raised cliff overlooking the ocean. His view is spectacular. This property may be a couple of miles from the actual ocean, but with a view like this, it is prime property.

A man in sunglasses watches us land with his arms crossed as he leans against a black Range Rover. His colorful Hawaiian-print shirt stands out from high above. It isn't until the helicopter door opens that the man pushes off his perch and tosses the lollipop stick he'd been chewing onto the ground.

"Welcome. I'm Wayne. Jack asked me to give you guys a lift back to his house."

"I thought we were landing at his house."

"San Diego city regulations." He clucks his tongue. "No go. We're about twenty minutes away. With traffic, it'll be more like forty minutes. Jack would've been here to get you himself, but he's still at the station. Mighty nice of you two to fly down."

"The police station?" Wayne nods in the affirmative. "Are the local police working the case now?"

"I don't think so. Unfortunately, he's probably as much of a suspect in their eyes as he is a father looking for his daughter. I told him to get a lawyer, but he's bullheaded."

Wayne reaches for the bags, and I give a quick shake of my head. "I've got it."

Alex mimics me. Growing up, they taught me to carry a woman's bag. But I also attended the Naval Academy and spent years in the Navy. I learned some women don't want a man to carry her bags. While I am okay with that, Wayne isn't. He chases her down and insists on carrying her bag. In her boots, the top of his head reaches her chin.

"Thanks for driving us," Alex says from the back seat as we pull away.

The light reflects off Wayne's Rolex watch. It's similar to the one Jack wore, if not the exact gold model. He's got curly dark hair, but it's short. I'm not sure if it's his hair or his Hawaiian shirt, but he reminds me of *Magnum PI* without the mustache. I haven't thought of that show in ages, but Wayne has a similar laid-back vibe.

"Not a problem," Wayne responds. "I hope you find her. She's a good kid. Like family."

I can't see his eyes, thanks to the Maui Jims, but with one hand on the wheel and an arm resting on the door, Wayne doesn't appear overly worried about Sophia. Jimmy Buffett plays through the radio, and Wayne taps his left foot to the beat. He's wearing khaki shorts and expensive leather loafers, and he's sporting a dad bod. But I'd guess he's not too much older than me, maybe mid- to late forties.

"Did you know Sophia well?" Dr. Rolfe asks.

"I don't think you'd say well. I mean, I've known Jack for a long damn time. Sullivan Arms was my first job out of college. Known Sophia her whole life. But, like, the way you know kids. Say hello. Things like, 'Dang, girl, you're getting tall.' I'd tell Jack he was gonna be in trouble when the boys came knocking. She'd laugh. Then she'd disappear. That's the way I knew her."

"Got it." Through the rearview mirror, I catch a glimpse of Dr. Rolfe's smile. She finds Wayne entertaining. With him, she's relaxed. "Did Jack ever mention he'd had problems with her?"

Wayne angles the rearview to get a better look at Alex.

"Not at all. She's a straight-A student. Never been in trouble. Goes to a fantastic, exclusive school. She's got it all."

I don't have to see Alex to know she doesn't interpret his response as good news. It leaves us with two avenues. If he's correct, then she was abducted, because fifteen-year-olds don't run away from great homes.

But by Wayne's own admittance, he only knows her in passing. He's not a highly reliable source.

"What about you two? What's your story?" Wayne's still got one arm draped over the wheel, and he's slouched back in the seat. I get the sense he doesn't care about our answer; he's just filling the silence.

"Jack and I were in the Naval Academy together."

"You know, I always forget he pulled that stint." He looks in the rearview. "And you?"

"Family friend."

"I saw you at the funeral." Wayne's focus centers on the back seat, and red brake lights shine. I slam my palm against the dashboard.

"Wayne." He glances forward.

"Damn slower drivers." He peels out one lane over, and we zoom past the braking sedan.

"Cassandra stayed with us when she studied abroad."

"Ah..." He readjusts the rearview so he can better see Dr. Rolfe. "You're the one who has that criminal profiler dad. Like a regular Sherlock Holmes."

"He'd like to hear you say that."

"Jack's mentioned him. So, you working with anyone? Or on your own?"

"It's just us."

"No FBI?" Wayne asks.

"No. Do you have kids, Wayne?"

"The wifey and I never did have kids. Good thing, too. I work so much I would hardly know 'em." He points out the window. "Now, see over there? If you get a chance, since you're Navy, that exit right there will take you to the USS *Midway* Museum. It's Navy. Tourists love that shit."

Forty-two minutes later, the SUV rolls into a gated neighborhood. A security officer mans the gate.

"Is that guard twenty-four-seven?" I ask.

"Yep. I live in this neighborhood, too. A couple of blocks away, near the clubhouse."

"I'm guessing there's not much crime here," I say as we pass stately homes with manicured lawns.

"Nope. But word's spreading about Sophia. It's stirring up concern."

"Any wild theories?" I ask.

"Not that I've heard, but I'll ask my wife and let you know. I try to avoid all gossip, whereas she lives to spread it."

Minutes later, we come to a stop in front of an oceanfront mansion. The circular drive leads to an arched gate. Through the gate, oversize, formidable iron and glass front doors offer a view through the entire home and out over the breathtaking ocean beyond. Palm trees line the sides of the yard. The scent of fresh-cut grass overloads my nostrils the second I open the car door. In the distance, waves crash. A slight breeze carries a floral scent. A Grecian statue with a narrow fountain base stands midway between the entrance gate and the front door beyond.

Inside the front courtyard, an array of fuchsia pink bougainvillea vines and matching pink potted geraniums splash color against the white stucco walls, the trimmed, plush green grass, and a white stone path. I scan the eaves of the three-story home for cameras. One roving camera hangs from each corner. A doorbell beside the front door likely houses another camera, judging by the black plated glass. In the yard, beneath oversize yucca plants, are spherical metal objects. They could be yard lights or cameras. An extension of the driveway continues along the side of the massive home. I assume that leads to the garage and side entrance, and additional security cameras.

Wayne pushes open the front door and hustles inside. A moment later, he lifts a small, obese dog.

"Come on in." The dog in his arms squirms and growls. "Ignore Sasha. She thinks she's bigger than she is. She's a little bitch until you give her a snack. Then she's all lovey dovey."

"Hi there, Sasha," Dr. Rolfe coos to the dog in a singsong voice. The growling simmers.

"Jack calls her Pita, Sophia calls her Sasha. Dumb dog responds to either."

"You look like a Sasha to me. Not a Pita. How did he get Pita?" In response to the smooth, kind tones, the dog's lips unfurl and her tail wags.

"Pita stands for pain in the ass." Wayne closes the door behind us and sets the dog down. "You do have to watch her getting outside from the front. There's a gap in the corner over there that opens onto the side of the house. Path leads to the beach. She takes off for it, and once she hits the sand... Man. Even though she's a fat little thing, she's hard to catch. She loves that beach."

Sullivan's house befits an exorbitantly wealthy man. The foyer ceiling rises two stories high above marble floors and pristine white walls. A large glass elevator shaft centers the back wall, allowing unfettered views of the ocean. White orchids sit atop a round table in an ornate porcelain bowl. Everything is ornate. Lots of scrolls, gold, and flowers.

"Jack asked me to take you to your rooms. There are two rooms on the street side of the house. They don't offer a view, but they each have their own bathroom, and there's a small kitchen and den. The only way you can access it is through the side staircase that's right over there. There's another bedroom that's on the main floor with fantastic views. It's beside Sophia's room. There's a basement bedroom with access to the pool. It's off the game room. Jack said to give you the choice."

"The two rooms in the back next to each other will work."

Alex's answer takes me by surprise. If she and Jack had anything going on, she wouldn't want a room next to mine. But, given I prefer to keep my team together, I can't fault her logic. Not that she's on my team. If this goes well, we won't even stay the night.

"Come on, guys. I've got to get back to the office." We obediently follow Wayne as he strolls through the house.

"What do you do?" Alex asks Wayne.

"Oh, I'm marketing, but I'm a wearer of all the hats. I've worked with the Sullivans for a long time. Once you guys get settled in, feel free to explore the house."

"Where is Sophia's bedroom? That's where I'd like to start," Dr. Rolfe says.

"Walk past the dining room, kitchen, and all that, and there are two bedrooms off to the side. The master bedroom is on the third floor, same as you, but you can only access the master through the front staircase. The only way you can get up to his level is to go down to the main level, then back up that front staircase. Or the elevator. Every floor opens up onto a deck. I'd give you the tour, but I've really got to skedaddle."

"Do you know, does he have security cameras?"

"I think he does." Wayne sniffs. Both hands rest on his hips. "I'd assume he does. You'd have to ask him."

"Any other employees on the grounds?"

Wayne chuckles. "Yeah, you'd expect a butler or something, right? Nah, that's not Jack's speed. There are some rooms in this house that feel like an old lady lives here, but it's just because he bought it furnished and hasn't been around enough to prioritize decorating. The library. The formal living room. You'll know you're in a room they spend time in if it's not overdone. My wife keeps asking when he's gonna remodel the kitchen. It's French country. Looks fine to me, but my wife says it dates the place. Anyway, you guys can take a look around and form your own opinions." Two steps later, Wayne stops. "He has a cleaning service. I don't know when they're scheduled, but they do have a key. And there's a gardener. If he's like mine, he shows up whenever. And a pool cleaner. I use his pool cleaner. He referred him to me. Good guy. Small company. I think he hired someone to cook for a while, but I seem to remember she quit. I could be wrong. Anyway, Jack'll be home as soon as he can."

The small apartment to the front of the house had been designed as an in-law suite. The front space includes a small but comfortable sitting area, a full kitchen, and a kitchen table. Two doors lead to bedrooms with private bathrooms. One door in the kitchen opens onto a large balcony with views over a neighboring house. Below the balcony is the driveway extension and the garage doors. At the end of the driveway there is a small wooden gate with a latch and no lock. One door provides access to the in-law suite and one staircase. The windows in the living area and the bedrooms offer views of palms and the manicured courtyards.

I drop my bag on the sofa. These rooms will not be helpful. "You wanna go look around?"

Dr. Rolfe removes her blazer and hangs it over her suitcase. White silk blouses over a leather belt. Silky dark hair covers half her back and spills over her narrow shoulders. Her jeans shape her ass nicely. If this is the kind of outfit she wears to teach, then I can only imagine the side comments from students. I most definitely never had a professor who looked like her. And yet again I question Sullivan's true motivation in leaning on her for this case.

She opens her tote bag and lifts a 35mm camera and hangs the strap over her neck. She gets a notepad and pen, slips her phone into her back pocket, and says, "Let's go."

Alex grips the stairwell with her right hand as we descend. "I don't think I'd want marble stairs. Would you? If you fell, it would hurt."

"Do you fall down stairs frequently?"

"I can be a mite clumsy. But so can anyone. I bet these stairs are slippery if you have wet feet. They have a pool and an ocean out front."

"You don't approve of the flooring. Noted." *Huh. She'll drive a car down a runway, but she has an issue with flooring.*

"I knew Jack was wealthy, but I didn't realize how wealthy. Is this family money?"

"He inherited a trust fund at twenty-five. The size of the fund expanded at age thirty. According to *Forbes*, his current estimated wealth far exceeds his trust fund. I don't know how accurate *Forbes* is, but personally, I would've expected a bigger estate based on his estimated net worth."

"If I remember correctly, he bought this place after Cassandra's death. He wanted to be close to Sophia's school. He didn't want to uproot her."

"Well, then, why didn't he move into Cassandra's house when she died?"

"I don't know. I'm going to guess she didn't have a twenty-eight-million-dollar mansion. This might be smaller than what you would expect, but it's still more posh than I'd expect his ex-wife owned."

"How'd you learn the value of this house?"

"Searched it online." *Of course she did.*

We stop in the kitchen, and I scan the back yard, the wall to the beach, and the narrow fenced in trail leading to the public beachfront.

"I'm going to survey the perimeter. I want to note all the cameras and entry points. When I access the security footage and send it to my team, I want to give them priorities. I'll meet you back in her bedroom?"

"Yes." Her eyebrows draw inward. "Touch nothing that might be evidence. Do you have gloves?"

"Dr. Rolfe." *This woman.*

"Call me Alex."

"Fine. Alex..."

I don't know how to finish with a professional conclusion. I am not inexperienced. She is the one who is inexperienced and acting like she's on an episode of *Sherlock Holmes*, presumably pretending to be her father. The woman is Jack Sullivan's to deal with. I exit the room, intent on my mission.

CHAPTER 5

22 Hours Missing

Alex

A floor-to-ceiling window with a wide-open view of ocean and crisp cerulean sky stops me in the doorway. Thick dark drapes frame the window and butt up against the corners, seamlessly blending into the wall. A thick platinum duvet and matching bespoke custom velvet pillows befitting royalty perch atop an ornate, painted, silver queen-size bed. A gorgeous crystal lamp sits atop a mirrored side table with a small bouquet of pale pink peonies. Thick white carpet covers the floor. The walls shimmer in barely there silver wallpaper. The view of ocean as far as the eye can see is breathtaking. The furniture belongs in a high-end design magazine. The effect stuns. But for a teen?

This must be the guest room.

I step down the hall to the next ten-foot open door. Like the other bedroom, thick drapes border an expansive window with an equally stunning view. Only this room doesn't have a floor-length mirror. Instead of modern, the bed frame with its detailed swirls and curved wood and off-white speckled paint treatment strikes me as French country, similar to the kitchen. Remembering what Wayne said about the rooms they didn't live in being the prior owners' designs, I return to the first room.

Neither of these rooms, gorgeous as they are, feels lived in. Both could function as five-star hotel rooms. The one wall of the Pacific Ocean definitely draws the eye. But there's nothing personal. How would a teenager live in a place like this? Had Sophia been miserable? Should I have been more involved after Cassandra's death? Had it been wrong to take Jack at his word and believe he'd step up?

To my right, there is a closed ten-foot painted white door with a crystal knob. I assume it leads to the bathroom. I slip on rubber gloves and turn the knob. In a room so clean, with vacuum marks lining the plush carpet, the gloves may not be necessary. But I don't know what I'm walking into, and my dad drilled into me at a young age the prudence of gloves when entering a potential crime scene.

The door opens into a narrow room. A built-in desk and shelves occupy one wall from floor to ceiling. Above the desk hangs a bulletin board.

Signs of life.

A UCLA banner pinned from left to right covers the top left quadrant. Photos of Sophia and friends line the bottom and right side. Sophia's blonde curls shine in the photos, as do posed, wide smiles. Based on the eyeliner and lipstick, all the photos are recent with the exception of a line of black-and-white photos from a photobooth. She's noticeably younger in the photo, and she's with one friend making goofy, funny faces. My finger traces the curled edge of photo strip. It's clean, no dust.

A push pin holds two concert tickets to Taylor Swift on the far-right corner. In the center of the desk, a closed silver laptop is charging, and on top of it, neatly placed squarely in the middle of the laptop, rests the latest model iPhone. The phone is not plugged in, and I do not see a charger nearby.

Farther down, a pocket door reveals a stunning walk-in closet. The closet is about the size of my bedroom, and all the clothes hang so beautifully it might be mistaken for a boutique.

Talk about posh.

Each padded hanger is wrapped in silk, and a floor-to-ceiling section holds her shoes neatly displayed on slanted shelves. Beside those shoes are additional shelves with glass fronts. The bottom row holds boots. A small fresh flower arrangement with light pink roses is centered above a marble-topped island. A grand crystal chandelier hangs over the island with sparkling elegance.

Another pocket door leads to the luxurious bathroom I expected to find off the bedroom. The bathroom boasts all white marble with bold streaks, champagne gold hardware, and another elegant crystal chandelier over a gorgeous freestanding soaking tub. A square window offers a view of perfectly manicured bougainvillea vines carefully grown and sculpted to provide privacy. On the bathroom counter, a silver soft-haired paddle brush and a tortoiseshell comb are artistically laid out, along with a silver tray holding a perfume bottle with the words Janie Had A Gun. I lift it and smell. Sweet, fragrant, and subtle. Perfect for a teenager.

Sophia may not have been happy, but she lived a more luxurious life than ninety-nine percent of Americans, or people worldwide, for that matter. Her bedroom, bathroom, and closet are all a dream. A stunning, breathtaking, enviable dream.

Heavy footfalls sound outside the door. I glance around and realize I am trapped in this back room. I am probably as safe as I can possibly be, but I trust my training and rush out into the bedroom.

Ryan Wolfgang fills the doorway, not looking quite so enormous beneath the ten-foot door frame and twelve-foot ceilings. Judging from his expression as he scans Sophia's room, his impression is similar to mine. The room is unspeakably gorgeous.

"Anything?" he asks.

"It's..." I search for the most efficient description. "Pristine. There's no sign of a struggle. Nothing is out of place. I found her computer." I tilt my head, gesturing for him to follow me. "And her phone. It wasn't charging."

"He already mentioned he tracks her with her phone. Leaving it uncharged could have been planned."

"Did you find anything?"

"The grounds are as immaculate as the house. He has a security system, and there should be video."

Ryan reaches for Sophia's phone, and I touch his wrist to stop him. Static electricity shocks us.

"Ow. Sorry," I mutter, shaking my hand to ease the zap. He scowls. "Let me get photos first. Then you can touch."

This might not be a crime scene, but it might be helpful later on to reference exactly how we found everything.

"Although I bet the cleaning service has already been through here. There are vacuum lines on the carpet in her bedroom. If that's the case, this might not be where her phone was when she left it." *Bloody hell.* "We'll have to interview the cleaning service. See if they remember anything suspicious. Those concert tickets. It's only a couple of weeks away. If she ran away, don't you think she'd take her tickets?"

"If she's hiding from her dad? No. He has those seat numbers on his receipt."

"Why would you run away from all this?" My gaze falls on the open view into her luxurious closet and the sparkling crystal chandelier.

Of course, the suite is the stuff of dreams, but it doesn't feel authentic. It's possible that on her phone, or in her laptop, we will discover Sophia's personality and all the different things she loved. Maybe her desktop is a complete disaster, with fifty browser tabs open, a gazillion images, and everything in disarray.

Ryan's jaw flexes. He scans the area, floor to ceiling. Silent. Imposing. Unreadable.

"Ryan? You guys here?" Jack's voice echoes, as do the clicks of his dress shoes on marble. Wordlessly, Ryan exits the bedroom, and I follow him out into the hallway.

"How'd it go down at the station?" Ryan asks Jack.

"The police spent this morning meeting with Sophia's friends and faculty at the school. The chief has conceded this may not be a runaway situation. But he had a ton of questions for me. Wayne may have been right about me needing a lawyer, but..." With a shrug, he loosens his tie. "I think they eventually ran out of questions."

"They suspect your involvement?"

He stares out the window and gives another shrug. "Asked about my whereabouts and who could confirm. It's fine. I'm sure they have a list of steps to take. If clearing me gets them further down the list, so be it. I expect next time they'll come to the house if they have questions instead of requiring me to go to the station. I think my leaving town this morning pissed them off." Jack runs his fingers through his hair. He's lost the sharpness he had earlier. Lines run across his trousers from sitting, and his shirt is no longer neatly tucked in. "Did you find anything?"

"When was the last time the cleaning service came?" I ask.

Jack's gaze falls to me, and a flicker of bewilderment crosses his face. "Sylvia? She and her team come every weekday morning." Jack's brow wrinkles. "Damn." He looks pained. "They cleaned the room." He steps past us and peers inside. "But, seriously, even without them cleaning, Sophia kept it pretty neat. She's not your average messy teenager."

"With daily room service, who would be?" If a daily service came to my house, even my tiny closet might be tidy.

For the briefest of seconds, my gaze meets Ryan's, and the corners of his lips twitch. Those icy eyes unnerve me, but if my interpretation of that slight lip movement is correct, he agrees.

I change my focus to the expansive window to avoid staring. Those light irises draw one in and make it hard to look away. It's easy to see why his friends began calling him Wolf. Not only is it a shortened version of his surname, but his eyes match the namesake, and there's the intimidation factor.

"Alex will photograph the space. I'll bag Sophia's electronics and courier them back to my team. Do you have her passwords?"

"Yes. It's a rule we have. I have access to all of her accounts."

"Write them all down. My team will split them up and go through everything. Your security cameras. Where does the footage go?"

"I hire a company. It's not monitored, only recorded. If an alarm goes off, police come. Basic level of service."

"Give me their info. Our guys will go through the footage." Ryan scratches his head. "The police haven't asked?"

"No. Like I told you, they expect her to turn up. Now that they've spent a day talking to her friends and, well, my net worth registered, the chief is taking it more seriously. That first night, the officer on duty told me thousands are reported missing each year in San Diego, and the vast majority turn up within the first twenty-four hours." He glances at his watch. "We're approaching twenty-four hours. The shift today seemed to take it more seriously."

"Are they now considering it an abduction?" I ask.

"No. But they didn't seem as confident that she just snuck out for a night of fun."

"Has she snuck out before?" I ask.

"She's not that kind of kid. She'd never do that." He rubs his eyes. "I mean, I don't believe she would. She fought me hard on the curfew." He sighs. "Hell, maybe."

"What was her curfew?"

"Ten. She was only fifteen." Jack raises his hands, palms out in a classic defensive gesture. "I mean, if she went to the movies or something, she could stay out later. But if she was just on the beach, why did she need—" Jack stops himself. He sucks on his bottom lip, deep in thought.

Cassandra ran a tight ship, too. I want to tell him not to be hard on himself, that whatever's going on here isn't his fault, but I refrain. There are missing puzzle pieces.

"You have your phone on you, right?" Ryan asks. "If someone needs to reach you, the call would get through?"

"It's right here." Jack pats his dress coat pocket. "You're thinking ransom? Right?"

"It's a distinct possibility. Do you have a landline?"

"No. Telemarketers were the only people who called it. Disconnected it about a year ago. But I assume if they can get my daughter, they can get my cell number."

"They'll find a way to reach you. Be sure to check your email."

"Do you think I should have hired personal security?" Jack pivots, peering up at Ryan. The two men eye each other. Jack is a good four inches shorter than Ryan, barely taller than I am. But both men intimidate with stern expressions and take-no-shit attitudes.

"I never said that," Ryan responds after a beat of silence.

"You own a security firm. You obviously believe in it. I just... I wanted her to live a normal life. That's what Cassandra wanted." I glance around this majestic home, taking in Jack's version of normal.

The low hum of a phone vibrating intrudes. Jack's eyes widen as he lifts a cell phone out of his pocket. Redness and puffy circles hint at his lack of sleep. Jack holds the screen out for an inquisitive Ryan to see.

"It's work. I've got to take this. I'll be in the office. It's on the other end of the house."

He steps away, leaving Ryan and me at the entrance to Sophia's bedroom. After taking photos of her desktop, I hand Sophia's electronics to Ryan.

"Your staff knows not to do anything that will destroy the history, right?"

"Yes." His permafrown remains rooted in place.

I'm not here to make friends. Jack asked me to help, and that's what I will do to the best of my ability. I focus on her desk, starting with the file drawer. I search for magazine articles, jotted notes in the margins of books, teacher feedback on assignments, anything that might provide insight into her state of mind.

A warmth spans my back, from the base of my neck down my spine. I suck in my breath and brave a glance upward, up the trousers to the broad, expansive chest of the oversized wolf man. Those ice-blue eyes watch. Scrutinize. But he doesn't offer a critique. My throat tightens. As he steps over my calves, his leg brushes my ass. A fission of energy climbs my spine. The file folder I'm holding bends as my fingers curl.

His phone vibrates. He checks it. "I have to head into town. I'll courier the electronics to my team. I should be back within two hours."

The click of shoes on marble diminishes, and I breathe more easily. I zero in on a red scrawled A- and a scribble from a teacher that reads, "Nicely done. Interesting tie-in to extramarital affairs." It's a term paper on *The Scarlet Letter*. Sophia texted me about this book. She'd been shocked how they treated women. I continue searching through a sea of stellar grades. With every new folder, I give myself a moment with Sophia's smiles pinned to her bulletin board.

As a teenager, she wears her hair longer. But when younger, her hair barely reached her shoulders, and I remember struggling with those curls.

"It doesn't matter how it looks," Sophia told me, perched between my legs on the bed. "I like how it feels."

"Ah, might you fancy a head scratch?"

"A what?" She'd giggled and grinned, and the metal on her braces gleamed. She'd gotten them at the youthful age of ten, or at least, that was what I deemed young.

She closed her eyes and eventually spread out on the bed, her head in my lap, as my nails scratched her scalp. The noises she made had me laughing.

"You sound like a purring kitten."

"Just keep doing it, please."

Cassie returned from her dinner with a friend to find her daughter passed out with my thigh as her pillow. She'd lifted her up and carried her away like a princess, settling her into bed with a stuffed bunny and a silk blankie. Yes, she had braces, but she clung to the things she loved.

CHAPTER 6

25 Hours Missing

Ryan

The woman sitting behind the reception desk peers up at me over the rim of her spectacles.

"I'm here to see Indigo Wolfgang."

She pauses, glances down at her desk, then swallows. "You know, visiting hours are almost over." The clock on the wall supports her statement. "You would only have ten minutes."

"I didn't expect to be in the area. Can I see her?"

"She's probably already on her way to be seated for dinner. If we call for her now, we risk getting her off schedule."

The clock behind the woman's head tells me we are now down to eight minutes.

"Can I see Dr. Ortega?"

"Let me see if she's in. She may have left for the day."

"She texted me. Said she'd like to speak to me."

"And your name is?"

"Ryan Wolfgang."

She adjusts her spectacles and reads something on the desk. "You are on the list," she says, more to herself than to me.

She picks up a phone and dials. Four clicks on the nineties-style keypad tell me she dialed an internal number.

"Yes, Dr. Ortega?" The woman eyes me as she speaks. "Mr. Ryan Wolfgang is here to see you. He's on Indigo Wolfgang's list. I mentioned you might be going home for the day." There's a beat of silence. "Yes. Thank you."

She sets the handset down with a click. "She'll be down in a moment. You can sit right over there while you wait."

I choose to stand by a window that overlooks a lush lawn. Paths laid in brick crisscross the sloping land. From this location, you can't see the fenced perimeter. This is Indigo's third facility. Twice I thought we were through the worst of it. Twice I believed she conquered her demons.

Heels on tile announce a person approaching. I first met Dr. Ortega when my sister agreed to try another treatment facility.

Experimentation with meth had been her first step past alcohol. Her teeth and skin bear that tale. Apparently, my financial support during her college years had been too generous. She sought higher-grade drugs. Cocaine, then heroin.

I no longer give my sister money. I refuse to waste time thinking about what she did to earn the funds for this latest spiral.

She's suffering. A month ago, she attempted suicide. I believe there is more at play than a drug addiction. But I don't want to feed my theory into a psychiatrist's head. I want the diagnosis to be true and accurate.

"Mr. Wolfgang."

Dr. Ortega tucks both hands into her pockets. Her purple silk blouse folds neatly into brown, pleated slacks. Her hair is up in a bun. She's about five foot four, and I estimate she is in her fifties. She's experienced and well regarded by the medical community.

"Thank you for meeting with me. How is she doing?"

"You mean, since you visited a few days ago?" Red lipstick stains her front tooth.

"Yes."

"You can call and check on her if you like." I nod. We're in a public lobby. Due to privacy laws, she won't share much where we can be overheard. I want answers. I want solutions. But she texted me. "When you visit with your sister, how does it go?"

She looks at me in a way that says she knows exactly how it goes. And for the first time, I wonder if my sister and I are observed during visitation periods. At first, she couldn't have visitors. She earned the privilege, but she doesn't want me to visit. She's twelve years younger, and I barely know her. But she's my blood relative, and our mother may have turned her back on Indie, but I don't work that way.

"Are your visits...emotional?"

"No." Outside, a man in scrubs approaches. His badge swings from his neck. "She doesn't say much."

"She may not be ready yet." Dr. Ortega attempts kindness. "There are no family illnesses documented on her health history. Is that accurate?"

"Nothing diagnosed on our mother's side." Suspected, but not diagnosed. I mentioned this during intake. "I don't know anything about her father's side. We have different fathers."

"That's all I wanted to ask you." She looks apologetic. "I didn't mean for you to come straight out here. I meant for us to speak on the phone. I'm sorry if I alarmed you."

The doors open, and the orderly speaks to Dr. Ortega. She offers a professional smile that doesn't reach her eyes and lets me know she needs to go, but if I would like to schedule an appointment with her, I am welcome to do so.

I hate this. I hate everything about this situation. I hate how my sister stares at me with her sad brown eyes. But most of all, I hate this helpless sensation. There is no action plan to follow. This facility, right here, is all I can do. And rehab failed twice before.

I open the Uber app to request a car. The car is two minutes away. I scan my texts as I stroll to the gated entrance.

Erik: Call me.

A flash of hope my techie partner at Arrow found something effectively pulls me up like a safety line. I can't do anything more for my sister. But I can find my friend's daughter.

Erik, the head of our IT team, spearheads the surveillance team. He lives up north in Napa. Our team lives in locations all over the world. Having a workforce in time zones around the globe gives us an advantage when we need work completed around the clock.

"Hey," he says. Instrumental jazz music plays in the background.

"What's up?"

"Wanted you to know we've searched her cloud-based messages and emails. Didn't find anything about running away. For that matter, she sounds like a well-adjusted, happy kid. When we receive her hardware, we'll see if she uses an app called SnapChat."

"Erik. I'm not ancient. I've heard of it."

"Then you know we won't have access to those conversations. So far, we've got nothing."

"Anything on the security cams?"

"The security company hasn't given us access yet."

"Seriously?"

"He's using a crap company with hourly IT. Said we'd have access tomorrow." Unbelievable. "Given the situation, we hacked in and are accessing the feeds that are stored on the server."

Our call ends as I climb into the back seat of a gray Chevy Impala. I lean back and consider the layout of the house. If someone wanted to break in, the public beach would be the easiest access. That would be the same if a person wanted to sneak out. A visual of the side path comes to mind. The gate with a latch. And past the gate, the racks of surfboards and paddleboards, then a higher gate with a lock on the inside.

Surfboards and paddleboards. Does his daughter surf? Could she have gone out on her own to surf after dinner?

CHAPTER 7

26 Hours Missing

Alex

The flower-patterned file folder requires a tug to loosen it from the back. It bulges open, the contents stouter than the school papers in the neatly labeled folders, titled by subject. Printed photos overfill the folder.

A teen having printed photos qualifies as an enigma. I can't remember the last time I printed my photos. I think I've only done it from sites that allow me to create my own holiday cards or for frames. I sit back against the wall, legs out before me.

The first photo is of Cassandra holding a baby bundled in a pink blanket. Cassandra's hair is uncharacteristically a mess, and her skin is pale, but she's wearing a tender smile. An expression of wonder brightens her face. The second photo is of Cassandra and Jack pushing a red stroller down a sidewalk. They both look so young. His hand overlaps hers on the stroller, but they are smiling for the camera. And then it hits me. I think my dad took that photo. I remember that day.

I thumb through the remaining photos. All photos from Sophia's childhood. A happy childhood, judging from her smiles and sparkling eyes. My bet is these are photos she inherited from her mother. Sophia's generation doesn't print out photos, but I bet Cassandra, as a new mom, did.

The last photograph is of Cassandra and Jack. They still look young. Jack's dark hair is lower on his forehead, and Cassandra's is pulled back, and they are holding champagne glasses. Cassandra wears a sparkly strapless number, and Jack is in a tuxedo. The background is blurry. They look happy, but then again, they are posing for the camera. That's the trouble with photographs. The truth a photograph presents is one-dimensional. And we humans are multi-faceted.

Footfalls announce the arrival of someone. It's late. My ass tingles from being pressed against the hard marble floor. I move to get up, rolling forward onto my knees and hands. Two large black shoes come into view. My gaze travels upward. Light blue eyes stare down at me. Ryan's suntanned hands spread across his hips, and his head slightly tilts. Based on his posture, I'd say he's unsure what I'm doing, and he's ready to pass judgment.

"Been going through folders and journals." I scramble up off the ground. "What time is it?" I ask the question as I check my wrist. *Jeez, I've been at it for hours.*

"Find anything?"

"Nothing to help us."

A sense of defeat suffocates me. Absolutely nothing is out of order. If she ran away, I would expect to find something. A sad drawing. Dark sketches. Hints in her journal. But I read all her journal entries. They are essentially a recording of the weather.

It's as if someone told her she had to journal, and she wanted to be obedient, but didn't have the time or a desire to keep a journal going, so she kept pages and pages of entries along the lines of, "Chilly this evening. Clear day. Tomorrow there is a chance of rain." Years of weather entries with the occasional, "Tomorrow Christmas vacation begins. Can't wait." She didn't journal or record anything on the day Cassandra died or for the month after. Then her weather mentions resumed.

"What about you? Anything?" What has Ryan been doing? Jack returned and asked, so I know he wasn't with Jack.

"Nothing so far. My team is still going through her electronics and social media. And security footage."

Security footage. A twinge of hope flickers. "We should be able to see her leave."

"If she went out the front door or the side door. He doesn't have a camera on the back deck or over any of the sliding glass back doors." His expression gives away exactly what he thinks about that. And any hope I have extinguishes. If she left on her own, she'd probably go out the back door. "Do you know if she surfed?"

"She did. Cassandra posted photos of her holding a surfboard. Years ago. I don't know if she still surfs."

His lips bunch. He doesn't seem to like this information. Awareness dawns.

"Do you think she might've gone surfing? At night?"

"If she did, her body would have probably washed ashore today. Go on and go to sleep. I'm going to find Jack, and then I'll be up. In the morning, we can visit the school."

"It's not looking like she ran away." I say it softly. It's not a question. It's the reality. I brush aside the surfing theory.

"No, it's not," he agrees, but he doesn't stand around talking about it. He leaves, presumably to find Jack.

The white shell of the moon casts little light over the ocean in the early hours of the morning. Darkness reigns, with hints of orange awakenings flirting to the east. Remnant stars scatter across the brightening sky.

Ryan's strong arms slice into the water seamlessly. His back arches as he approaches the wall, flips, and kicks off the wall in one fluid movement. He pushes off with enough force to shoot his massive form almost halfway back across the rectangular pool. His muscular back and shoulders remind me of an Olympic swimmer. Power, grace, and speed intertwine. He wears goggles but no swim cap. It isn't hard to imagine him tackling the wild ocean, cutting effortlessly through waves.

I snuggle into the white fluffy robe I found hanging in my closet and breathe in my coffee. I'd planned on swimming laps myself and had been surprised to find the pool already occupied. Room exists for me to swim laps, too, but his speed and power intimidate me. I am a good swimmer, but I'd be lost in his wake. If I were a good friend to Sabrina, I would video him. She's the one with a military and federal agent fetish.

When I woke, I discovered coffee brewing and carried a steaming mug out to the pool. I like to drink a cup before exercise. I'd wondered if he returned to his room last night, and then I found him.

Off in the distance, the waves crash, seagulls squawk, and a lone early morning walker passes on the sand close to the ocean's edge. What a life the Sullivans lead. The beauty and luxury are mind-boggling. How many families possess an enormous swimming pool overlooking the Pacific Ocean in one of the wealthiest gated San Diego neighborhoods? Few. The real estate listing for this address used the word *mansion* in the description. It's easy to imagine Sophia inviting friends over for pool parties or to simply hang out in decadence.

Sure, the pristine nature of her bedroom speaks to potential issues. Maybe her life wasn't full. Maybe Sullivan is an overbearing single parent without Cassie to soften his expectations. Or, hell, maybe that's just what a kid's room looks like with cleaning service five days a week. Regardless, the nagging in the pit of my stomach warns something isn't right. My father's deep voice resonates. *You need to look beyond the obvious.*

"You're up early." Ryan's deep timbre shakes me out of my thoughts.

"Early riser." I hold the mug up in a morning salute. "Thanks for making coffee."

"Is it even five yet?"

"Just turned. Guess you're an early riser, too?"

"Military. What's your excuse?" Ryan rips off his goggles and wipes water droplets off his forehead. He hoists himself up, over the edge.

The predawn light highlights chiseled biceps and solid eight-pack abs. *Oh, my.* I sip my coffee to thwart drool. Lordy, the man has abs of steel, and with water dripping down carved muscles... I avert my gaze as he grabs a towel off a nearby chair and wraps it around his waist.

I have no business gawking. This exact reason is why business experts say colleagues shouldn't be around each other in swimsuits. But, bloody hell, if I could sneak a photo, Sabrina would love me forever.

"Did you not sleep well?" He bumps the end of my lounge chair with his leg.

It takes a few seconds for my brain to kick into gear. *Why am I an early riser?*

"No, um. It's just the way I am. Especially in a new place. And when I have a lot on my mind."

"Well, come on back. I'll fix you an omelet and we can do a situation review."

"Unless I've missed something, we're in the same place we were yesterday. Nowhere." I rise and follow Ryan back to the house.

"The surveillance night shift worked last night," he says.

"Did they find anything?"

"As of when I woke, no. Let's go back and see."

"You left your phone in your room?"

"It's not like I'd hear it when I'm swimming."

Obviously.

The sliding glass doors open automatically on our approach.

"There's an unlocked gate from a public beach to enter this property. The sliding doors open automatically when approached from the ground level. There are a million ways you could approach the house under the eaves of the deck and not be picked up by one of the handful of security cameras hanging from the third floor of the house. The only way someone might have difficulty breaking in is if they decided to go through the front door."

"You don't sound impressed with his system."

"I'm not. After we find her, he needs an overhaul."

"You think we'll find her?"

"We will." He brokers no option for failure.

For the school year she lived with us, Cassandra had been like a sister to me. I'd looked up to her, shared my secrets with her. I keep thinking of Cassandra and imagining how she would react now and what she would want us to do. I imagine her combing the beaches, standing in front of a podium talking to the press, crying, pleading for her daughter to come home. But of course, if she were alive, this would've never happened. Last night, Jack came across like a fragile dam on the brink of collapse. Not too different from the man I remember at Cassandra's funeral. Did he never recover from Cassandra's death?

Back in our guest quarters, Ryan opens the refrigerator, and I peer over his shoulder.

"You think he keeps food in this refrigerator all the time?" This guest refrigerator is better stocked than my refrigerator at home.

"My guess is his so-called cleaning service is also a property management service, and they keep everything stocked. I doubt Sullivan has any idea we have coffee, much less food. He pays someone to think about those things."

"Like a plush robe in the guest closet?"

"Exactly. I didn't bring swim trunks. There were a variety of options in the drawers."

"Same." I untie the white sash, and the robe falls open, exposing a black one-piece designed for lap swimming. There had been three full drawers of brand-new suits with brand tags attached, no prices, and a cute card read, "Be our guest, we insist. The pool and ocean await."

The bathing suit wasn't sexy, but the generous cut would have been fantastic for swimming laps. The shocking bit had been that Jack stocked a size for long torsos. When I saw that, my first thought had been that Cassandra had thought of me when she stocked her guest drawers, but that was a silly, egocentric thought. Cassandra never lived here.

"What are you thinking about cooking?"

Ryan's shoulder turns into mine. My thick robe is between us, but heat somehow permeates. I lift my chin. Icy blue eyes gaze down, but not into my eyes. His gaze falls lower, and his chest lifts as his lungs pull in air. I follow his gaze and blink in embarrassment at the sight of my perfectly outlined nipples through the smooth Lycra.

I step back, cross my legs, and tumble backward. My hand instinctively pushes back to catch my fall, but a steadfast arm swoops in. I blink again, pressed against his bare, brick-like chest. He smells of chlorine, and I lean closer as if that's an attractive smell. Never before have I cared for it, but on his skin, I quite fancy the stiff, clean aroma.

An undercurrent flows between us, filling the mere inches between our chests and sucking the oxygen from my brain. I feel positively dainty next to his broad shoulders and height. My last boyfriend had been one inch shorter and about my width. He made me feel Amazonian.

Ryan's close. An inch of space separates us. He's close enough the tip of my nose could graze his jaw. And he's only holding me because I am a klutz who tripped over her own oversized foot. I push away with so much force I can't halt the forward movement and bang my knee into a cabinet.

"Fuck."

"Jack mentioned you're clumsy." His gaze scans my body, and one knee reflexively bends over the other.

"He did what?" I mean, yes, I'm likely to have a bruise somewhere on my body, often on my thighs from the corners of tables, but why would Jack ever comment on it?

"I asked him if there was something going on between the two of you."

My mouth gapes open. "Why?"

"Situation exploration."

I wrap the robe over my torso as I piece together what he's saying. "What does that mean?"

"Wanted to understand the lay of the land." Those ice blues meet me head on. In other words, he wanted to know why Jack has me here. But…

"He said I'm clumsy?" *Ouch.*

"He said he'd known you since you were ten. Something about you haven't changed much since then. I guess you were tall at ten?"

Compared to others my age, I've always been gangly, but... "And he said I'm a klutz?"

A low chuckle rumbles from his massive, sculpted chest. The funny bits warranting a chuckle elude me.

"I'm going to get a shower," I tell him as I rush to my bedroom haven. I need distance. "Won't be long."

"I'll shower, too."

"Oh, should I wait?" I pause in the doorway. "Think there's enough hot?"

"Water? Don't worry. I'll be taking a cold one."

CHAPTER 8

40 Hours Missing

Alex

When I exit my bedroom, one glance at Ryan confirms he likes cold, short showers. A stern expression joins those icy blue eyes to convey a high degree of annoyance. One lone plate sits on the table. He has presumably showered, dressed, cooked breakfast, and finished eating. For the second time in under twenty-four hours, I have forced him to wait.

"It might be cold now." He returns his attention to his laptop.

I pick up the plate and down half the omelet in the course of four steps to the counter. I dump the rest into the trash, rinse the plate, set it in the dishwasher, and spin around while wiping my palms on my thighs.

"I'm ready," I announce.

"Did you not eat?" His brow scrunches in bewilderment. Or

the flex of his jaw combined with the wrinkled brow could portray an intensified annoyance. Ryan is rather difficult to read. My father trained me to pay attention to body language. Body language sometimes tells us more than words. Latency and pitch in tone of voice can also reveal so much. It's a fascinating science, really, body language.

"I ate. It was good."

"In under thirty seconds?" He's become quite growly since showering.

"I'm a fast eater. You looked ready. I didn't want to make you wait." I cross my arms and glare at the man. *You looked like you were going to scold me. What the hell else should I have done?*

He says something under his breath that I can't quite hear, but the tone further confirms my annoyance theory. He pauses at the doorway, waiting for me to pass through first. His annoyance raises my annoyance level, and by the time we've descended the stairs, my arms are crossed and I need to look anywhere else but at him.

When we arrive in the main house kitchen, Jack's back is to us as he looks out over the pool and ocean. He gives no sign he hears us approach. His arms are crossed, and his shoulders curve inward. All my Ryan annoyance dissipates instantly.

Jack looks broken. More so than yesterday. He seems to have shrunk since we met at Arrow's office two days ago. The growth along his unshaven face has filled in further with tones of salt and pepper. The added dash of gray ages him, as do the deep wrinkles around his bloodshot eyes.

"Morning," I say softly. "Do you need some coffee?"

Jack slowly turns. There is a coffee mug in his hand.

"I have no idea how many paddleboards or surfboards we own. I went through receipts..." He trails off.

"It's okay," Ryan says. "I mentioned the possibility to Jeff Hernandez at the SDPD. He said they'd alert the Coast Guard and keep an eye out for any unclaimed boards that float ashore. Sounded like they'd already considered the possibility. It's a routine consideration for them."

"Does she still surf?" I ask Jack.

"Sometimes. There's a sandbar not too far out. You have to hike to find the better waves on this stretch of beach. She prefers paddleboarding. But I've never known her to do it at night."

Ryan's large thumbs work his phone. Texting someone.

"We're going to visit the school this morning," I say, but as I say it, I suspect Ryan informed Jack of our plans last night when they discussed the surfboards and, apparently, me.

"Principal Estevez said you can meet with students. A faculty member needs to be present. He gathered parental permissions from everyone already. Except for one kid. Zane Oglethorpe. His parents want a lawyer present."

"A lawyer? Doesn't that—"

"Before you go and think that means something...his dad is a congressman." Jack waves his hand dismissively. "Oglethorpe's crazy risk averse with an election coming up. He's running for state senator. It's the dad, not the kid." Jack pinches the bridge of his nose and closes his eyes.

A faint humming sound comes from the kitchen island. Jack charges to the counter and lifts a cell phone. He glances at the screen, and the life in his eyes dims.

"Hey. No news." Jack holds the phone away from his mouth and addresses us. "It's my brother. I'm going to take it in my office. If Wayne comes over, will you send him in? He's taking over for me this week but needs me to sign some things."

Jack doesn't wait for a response as he heads out of the kitchen and to the room he spends the most time in. My gaze follows him, and I remember those photographs. So much has changed since those youthful, happy photographs. Nowhere in the house do they have candids. His daughter had those happy times filed away. Is it possible it hurt to look at pictures of the past?

"Let's go to the school. Maybe we can talk to some of her friends before classes start." Ryan's command brings me back to the kitchen.

The click of our shoes echoes through the tall entry. Had Sophia been lonely? Had she been miserable in this formal, multi-million-dollar estate?

In the car on the way to the school, my left toe taps mindlessly against the floorboard of the automobile Jack loaned us. Neither Ryan nor I turn on the radio. Somber emotions cloud the horizon like a rolling, dense fog.

Sophia's been missing for two days, and it's as if she vanished. We have no good theories. Even if she got fed up with her father, I can't imagine her staying away this long. The Sophia I knew would want to let him know she was okay. At Cassandra's funeral, they may have been technically strangers, but there was still love between the two of them. He's her father. She has to love him.

Look beyond the obvious.

Outside the car, the clear blue sky and palm trees conflict with the swirl of confusion and worry in my head. It's surreal. The manicured lawns feel like utopia, and yet a fifteen-year-old girl is missing. This afternoon we will cross the forty-eight-hour threshold.

"If you would like to turn the radio on, please do," Ryan says.

I don't want to mess with the radio. What I want is a plan. When Jack asked me to help, I truly believed it had to be a misunderstanding, a teenage act of defiance, and we'd find her. And I said I would help. Sure, I want to be a criminal profiler. But at this stage, there is no criminal to profile. Unless we determine she has been abducted. And if that's the case, where would I start?

A stucco sign with a tiled roof and golden letters spelling

Palisades Day School comes into view. The road curves past the entrance sign, and small directional plaques lead us to the admissions building where Jack instructed us to go.

"What do you think is the best way to tackle this? We have about fifty kids to interview."

"Unless one of them can't look us in the eye or seems unusually emotional, I expect it's going to go pretty quickly. If the teachers let us, you can video our interviews. The Arrow team can go through and compare with the police interviews. See if there's any variance. But I'm not hopeful."

"That's your opinion from the groups?" Arrow has been monitoring the Searching for Sophia group chat and the private Facebook group a classmate created.

"Yes." Ryan taps his index finger against the steering wheel. The beat of his finger oddly matches the tap of my toe.

"You think this is a waste of time?"

He side-eyes me. His sunglasses hide his irises, but the tilt of his head conveys condescension. "Waste? No. It's a necessary step. Local police have already met with her close friends and teachers. But, given we have no clues, it's worth backtracking. If one of these kids knows anything, maybe one of them will come forward."

It is possible. If a student knows something, it's conceivable one day in, it didn't seem real. Maybe with two days missing, concern will override any fear.

Look beyond the obvious.

These kids could lead us down a very different path. This day and age, dangers can look seemingly benign in emails or chat groups.

"If we don't learn anything at the school, what do you see as our next steps?" This fear gnaws at me. I fear an absence of next steps.

"We accessed street-cam footage. Our team will review the

footage today. No matter how she left the house, at some point she had to come onto the streets."

"Unless she went paddleboarding."

"I'm focusing on the angles we can do something about. On the off chance she's somewhere around the beach, I've got a couple of men searching the area. Yes, volunteers already did it, but I hired some folks who specialize in tracking."

"You don't sound optimistic." Or maybe he does. His voice projection is business normal. Maybe I am projecting.

"No?" His angular jaw flexes while his eyes remain focused on the road.

I shake my head.

"Are you optimistic?" he asks.

I let out my frustration in a sigh. "No. I was really hoping for a crime scene. A struggle. Or fingerprints."

"Did you find any prints at all?"

I dusted for prints yesterday afternoon while he was out and about.

"A few of her prints. The cleaning service is thorough. I mean, think about it. There weren't even footprints on her carpet."

Blue skies fill the horizon. Rain would better fit my mood. That is one thing my dad has going for him. He is bound to have some dreary weather when working on his cases.

"When do you think you'll head back to Santa Barbara?" Ryan asks as he pulls into a parking space.

"This afternoon. Unless we come up with another lead. I mean...unless you see a reason to stay. I'm hoping your IT team comes up with something."

"You and me both."

When Ryan exits the car, he releases a high-pitched whistle.

"It looks like a TV set," I say in agreement. The pristine campus, perfectly manicured lawn and flowerbeds, and wood-carved directional signs all speak to an abundance of money. "This reminds me of UCSB."

"Definitely well-funded," Ryan comments under his breath. Three students in plaid skirts and starched white blouses pass by on a distant sidewalk.

"Uniform school." I catalog the details. Maybe Sophia hated uniforms? But no, I push the random idea out of my mind.

Grasping at straws won't help. The Sophia I remembered didn't have an issue with uniforms and wouldn't have run away because of a mundane issue. She had a good head on her shoulders.

The woman behind the front desk greets us with a pleasant, glossy smile.

"Hello. Welcome to Palisades Day. How can I help you?"

"Principal Esteban is expecting us. We're here to talk to students about Sophia Sullivan." The woman's smile falls. Her palm flattens against her chest, and an eye-catching diamond sparkles on her ring finger.

"That poor girl. Mr. Sullivan must be beside himself. Yes, come right this way. We have a room set up for you. I hope one of these students can help you."

"We'll also meet with any faculty who knew her well or might have some information."

"We discussed it in the staff meeting after school yesterday. No one...I mean, of course our faculty will talk to you. But at least as of yesterday afternoon, no one could think of anything useful to share. She was a happy student. She landed a lead role in the spring production. For her age, it was a big deal. Sophie in *Mamma Mia*." She leads us into a conference room with an oblong table and six chairs. Before leaving with a promise to call the principal and bring students over, she adds, "I hope you find her soon. She's a great kid."

Sophia's bestie, a girl I've heard lots about over the last couple of years, Lauren Hill, is the first student we meet. She's in the school uniform. Her brown, shoulder-length hair is pulled back in a barrette on one side, and she sports platform Converse shoes. She gets teary when we talk to her. Her body posture is open, and her hands remain away from her mouth and ears during our conversation. Her cheeks flush when I ask about a love interest, but she looks me straight in the eye. If anything, she's flustered I am asking about a boy. She leans forward when she swears that this is not something Sophia would plan. The pitch of her tone rises. She's sincere, and she's frustrated because she believes we're off course.

Zane Oglethorpe is the fourth student we meet. Like the others, he is in uniform. His white button-down shirt is half untucked, the collar is unbuttoned, and his tie is loosened at the neck. He has a bit of a bad-boy vibe, partially due to the unkempt uniform, and partially due to the brown hair that flops over his forehead. Every minute or so he jerks his head to toss the hair off his forehead, but it falls right back in place.

Zane's lawyer extends his hand and introduces both of them. He's a short, friendly looking man in a suit. He's the first to sit, and it occurs to me someone probably coached him to encourage everyone to sit when possible to level the perceived playing field.

"We're sorry to hear about Miss Sullivan. My client is willing to answer any questions you may have."

The lawyer positions himself beside Zane and looks him in the eye. There's a silent communication passed between the two, and I get the distinct impression he is not authorized to answer any question. I exchange a glance with Ryan, and he nods for me to proceed.

"We're really gathering her friends to ask if you might have any idea where she might—"

"No. None." Zane blurts his answer. His hands remain by his side.

"Have you seen her talking—"

"No."

"Are you good friends with her?" I didn't ask the others that, but he's the first student to interrupt me, and the attitude puzzles me.

He shrugs. His gaze travels upward to the ceiling. "We're friends."

"Are you in any of her group chats?" We obviously know the answer, but now I want to know how honest he will be.

"Yes."

"Do you ever talk to her privately? Or do you only text?"

"Why?" His lawyer's hand brushes his wrist, and Zane exhales. "We mostly text. Sometimes we meet up on the beach."

"Oh?"

"I live a few houses down." His shoulders lift again. "Sure. A lot of us hang out on the beach." Another exhale. His gaze falls. "But she's not there. I volunteered in the search group." His gaze lifts. "She didn't run away. I know everybody thinks that, but that's not what happened. You need to fucking do your job and find her."

"Zane," his lawyer admonishes.

At the conclusion of our meeting, Zane stands and looks directly into my eyes. "You don't need to waste time here. No one here has any leads for you. She's a good person. And she would never do this to her father or her friends. Not willingly."

Unfortunately, over the next two hours, we hear more of the same from faculty and students alike. There are no issues, no warning signs, no suspicions. A few teachers suspected she missed her mother, but she had adjusted and continued to thrive both academically and socially. Every single student and faculty member passes my body language lie detector analysis with flying colors.

Body language is a science, but it's not infallible in a five-minute interview. Still, I'd expect some hint of nervousness or worry from a culpable person. Especially a teenage student.

As we exit the front doors to the school, Ryan grumbles, "That was useless."

As we cross the lawn, we pass a gaggle of students giggling. None of the students are ones we interviewed. I doubt they know why we are here. One uniformed male student points in our direction, and I could swear he says the word *amazon*. Are the kids here mean? Was Sophia bullied?

Ryan opens the passenger door for me and hands me his phone.

"Erik texted over a compilation of some of her posts and videos that hint at melancholy. I just glanced through them, and they look like a teenager doing a pouty face to me. But check them out. You might have a different perspective."

I scroll through the photos as Ryan starts the car.

"Yeah, these are all fashion-model poses." In some pics she pushes glossy lips out in an exaggerated pout, but combined with the dramatic eyeshadow, it looks like she'd been goofing around taking selfies. "I agree with you. These are meaningless. Especially when mixed in with all her happy posts."

"Did you check over her social media?"

"Last night. I've followed her on Facebook, Instagram, and TikTok since around the time of the funeral. I'm not on SnapChat. She and I communicate on WhatsApp. She mainly uses Instagram. From what I can tell, she doesn't post a lot of TikTok videos, but that doesn't mean she's not on it a lot."

"Your degrees are in criminal justice, right?" Ryan flicks his blinker.

Click. Click.

"I have a PhD and a master's in criminology. My undergraduate work was in biology and psychology." The change in the direction of our conversation has me sitting up straighter.

"Okay, so, did you come across any studies on the reasons kids run away?"

Oh. That's where he's going.

"Well, the number one reason is abuse. There's no reason, from what I've seen, to suspect that here. Or love. What a young girl might mistake for love. But again, all her friends consistently told us she's not dating anyone. Alcohol or drug abuse. There's no evidence that supports any of those possibilities. A lot of the top reasons don't fit here at all. Death in the family, but it's been three years. New child in the family. Doesn't fit. Jack said he's not dating anyone. Feeling unloved. It's possible. The absence of personality in her bedroom feels cold to me. But I didn't get the sense from any of her friends that she's unhappy. Did you?"

Ryan focuses on the road, and I interpret his stoic silence to equal agreement.

"I mean, we haven't said it, but human trafficking is a growing issue. What if she was out on that beach for an evening stroll and someone grabbed her, not having any idea who she is?"

"I'm thinking that's more likely. We haven't come across any reason for her to leave of her own volition. And we don't have a ransom yet."

It's insanely frustrating. We have no leads.

"Do you think we'll head back this afternoon?" I ask.

"You need to get back, don't you?"

"If we're needed here, I can stay." I watch as a woman leads a tiny white fluffy dog down the sidewalk, and I think of Trace. I shoot off a text to my neighbor, Jenny, checking in.

"I hate to say it, but I think we're running out of things to do, at least until surveillance picks something up. We can fly back this afternoon. It's not a big deal to return tomorrow if needed." Ryan glances at me, and I nod. "Would you be interested in getting dinner tonight?"

His question throws me for a whirl. His body position driving the car gives nothing away. *Dinner?*

"We can talk about the case," he amends.

"Over dinner?" I need the clarification.

He nods. *Holy shit.*

Dinner. But it's not a date. It's to discuss work. Sabrina pipes up in my inner ear. "Don't be a dork. You have no business to discuss. It's a date."

Dear old Dad would frown on the idea. He believes romantic relationships could interfere with police work and case studies. In one of his criminology classes, he dedicates an entire class to all the reasons fraternization between colleagues during a case should not be allowed. The lecture logic follows chain of command issues and future career risk if a relationship goes bad.

But I am not a police officer. Working with Arrow represents a career opportunity, and if things don't go well, then I might be sabotaging that career opportunity.

But I'm getting way ahead of myself. He didn't specifically ask me on a date. We're not going to give up on Sophia. We will brainstorm leads. We can't give up after forty-eight hours. Brainstorming theories and possibilities while eating is quite logical. My dad had colleagues over for pizza or shepherd's pie more than once over the years while working a case.

Half the time, Ryan doesn't seem to have a high opinion of me. But then he did take the odd cold shower. Maybe he is asking me out. Which is fine. But is it fine? On the off chance he is asking me out, I should set the ground rules.

"For clarity, while we are working on this case, it...we..."

He sucks on the side of his lower lip, looking borderline amused. "Are you stuttering?" The man smiles. Or smirks. Yes, he smirks. And it irks me. The man is attractive, but he's not nice. Attractive-but-asshole is not my type. My type is academic sweetheart. A goof with a giant heart. I don't want to go on a date with this man.

"Mr. Wolfgang, it's hard enough to earn respect in this industry as a woman. Please don't tease me. Treat me as a colleague." My response would make Dad proud.

"Absolutely. I hope I didn't step out of line. Forget I said anything." His stoic expression returns. An awkward silence fills the space between us for the rest of the short car ride.

"How did it go?" Jack stands in the garage as we exit the vehicle.

Ryan grunts. The near growl tells Jack everything.

Jack's phone rings. He checks the screen and answers. "I signed everything." There's a pause. "Wayne has it all." He glances between Ryan and me. "Yes, I understand." He lets out a sigh. "Can we not do this? I agree. Let me focus on my daughter."

"What was that?" Ryan asks.

My gaze falls to the ground to lend a modicum of privacy.

"My uncle. I'm taking a temporary leave from the company. It's standard procedure in cases like..." He vigorously scratches the back of his head as he steps to the side door of the house. "Let's go talk about next steps."

CHAPTER 9

48 Hours Missing

Ryan

Jack scribbles a phone number on a piece of paper. He has the look of a man on the brink of dissolution, hair unruly, face unshaven, clothes wrinkled, and red-rimmed eyes.

"When you're ready to go, call this number for a car service. Wayne isn't available today to drive you back. He's stepping in." He balls his hands into fists and presses down on them, supporting his weight as he leans over the desk. "I don't know what I'd do without him." He raises his head, and his wretched gaze falls on me. "You too, Ryan. Thank you."

"I haven't done anything."

"You came. And your team..." There's a question and a plea in the way his eyes crinkle at the sides.

"You can thank me when we find her."

Jack's eyelids close. I interpret it as gratitude, but it could be prayer. When men lose hope, regardless of religious affiliation, they pray. Visit any battlefield and you'll witness this truth.

"You know, back at the academy, you were pretty much the only upperclassman to give me the time of day." Jack's eyelids open slowly. There's a faraway look to his gaze, like he's mentally elsewhere. "Never forgot you. And I'm going to find your daughter."

"I was hoping you'd remember I helped you with that physics final."

That brings out a chuckle. In me, not in Jack. I suspect he doesn't have a smile in him.

"Thank you," he says and nods to emphasize the words. "I'd drive you guys, but I should stick around the house. The police might—"

"That's fine. I understand." The last thing the man needs to be worrying about is transporting us.

I am two steps outside the office when he calls out, "And Ryan? Thanks for working with Alex. Cassandra, her parents passed early on in our marriage. She doesn't have a big family. Alex may not realize it, but she and her dad, in the ways that matter, were her family. She'd want them to be involved." He folds his arms across his chest. His gaze falls to some point on the floor. "Alex would be her first call. Cassandra believes she's brilliant. So, thank you."

The present tense associated with his dead ex-wife isn't lost on me, but it's not the type of thing one corrects. Especially on a day like today.

Frustration seeps out of every pore as I clomp up the stairs. Leaving with no clues feels like ringing the god damn bell. I made it through BUD/S, the SEAL training nightmare, without ringing it. And yet here I am. But it isn't the same.

We have a dozen agents working the case around the clock. Going home doesn't mean giving up. It just means regrouping. Back in the guest suite, I fling the bedroom door open and freeze.

Alex stands at the end of the bed. She's wearing a sheer crimson bra and matching lace thong. *Christ.* Her dark hair skims her shoulders, and those dark eyes lock on me. Mere seconds tick past, yet I memorize every single curve, her flat, smooth stomach, the shadow of her belly button, and those long, lean, sensational legs. I have always been a leg guy, and this woman defines legs for miles. The sheer bra hints at the darker shade of her areolas, and the fabric lifts her breasts, breasts I had dismissed as small, but before me, dressed in red lace, I ache to taste.

Feminine, graceful fingers stroke her clavicle, and the movement breaks my frozen trance.

"Ah, sorry...wrong room."

One arm crosses over her breasts and one knee bends over the other, demurely covering herself, the same sexy move she pulled this morning. The slope of her hip and thigh draw attention to the juncture between those lengthy thighs.

"I was just changing. For the flight."

"Right." *Move. Back out of the room.*

"You saw me in my bathing suit earlier today. This isn't much different." A timid smile flickers.

"Right."

She looked sexy as fuck in that one piece too, but red lingerie is an entirely different scenario. She lifts a pair of jeans from the bed and shakes them out.

"Are you going to watch me get dressed?" She glances over her shoulder, sending her silky hair cascading down her back.

"No. Sorry." My gaze drops to the floor, but her exposed curves remain singed in my mind.

As I pull the door closed, I take stock. There's no need to

check my pulse. I am fully aware I have an elevated heartrate. And the semi I am sporting needs adjusting. Fuck. I'd known she was good looking, but holy mother. Fire engine red lingerie.

And Jack seemed shocked when I asked him if he was dating her. What did he say? *She's not my type*. I'd call bullshit, except for his explanation of knowing her as an awkward kid. Plus, Victoria's Secret models could parade through Jack's home and he wouldn't notice. Hell, a runway-worthy knockout stayed in his home last night and he remained oblivious.

But I already asked her to dinner. She said no. I'm not a fucking horny teen. We are working a case. Our mutual friend's daughter is missing.

Fuck. I wish I hadn't opened the wrong bedroom door. I do not need to be thinking about what her lingerie looks like from here on out. And I wish she'd been timid. I wish she had ducked down instead of standing there and letting me soak her into my subconscious. But of course, like she said, lingerie is like her bathing suit. A bathing suit that sent me into a cold shower. I need to get a grip.

My phone vibrates as I zip up my duffel.

"Erik." Work is exactly what I need to get my mind back on track.

"She slipped out of the house at ten forty-five on Monday night. Just texted you a video clip from the side of the house video cam."

"You're positive it's Sophia?"

"No markings of a deep fake, if that's what you're asking," Erik answers.

Deep-fake technology has improved to the degree that sometimes even film executives can be duped.

"Hold. Let me watch it."

I flick over and play the video he texted. The feed is grainy. The angle is from high above and covers the side path and the side door. Her hair is pulled back in a low ponytail, and she's wearing a small black leather backpack, a short-sleeve shirt, and shorts. She's dressed to meet someone, not to go paddleboarding or surfing. And she's alone.

Damn. I'd prefer a ransom.

"Have we learned anything from her electronics?"

If she planned this, there has to be something we haven't found.

"Not yet. Nothing at all on Monday or for the past week. I've got a dozen people combing through the past year of her life and building a timeline. But if she coordinated meeting up with someone, it's looking like she did it on a burner we don't have access to."

"What fifteen-year-old has a burner phone?"

"I checked to see if she had mirrored an account. Like set it up so her father wouldn't find it. There's nothing like that on her phone or computer. That just leaves a device we don't have access to. Maybe she kept a phone her dad didn't know about. Would she have the money to pay the bill?"

"My guess is she has the money to buy anything she wants."

"I'll keep everyone on this, but if she left to meet someone, she coordinated through a device we don't have access to."

"Thanks. Hey, can you do me a favor?"

"Hit me."

"Just...go over that security footage with a fine-tooth comb. This isn't adding up."

"Or you just don't like what it's adding up to." Erik is always direct. I like that about him. But I dislike what he's insinuating.

"What does that mean?"

"Trevor said this is one of your old Navy buds."

"So?"

"Forget it. There's nothing to implicate him. Other than it looks like his daughter didn't want to keep living with him."

When the call disconnects, I re-watch the video. I hadn't wanted to live with my parents. Trevor hadn't wanted to keep living with his. But Trevor and I both stayed under heavy hands until we could leave. Trevor left at age seventeen for the Navy. I waited until high school graduation. But neither of us ran. Does Jack have a heavy hand? When they fight, could he hit her? I don't think so. Maybe she kept any issues close to the vest, in the same way Jack is keeping his daughter's disappearance out of the media.

Alex sits on the sofa in the suite, her suitcase upright beside her. She's texting back and forth with someone. She's smiling softly, entertained by her correspondence. As if aware I'm watching her, her gaze lifts.

"Erik called." I approach her, my phone held out. "We found security video that shows her leaving. By herself. On her own."

She watches it, and I peer over. This time I notice a long palm branch flutter in the breeze. Her head is down, as if she's aware of the camera above her head.

"Let's go show Jack," she says.

"That's at ten forty-five Monday night," I tell Jack, after he watches the video.

"That doesn't make sense," Jack says. "I was home by ten. I searched everywhere for her."

Alex's lips scrunch together. Her brow wrinkles. She appears uneasy, and I give an encouraging nod. Whatever she's thinking, we need her to say it.

"In this house?" she asks. "If she wanted to hide, she could. Easily." She sounds apologetic.

Jack's head hits the back of his office chair, and his eyelids fall shut. I can only imagine what he must be feeling. I expect he is battling a sense of failure. How devastating would it be to have your child willingly leave you? And leave you with no idea where she'd gone or that she was okay?

Alex stands. Sadness wafts off her. She brushes her dark hair out of her face. And her expression transitions to one of business. I recognize that move. *When the emotion gets tough, focus on steps forward.*

"You said they mirrored her accounts?" she asks me.

"Yes. You can see everything on the portal. Erik sent you a link."

"I'm going to go check everything. See if I can figure out where she went."

"I have a team doing that."

"I know. But they don't know Sophia. Her passport. Do you have it?"

Jack gets up and opens a cabinet door. Behind the door is a small fireproof safe. He unlocks it and lifts a navy passport.

"It's here. She knows where I keep it, so if she wanted it, she could have accessed it," Jack says.

"This doesn't make sense." Jack leans against the office wall and stares down at his feet. "I mean, you can disagree about a curfew, but you don't run away."

"Did you ever hit her?" Jack's head snaps up. Agonized. Distraught. He hates hearing that question as much as I hate asking it.

"Never. Not once. She's never been spanked. Cassie was completely against it." He shakes his head, gazing out over the horizon. "When I said we had disagreements, I didn't mean like that. The Sullivans don't yell. We are reserved. We discuss. And I can promise you, I would never lift a hand to my daughter. Ever. I wasn't a great dad. Not until Cassandra died. But when she came to live with me, I stopped business travel. Hell, that first year, I barely worked. I stepped down as CEO so I could be here for her transition. I mean, Cassandra's death...it knocked us both off our feet. The next year, I returned to work. Spent a ton of time locked away in the office." He looks directly at me. Solemn. Meditative. "Clearly, she was unhappy. But I never hit her."

"Had to ask." It's an awful question, but an important one. One I'm sure the SDPD has already asked, but I needed to see his reaction. "My team is combing through her online life, but so far, we haven't come up with any leads. We suspect she had a burner phone or some alternative electronic device she was using."

"Why?"

"I think it's unlikely she left here to go for a walk alone on the beach. She had to have been meeting up with someone."

"She could have coordinated at school, right? You know, the old-fashioned way? Spoke to someone?"

"True. Although all her close friends from school are still at home and seem concerned."

"I feel so helpless." The back of Jack's head thuds against the wall. He doesn't flinch.

"I think it's time to put it all over the news," I tell him. "Have the world searching for her."

"No." He stares me down, jaw flexed. "No. Absolutely not. It's clear she ran on her own volition. You put that in front of the media, they're all over it. Not just now, but for the rest of her life. They'll be hounding her, looking for a juicy story about a rich girl gone astray. No. Way."

"How'd the search party go earlier?" I ask to deflect to a safer topic.

"Her friends took us everywhere they hang out. All the places on the beach and..." He flexes his hand. "What if she went out to meet someone and something happened?"

"It's a possibility. And another reason to get the word out. If someone has her, and they by chance don't know her father's net worth, it might be worth it to let them know."

"I'll think about it." He turns his back to me, crosses his arms, and blindly stares out the window.

"I have a file on the portal of the photos off her phone. Can you go through them? I need you to flag anyone you don't recognize."

"Definitely." He swivels his office chair around, sits, and pulls up to his keyboard. "Did you send me a link?"

There is hope in his question. I understand. Having an actionable task is infinitely better than swimming through watery emotions.

CHAPTER 10

49 Hours Missing

Alex

Buildings dot the landscape as far as the eye can see. Even up in the hills, homes peek out between dots of green and rocky peaks. Through the curved helicopter window, a long white coastline stretches before us, and bright white crests speckle the mass of navy blue. Just another day in beautiful Southern California.

Is Sophia in one of the cars flying down the 101? Is she getting stoned on the beach and enjoying newfound freedom? Maybe having sex with some older man who convinced her this is the only way they could be together? Or is she the latest human trafficking victim, bound in a large container headed off to the highest bidder?

"How long have you lived here?" Ryan's mundane question brings me back to the cabin. After leaving Jack's, silence has dominated.

"Not long. Less than a year. What about you?"

"Santa Barbara? Less than a year." His frown softens. Piloting a helicopter suits him. He's in charge, a machine under his control, the world beneath him. "Did you love being a student?"

"What?" I field plenty of questions about my chosen coursework, but few about being a student.

"That's a long time to go to school. I've always wondered why people do that. I mean, I get doctors. There's a lot to learn to do the job. But those who essentially become full-time students, I've always wondered what makes you tick. There's not that much money, is there? How long do you have to work before you break even on all the tuition?"

My laugh spills out. There is a slight playback in my headset, and my laugh sounds godawful. I choke the laugh down, self-conscious of the unattractive noise. But when I glance at Ryan, the corners of those growly lips are up, amused for once.

"My father is an academic. I can't remember a time when I questioned if I would pursue a doctorate. I don't think my father did either."

"So he's big shit?" He turns his head, and his ice-blue irises study me. "That's what Jack said."

The informal language contrasts with Ryan's demeanor, and another laugh escapes, but that awful, windy headset playback shuts it down fast.

"Yes. That's one way of putting it."

"So big you had to move to a different continent to escape his shadow?"

I let out a confirming sigh, which comes across like a wind funnel in the headset microphone.

"Everyone knows my father. There isn't a continent I could move to where his reputation wouldn't precede me."

"I've never heard of him."

"I mean, in academic circles." I rest my head against the headrest. "Where did you go to school?"

"Naval Academy. Four years. Did not remotely feel the need to continue my education."

"No master's?"

"Nope. And I could have. There are guys in the military who go on, get an MBA. Some go to medical or dental school."

"But not you?"

"No."

"What made you choose military?"

"I wanted to fight the bad guys." He stares straight ahead, but his face softens. He looks more human, less soldier. "The towers falling proved bad guys existed in the world."

"As a kid, I had a morbid fascination with serial killers. Jack the Ripper and the like. I've never doubted that there were darker sides of the human condition." Silence returns, and I reposition myself in the seat. "Well, you seem to do well with your business. And you still go after bad guys. And, as you pointed out, you're not saddled with massive student loans. But neither am I. I have dual citizenship. The government covers undergraduate coursework. My postgraduate coursework carried fees, but my father is a professor at the University of Edinburgh. I have debt, don't get me wrong. It's hard to go ten years as a student and not accumulate debt. But I'm not as bad off as, say, my American counterparts."

"Do you miss being a student?"

"Aren't we all students? Students of life?" The philosophical question posed by my academic friends feels trite, so I add, "There's always something new to learn."

"True," he agrees. "But I'd prefer to hire those who spent ten years learning than spend ten years taking tests and writing papers."

A vibration pulses in my back pocket. I lean forward to retrieve my phone.

Timothy: How's the case going? Nothing on the news yet.

Right below Timothy's text, I notice a text from Sabrina.

Sabrina: Are you working with FBI agents? Ask them to meet us out for beers. Please! Please! Pretty please!

I respond to Timothy first.

Me to Timothy: Still going. Client keeping it out of the news. How did class go?

Me to Sabrina: No FBI.

Now that we know she's a runaway, I'm not sure the FBI will agree to get involved.

Sabrina: But cops? The Arrow men?

. . .

A visual flashes of Ryan coming out of the pool, water droplets gliding over his taut muscles. Ryan would prefer to date someone like Sabrina. She's curvy, feminine, and flirty.

"Do you mind if I take a photo of the inside of the helicopter? For my friends?"

"Go ahead."

I snap a photo of the dashboard, then angle to get a photo of Ryan, or as his friends call him, Wolf. I check the screen and see my angle didn't quite do those arms justice, and lean back to get a better profile shot. Satisfied, I send the photo off.

Me to Sabrina: Here you go.

Sabrina: Holy. Shit balls.

Dad: Checking in. Any news on Sophia?

Me to Dad: Security video shows her leaving. Of her own volition.

Dad: A crime may not have occurred, but you can approach it like a crime. Kids don't run without someone knowing. Find the person who knows.

Pearls of wisdom from Dr. Rolfe. *Gee, thanks, Dad.*

. . .

Timothy: Class went well. When are you back? Want to grab a beer?

Timothy: To go over everything?

"Everything okay?" Ryan's question bears the hint of a reprimand. Feeling rather rude, I flip the phone over so I'm not tempted to continue texting.

"Yeah. Just my TA checking in."

"You sent your TA a picture of me?"

If there were a table in front of me, I would duck under it. But there's no table. I forget he's probably got great peripheral vision. Hell, he might have read my texts.

"A friend. Guys in uniform are her thing." He's mostly unreadable, although there is a slight crinkle of the skin near his eye on the edge of his sunglasses.

"What's your thing?"

"Ah..." Should I tell him I like height? It's such a shallow thing to admit. But I do. Besides, most men who are shorter don't have an interest in me. So perhaps it's a learned preference.

"Your ex-boyfriends. Any patterns?"

"Academics?" I shrug. Study partners who became drinking buddies and became more.

"What about you?" The desire to slap my forehead for asking that question has my right hand gripping the edge of the seat cushion to prevent the out-of-control part of my brain from taking over and doing so.

"No type." He rubs his nose immediately. A hand-to-face gesture. *What a liar*.

I shift to look out of the ocean so he can't observe my uncontrolled smirk. He so has a type, but he doesn't feel comfortable telling me.

"So, do you need to fly all around for your clients? Is that why you own a helicopter?"

"I fly to San Diego regularly. I'm from there."

"Oh. Was your neighborhood like Sophia's?"

"Not at all. I'd never been to the Sullivans' neighborhood before in my life. No, you could pack about fifteen homes on Sullivan's property. Maybe more. That's the San Diego I know. Postage stamp–sized yards, ridiculous prices in what we called transitional neighborhoods, meaning there'd be a shit hole next to an oversized new build. I lived about a mile from the beach. Biked it every day. Still a good life, even in a small house without a view."

"You must have liked it if you always go back."

"No." His cursory response catches my attention. "Let's just say childhood memories have nothing to do with my frequent returns to San Diego."

I detect a hint of disgust as he spits out the city name, and his stern expression warns he's done with that topic.

The band on the end of his short sleeves snugly wraps his bicep. His forearms flex as he maneuvers the controls. He's wearing an enormous watch, the kind you could use for scuba diving. The thick plastic band accentuates that strong forearm, thick wrists, and large hands. Dark, curly arm hair underscores his strength.

Sabrina would go wild for a snapshot from this angle. "Forearm candy," she calls it.

I stare out the window, forcing myself to take in the view outside the helicopter to avoid getting caught staring at the pilot.

"How do boyfriends feel about you choosing a career hunting killers?"

"Excuse me?"

"That's what you want to do, right? I read up on you a bit. You're positioning yourself as a criminal profiler."

"Potentially. I don't want to leave academia. I love campus life. Being around students. Research. I'm at the beginning of my career, but I don't see myself as a criminal hunter. It's more an interest in the criminal mind. Which, if you study it, isn't quite as different from a law-abiding mind as we like to believe."

"That's an interesting perspective. So, your boyfriend, he's okay with it?"

"There's no boyfriend." A smile threatens, and I turn my head further to the side. "And if there were, he would be okay with it."

I dare a glance over my shoulder, and Wolf grins. A ridiculous, completely absurd warmth spreads through my whole being. Alas, we work together. I can imagine my father's abhorrence if he got wind that I dated a colleague. He would never tolerate unprofessional conduct on a case he contributed to. And besides, as soon as Ryan meets Sabrina, he'll be into her.

I flip over my phone and access the link Erik, Arrow's tech guy, sent. Travel time should be used to catch up on work. I need to focus on finding Sophia. On my consulting case. Yet here I am behaving like Sabrina. Boy-crazed, flirty, and silly.

I don't stop reading until we land and the rotor blades slow. When Ryan removes his headset, I follow suit.

"Do you need any help?" I ask.

"With?" There's no innuendo in his question, but like a ridiculous girl, my face warms and most likely tinges red.

"The helicopter? Do you have to do stuff to it?"

"I got it." He grins. In his office, he never smiled, but I'm seeing it more and more. It's a good look on him. His smiles warm those icy eyes.

A man steps out of the building off in the distance, and Ryan waves. He holds his hand out for me as I get down from the helicopter. His warm hand is enormous, as are his fingers. When Sabrina meets him, without a doubt, she'll bring up the meaning of big hands.

"Well..." I stand awkwardly in front of the helicopter. Because my brain has gone berserk. I need to focus on finding Sophia. We don't have any good next steps.

"I'll let you know if we find any leads," Ryan says dismissively. The trip back has concluded.

"Sounds good." With a tug on my suitcase and gratitude for the lift, I return to the parking lot.

I am not sure what I can do, other than read up on other missing persons cases. Runaway cases. Maybe something will resonate. Maybe I'll see something we haven't looked into that helped solve another case.

As I approach my car, I do a double take. My rinky-dink tire is no more. A brand-new Michelin tire holds up my bug.

I find Ryan strapping a cover over his helicopter with help from the man he waved to earlier.

"Did you have my tire replaced?"

"Yep."

"Why?"

"You needed a new tire."

"But..." I don't know what to say. It's not like I'm going to insist on getting my old tire back. "How much do I owe you?"

"Nada. You're on our team. We take care of our own." He ducks below the back rotor and steps close. "What are you doing tonight?"

"I'm, ah...meeting a friend out. I have to pick up my dog. Take him for a long walk. Check in on campus. Then later, go out." I'm stumped on his fixing my bloody tire and therefore a mumbling mess vomiting out unnecessary minutiae.

"Have a good night. I'll let you know if we pick up any leads."

He disappears to the far side of the helicopter. I back away, my brain mush. The growly man fixed my tire.

"Thank you." The weak expression isn't quite enough.

CHAPTER 11

112 Hours Missing

Ryan

Pre-dawn stillness reigns over Haley Street. The bright yellow bungalow sits at the corner of an intersection with no parking allowed along the front and side, so I drive into the narrow driveway and park. On this spring morning, sunrise won't occur for another hour, but there are traces of gold along the horizon to the east.

Locating Alex's address had been easy. One online search easily accomplished the task. I searched out of curiosity, looking to see how protective of her privacy she is. The answer had been not at all. She set her Instagram and Facebook as public accounts. She is trusting, and the bright yellow painted brick of her bungalow corroborates my conclusion. The young professor studies the darkest side of human nature and yet maintains a sunny outlook. Having fought in battles and witnessed men blown to shreds, I both admire that ability in her and wonder over her naivety.

With practiced ease, I stack one coffee cup on top of the other and tap lightly on her front door. She said she wakes early, but knocking shortly after six on a Saturday morning constitutes a gamble. A shrill, loud bark erupts.

She doesn't ask who is at the door before swinging it open. Annoyance at her lack of situational awareness surfaces, and I push past Alex into her den. She holds a coffee mug in her hand, so I keep my extra.

"Is everything okay?"

A small, curly haired, brown dog barks and jumps, his nails scratching my unprotected calves. It's the weekend, and my shorts and running shoes offer no protection from the yapper.

"Trace, down."

The little dog disregards her command, so I bend down and offer my hand. The barking ceases as the tip of his nose wiggles while he sniffs.

"How'd you know it was me?"

She lives in an exposed house on what I imagine is a busy intersection during most of the day, and she didn't check the peephole.

"I—"

"What would you have done if I charged in?"

She closes the door and twists the lock. "If you must know, I saw you through the window as I approached the door. Is everything okay? Or is early morning coffee delivery a standard service for Arrow consultants? Sort of like tire replacement?"

"Sullivan's PR person has been effective at getting the word out. Sophia's disappearance is in *USA Today*, and it's all over the news. And he released your name as a consultant on the case."

"Oh." Alex glances back out the window. "What made him change his mind about the press?"

"Our lack of next steps."

"Why mention me? Is that standard?"

"I asked him that exact question, and he said his PR person said it emphasizes he's using all resources, including private means, to locate his daughter. He ultimately agreed to it because he assumed it would help your career."

"He's not wrong." Her brow furrows, and I wonder if she is worried about a media storm. We've already received a few media inquiries at Arrow, all messages left overnight.

"Well, I wanted to give you a heads-up." The dog is calmer, so I rise from my crouched position.

"You could have texted me." She tilts her head and narrows her eyes. Her body language is clear. She's not buying my story.

"Yes, but that would have made coffee delivery challenging. Uber Eats isn't available this early."

Her tank top clings to her breasts, and the thin material does little to hide the perky nipples. An untied silk robe hangs loosely from her shoulders, and her pajama shorts expose those long, sexy legs. Thick cream socks cover her feet and rise to her defined calves. Her Saturday morning outfit is both adorable and sexy, a combination I didn't know existed.

"Have you eaten breakfast?" she asks.

"I had a shake. I take it you don't need the coffee?"

"I'll take it. Come on back."

"This is a cute place." I'm not a fan of the lemon yellow on the outside, but inside, the off-white stucco walls and large windows frame a welcoming warmth. A lumpy, well-worn sofa and low coffee table sit across from the windows looking out on the street. Brightly colored paintings hang on the walls. Potted plants crowd the corners and tabletops.

"Thanks. I moved in less than six months ago." I follow her through a doorway, ducking to avoid hitting my head on the low archway, into a narrow kitchen with white-painted cabinets and a wide porcelain sink centered below a window. Through the window, you can see the driveway, a car, a wooden fence, and her neighbor's house, but the fence blocks any view into the house next door. A side door next to the refrigerator provides one of two entrance points. A small, ineffective brass lock sits above the doorknob. "Soon, I plan to paint the outside. It's a small bungalow, but it's perfect for one person. And I can walk to State Street."

"Did you consider living closer to campus?" I only ask because my impression of lifelong academics is that they prefer to live near campus.

She backs up against the kitchen counter and lifts a half-eaten muffin from a napkin.

"I guess I looked everywhere. But I like this area. There are some others from the university who live around here. It's a good neighborhood. Where do you live?"

"Near my office."

"Oh. So, close, then?"

"Yeah, an easy jog."

She takes a bite of her muffin. A few crumbs remain on her lips. An urge to run my thumb across her lips and brush the remnants away comes out of nowhere. I shove my hand into my shorts pocket.

"Are you sure I can't get you anything to eat? Why don't you sit?" She gestures to the small round kitchen table with two chairs pushed into the corner.

"I ate earlier. But thanks." If she had bananas, I'd take one of those for the potassium. But I've already had my protein shake. I pull out one chair and sit. "Jack is hoping the FBI will get involved."

"I can understand him wanting to bring in as many people as possible. But I don't think the FBI will touch a runaway case, no matter how much money he has."

"My contacts are saying the same thing. But I do have one agent from the LA office who agreed to come out this morning and go over the case. I thought you might like to be there."

"Really?" Alex's eyes widen. "Now?"

"He's going to arrive around eight. He's in town for the weekend. Personal friends or something."

"Great." She shoves the rest of her English muffin into her mouth. "Let me go get ready."

"We've got time. It's no rush." I should've waited a little longer to stop by her house, but I woke at four, unable to sleep. I worked out, showered, and was the first customer at the small coffee shop around the corner. I didn't have much of a plan. Only a few things to talk to her about and a desire to be certain she wasn't bothered by the media, coupled with the knowledge she's an early riser.

A short hallway off the kitchen leads to her bedroom. From my kitchen chair, I have a clear view of the solid wood, cream-colored painted door. A half-inch gap below the door lets sound flow freely. Drawers open and close and shadows pass below the gap. The yappy dog followed her into the room, so I sit there, elbows on my thighs, hands clasped.

She exits the room wearing a long skirt and a form-fitting tee. The white cotton skims the skirt's flat waistband, and when she lifts her arms to drape a necklace over her head, she reveals a tantalizing strip of skin.

"Are you single?" Her question throws me. Yesterday, I asked her, but she didn't bounce the question back to me.

"I am."

She lifts a photograph from her dresser and delivers it to me. Lights shimmer off of a toe ring as she passes through the kitchen.

"This is my friend Sabrina. She's the one I sent your photo to. The one with a thing for uniforms."

She leaves the frame in my hand and returns to her bedroom. She sits on the end of the bed and kicks a leg up to buckle on sandals. Long, fluid skirts flatter her svelte form.

"If you'd like to meet her, I can set that up."

The photograph is of Alex and a blonde girl. The angle of the photograph offers a nice view of cleavage. The top of the other girl's head reaches Alex's shoulder, and judging from the way her shoulders cave in, I'd bet Alex is crouching for the photo. The curvy blonde is objectively attractive and has a nice set of tits, but Alex steals the show with her angular features, dark hair, long lashes, and thick eyebrows. I set the frame down on the table.

"Are you trying to play matchmaker?"

Alex's face is hidden behind her knee. I asked Alex to dinner, and she shot me down. It's not a big deal, as I don't do relationships. But I'm certainly not going to pretend to be interested in one of Alex's friends.

"She's really great. Everyone loves her."

"What about you?"

"What about me?" Shoes fastened, she scoots off the bed.

"I'd rather take you to dinner." She studies me. I'm not sure what she's looking for, but I stare right back.

Our gazes deadlock. I will not back down. I'm not asking anything that isn't appropriate. Jack confirmed nothing is going on between the two of them. Her eyes flit to the frame.

"Me?" Disbelief colors the singular notion.

"Yes. You." I'd like to do a lot more than take her out to dinner.

"I don't think that's a good idea." She leans back against the doorframe. One arm crosses her stomach, one hand goes to her mouth, and her teeth scrape her thumbnail.

"Dinner isn't a good idea?" She's out of her mind. The sexual chemistry between us practically crackles, so intense her little dog glances back and forth between the two of us, as if questioning which one of us will lead the pack.

"I mean, it's just that, you know."

"No, Alex. I don't know."

"What would other people think?"

"What other people?"

"I mean, within Arrow. Or the FBI guy we're about to meet."

"I don't believe he'll question us about our dinner plans." She rolls her eyes and drops her hand from her mouth, where it lands on the curve of her hip. "You know what I mean."

Growing tired of this game, I stand and scoot the chair back under the table.

"Alex, I can assure you I wouldn't feel it necessary to tell anyone working on this case if you and I decided to have dinner. As a matter of fact, if you wanted to keep things between us private..." I let the word hang for a beat for maximum effect. Her tongue flicks over her lower lip. "I wouldn't have an issue with that."

I am too old for kiss-and-tell games. Trevor, my closest friend, never hears about my encounters.

"Just dinner, right?"

"Or more."

She drags one foot over the other, causing the fabric of her skirt to tighten around her thighs.

"I'm asking for us to see where it goes."

"Where what goes?" Her lips curve upward, but it's not quite a smile. No, it's a flirty tease.

"I've just got this hunch. And I've been trained to trust my gut."

"And your gut is telling you we should go to dinner?"

I nod. She reaches for her hair, gathers it to one side, and her fingers weave the dark locks into a braid. Braiding her hair could be a nervous tick. Or maybe she's buying time to respond as she weighs her options.

The hem of her shirt rises as she braids. She's truly sexy as fuck, but if she's only been around mild-mannered academics, it's conceivable she's clueless how beguiling she is. She flicks a piece of fabric off her wrist and straps it around the end of her braid.

I move on instinct. My thumb grazes the soft curve of her chin. She tilts her head up. I search those forest eyes for any hint of a response and sense an invitation. It's in those widening pupils, the way her body leans closer, the flush in her cheeks, and her quick, short breaths.

My lips cover hers, softly at first. I pause, searching her eyes, hoping to confirm I read her right. She reaches up, and her fingers snake behind my neck and into my hair. She gently pulls me to her. My lips brush hers, and I close my eyes. The slow kiss deepens, and her body melds perfectly against mine. She tastes of mint with subtle hints of rich coffee. My skin tingles, and my heartrate jolts into overdrive. She lets out a soft moan that goes straight to my dick. I grip her bottom, pressing her more firmly against me. She molds to my body as if someone designed her curves specifically for me.

My phone vibrates in my shorts pocket, a little too close to my throbbing erection. With a groan, I break the kiss and reach for the offending device. I hold her close with my other arm as I check out the text.

Erik: The Sullivan video is spliced. Possible deep fake.

Alex leans to see the message as I reread it.

"Does he mean the security video? What does spliced mean?" she asks.

I weave my fingers through hers, breathing deeply, willing my body under control. I need to call Erik back and get to Arrow's offices as quickly as possible.

"It means the video was planted. This isn't a runaway case. It's an abduction."

End of Part 1

CHAPTER 12

113 Hours Missing

Ryan

On a typical Saturday morning, no one mans the front desk at Arrow, but this morning a young man sits behind the glass reception window. He stands as we enter.

"Sir," he says.

"Caleb. You're here early."

"Erik asked me to cover down here. I'm just watching surveillance tapes. I can do that from any desk."

"Can you buzz us up?" I don't need him to. Ocular recognition will clear me, but if he buzzes, it's less hassle.

Caleb scratches behind his ear. "Ah, I'm supposed to check ID. I guess if she's with you..." We have a strict protocol outlined for confirming identification. If he let her up without asking, I could conceivably fire him. Or at least, that's the consequence for not checking ID outlined in the employee handbook Stella created.

"Her name is Dr. Alexandria Rolfe. Can you enter her into the system? Alex, do you have your license?"

"Oh, yes. I'm probably already in your system. I was here last week."

"Right. You are. But I thought I'm supposed to check ID anyway?" Caleb directs his question to me.

"If you know who it is, it's okay." It's good to see our system working. "But since you've pulled her up, can you give her full clearance? Dr. Rolfe can come and go without an appointment."

"Yes, sir."

Once the elevator doors close behind us, Alex leans against the back rail with a teasing smile. The playful expression has me wanting to press her up against the elevator wall. She's the perfect height. She could lift one thigh—

"Is he former military, too?" Clearly, her thoughts are not the same as mine.

"Caleb?" The elevator slows to a stop, and I face forward. "If I recall correctly, he did a few years in the military, plus military academy. He's a former LEO of some sort. He works for Erik and Kairi."

"What's an LEO?"

"Law enforcement officer."

When we round the corner, activity buzzes. Employees sit in cubicles watching video with headsets on. Erik steps out of the conference room and waves us over. "Come see this."

When we enter the conference room, Erik is back at his laptop, typing away.

Erik's fingers don't slow until black-and-white video footage of the side of Sullivan's home in San Diego shows on the monitor at the end of the room.

"Did you see that?" Erik asks.

The video shows a palm frond fluttering in the wind. Nighttime. I cross my arms. He stops the video.

"Look closely," he tells us and rewinds the video.

White lines at the top of the screen flick for a nanosecond. Inferior quality footage. Not unexpected, given the inferior surveillance system.

"Did you see it?" Erik asks.

"What am I supposed to see?" I step closer to the screen. The same palm leaf lifts in the wind.

"This is spliced. Someone went into the system and cut video from an earlier day, months earlier, and spliced it on the server. Fourteen hours' worth. The only reason we ever caught it is because I had multiple resources studying the footage. They were smart. They inserted a wide segment with little to no activity."

"So, where's the real footage?"

"Deleted. Swiped from the server. I suspected this might be a deep-fake video. But I was wrong. It's just spliced. They copied old footage."

Deep-fake video poses a tremendous risk to law enforcement. Not being able to trust what you see creates extensive ramifications. Splicing security video is another risk, and it's usually done with footage that shows no movement at all.

"We found this exact video four months earlier on the security tape. They copied it. They may have assumed we'd never look back that far. Or they may have copied it four months ago and assumed back-ups wouldn't be kept that long. Maybe thought deleting the file risked raising suspicion."

"So, she did sneak out late at night, just not recently?"

"The video from four months ago shows her returning an hour later."

"She probably met up with a friend."

"And it's possible Jack knew about it. There's nothing to confirm she was sneaking out. Who remembers what they allow their kid to do four months earlier? Or what they were wearing?" Alex points out.

"I've got to call Jack."

"Before you call him..." Erik rubs the bridge of his nose, shifting his glasses up to his forehead. His eyes are slightly bloodshot, a sign he's been staring at screens all night. "I did some background work." He holds up a defensive hand. "Just being thorough. There was a police investigation into Jack's wife's car wreck."

"And?" Alex's arms clasp her sides.

"Determined it was accidental. But there was an investigation open."

"And you're telling me because...?" If he found something, he needs to spit it out.

"I'm telling you so you have the background. Look, whoever did this has technical expertise. Assuming they don't work at the security company, then they had to hack into the servers. And it's conceivable they've been planning this for as long as four months. You said he hasn't received a ransom, right?"

"That's what he says," I answer. Alex's facial expression remains frozen. Her gaze drifts from Erik to the window outside.

"Do you trust him?" Erik asks me.

"Yes. Do I trust him not to get ahead of himself? Think he's better off not involving anyone in paying off a ransom? No. He has skills. It's his daughter. The guy lives and breathes guns. It's in his blood. His aim is as good as some SEAL snipers, with probably more hours on the range."

"What are you thinking?" Erik asks.

"It's possible he hasn't told us everything. Maybe he received a ransom and wanted to follow instructions." But he knows Arrow specializes in K&R. That scenario doesn't seem likely.

"That's not where I was going," Erik deadpans.

I hold my gaze on his glasses, giving him a silent command to continue.

He lifts one shoulder and leans back against his chair. "I don't have anything yet. I have people looking into Sullivan Arms' financials, the Board of Directors and executive team."

"What could someone gain from taking Sophia? If they aren't after a ransom?" Alex's question is a good one.

"What are futures looking like for Sullivan Arms stock? Did news of Sophia's disappearance impact stock price at all?"

Erik rubs the bridge of his nose, pushing his glasses up higher as he considers my question.

"Shiloh!" he shouts.

A young woman with bright blue hair twisted into pinwheels on the top of her head appears. The overhead lights reflect off her eyebrow and nose rings.

"Yeah?" She rocks back on the heels of heavy black boots. Rips cover her jeans, and her loose, unbuttoned flannel partially hides a faded cropped t-shirt.

"Can you pull stock price history for Sullivan Arms for the past five years? And set up an alert. I want to be notified of any sharp swings in the stock moving forward."

"Yep." She shoves her hands in her front pockets.

"What?" Erik asks her.

"I don't know if it means anything. But I'm working the deets on the company executives."

Erik tilts his head at her and gives her a wilting look. Patience isn't his strength. Since he's normally up in Napa, I don't often get to see him interact with his employees, but Shiloh appears unfazed.

"I got their photos off the company site. I ran facial recognition through the security footage, and a couple of these guys visit his house all the fucking time."

"He works from home," Erik says, and his fingers fall back to his keyboard.

"But there are a couple who come by when he's not home. To the point I started wondering if, ya know, there might be a little reverse age gap going on. You know, back when we thought she might have run away. So, I started cataloging the dates. I don't have names for all of the men, because, you know, they aren't all board members, but I'm filing the unknowns by face. If you want to see. I mean, the super-frequent visitors...I doubt there was any romantic action. The age gap would be pretty massive."

"Send me one photo of each unidentified visitor. We'll send to Sullivan for identification."

She spins on her heel and speeds out of the room.

"FBI will be getting involved." Erik states this as fact and directs his attention to me. "We've got two dozen working this. Let me know when to pull them."

"I've got an FBI contact stopping by this morning. We'll show him what we have. We stay on it until we're told otherwise. Let me call Sullivan again. When I called earlier, his friend Wayne answered. Said he made him shower."

Trevor raps on the door. "Guys. We've got an issue." He pauses, pointedly staring down Alex.

"It's okay. She's working with us," I tell him. Although I should have Stella send her an NDA.

"One of our security details in Syria. Bomb. One hour ago. Jagger's on a medivac. Critical condition. Our client is in a safe house, but the team is short. Stella is working on reassignments so we can get some coverage asap. I'm heading to Damascus."

Jagger hadn't been on my team, but we'd been over in

Afghanistan at the same time. *Fuck.* We should have never debated staffing up the project.

"What happened?" I ask.

Nothing in Syria would be considered a cushy assignment, but as far as assignments go, providing security for the family of a CIA officer shouldn't result in a tango with explosives.

"They were targeted. Not sure by who. I'm hearing AF."

"Israeli forces?" Also known as the "men of silence," AF are comparable to Navy SEALs, and they fight the war between wars on covert missions. If they wanted someone dead, then that sucked for the target. And the CIA officer would probably never share what he did to get placed on a hit list. The guy was supposed to be over there under cover as an expat businessman. Regardless, Arrow had a job to do. And an injured friend.

Stella, our HR director and Trevor's girlfriend, wraps her arm around Trevor's lower back. She peers up at him with concern and love.

"Backup is on the way to the safe house. Best I could do is commercial. We need to get you to the airport," Stella updates Trevor.

Sending Trevor off into a dangerous situation when he has his first real relationship, the kind that could last fifty years, hits me wrong.

"I should be the one going," I tell Trevor. "If we can get the FBI engaged today, then I could be on a plane tomorrow."

"You've got your hands full. I've got this," Trevor responds with characteristic aloofness. To Stella, he says, "I'll send updates."

"Don't take any unnecessary risks," I command. What I don't tell him is to get his ass back home in one piece.

Trevor gives me a quick nod in understanding and says, "You find that kid, then you can come join me." He winks, as cool as ever, and leads Stella away.

"Are they married?" Alex asks.

"For all practical purposes," I answer. "All right. I'm going to call Sullivan from my office." I pause. Alex has been mostly silent. "Do you think this is good news? The spliced video?"

Alex frowns. "Do you know what we call silent kidnappers?"

I shake my head, but an unsettled sensation stirs in my gut. I'm pretty sure I know where she's going with her answer.

"Killers." She chews her thumbnail, thoughtful. When her gaze lifts to look me in the eye, she adds, "Let's hope he's received a ransom."

CHAPTER 13

114 Hours Missing

Alex

My chaotic thoughts churn through the facts. There was an abduction. There should have been a crime scene. But I didn't find anything. Not even a suspect fingerprint. Are we dealing with professionals? And if yes, what does that mean? Why?

As unreadable as ever, Ryan commands the room. Every time my gaze travels to him, I jerk it back, down, or to a far corner. A slight tingle persists on my swollen lips. And it is truly ridiculous, because someone abducted Sophia. That's where I should focus. Dad counsels against fraternization for this reason. Divided attention reaps failure.

My phone vibrates, and a photo of my dad floats to the screen. It's a selfie of the two of us near the Dover cliffs. My hair blows wildly in the wind, partially covering his face, but he's smiling for the camera. What will he say when I confirm what he no doubt has already read in the news? It is an abduction, I was first on the crime scene, and I found nothing. Years of following him around, learning from him, and I fell for a cleaned room and a snippet of video. I hit decline.

Through the glass wall, Arrow employees sit at cubicles, the worst kind of cubicles, basically tables spread out in the middle of the room with no privacy walls. Heads are bent. Almost all of the employees wear headsets. Shiloh's neon pinwheels bob up and down as she works away at her station.

Whoever did this knew Jack. They knew who he uses for a security company. They probably knew he had a business dinner Monday evening. This is not random. But without a ransom, why? I want to see the photos of the frequent visitors to the house.

"Hi, Shiloh? I'm Alex. Do you mind showing me those photos?"

"Sure. Pull up a seat."

The chairs in the cubicle farm are on wheels, so I roll an empty one over to her desk.

"Where's the accent from?"

"Pick that up, did ya?" Since moving to California, I've become used to people asking where my accent is from. Sometimes I ask for guesses. I get a variety of responses. Some say Great Britain, but others will guess Australia or even South Africa. One of my students guessed New Zealand. "Scotland."

"Was immigration as much of a bitch as they say?"

"I have dual citizenship, so I wouldn't know. My mom was American, my dad Irish. Most of my childhood was in Edinburgh with summers in the US." My focus is on her monitor. She has multiple windows open. She's closing windows right and left via the mouse under her right hand. I've been told I leave too many windows in my browser open, but this girl takes the cake. My laptop would crash.

"That's still a lot of paperwork, right?"

"I wouldn't know. My parents handled it all when I was a kid."

"Huh. I have a friend who wants to come over. She says it's nearly impossible." Now she's opening folders. I clasp my hands between my thighs to control my jitters. "Are you gonna stay here or are you going back?"

"Planning on staying."

Prickles climb my spine. I glance over my shoulder and freeze. Ryan's penetrating icy blues send goosebumps scurrying along my arms.

"This guy has come by the most," Shiloh says. I break my gaze from Ryan and check out her screen. Disappointment pokes me.

"That's Wayne. Jack Sullivan's friend and neighbor."

"Figured he must be a close friend. He has a key. He's not a board member." The screenshot shows him at the front door, his hand suspended in air, reaching for the doorknob. Shiloh labels the folder "Wayne."

"His last name is Killington," I tell her, and she types.

"What else do you have?" Ryan asks.

She closes Wayne's folder, which appears to be chock full of security video clips, and opens the next folder.

The man in the frozen screenshot wears a suit and tie. He has dark hair. The screenshot is black and white, so it's not possible to discern colors.

"Do you have any images in color?"

"No. This guy's system is from the nineties."

I lean forward to get a better look at his face. He's an attractive man. I would guess he's in his early to mid-thirties, which is intriguing, because I would expect any employees visiting Jack's home would be executive level, and therefore older.

"I don't recognize him. Do you?" Ryan places one hand on the back of my chair and leans closer to the monitor.

"No. Send me your best screenshot of his face. I don't need video. Who's next?"

The next image shows a guy in baggy shorts, flip-flops, and a t-shirt. He's wearing sunglasses. His hair is lighter. Possibly blond. He's baby faced.

"That's one of her friends. We met him at the school."

"How many visitors need to be identified?"

"A lot. Sorry. I thought I pulled out her friends."

"Let's focus on the adults. Actually, Jack went through all the photos on her phone and identified them. You can cross reference with those. The file is on the server." Erik gestures for Ryan from the conference room doorway. "When you've got those photos, send them over. Let's create a list of all the house visitors, date, and time."

"You know we don't have any accurate video from Monday?"

"Yes. But it's worth looking to see who came by in the months leading up. Go back six months." His gaze sweeps over me, and I can't tell at all what he's thinking. Is he wondering why I am sitting with Shiloh? Does he want me to be doing something else? He leaves without a word to join Erik.

My gaze follows his broad shoulders and dark hair. He's wearing Saturday casual shorts and trainers, yet his vibe remains all business. A man on a mission. Which is a complete turn-on. The shirt covers those muscles, but I know exactly what those extensive shoulders and muscular back look like with water beading down like sweat droplets. His sculpted ass flexes with each step above powerful, muscular legs.

"He's hot." Shiloh's words bring my wayward mind back to our task at hand. "But those eyes are a little freaky."

"So, who's next?"

She pulls up a photo of a man I would guess is in his sixties in a golf shirt and slacks. I don't recognize him.

"Put that in our executive folder."

"How do you know he's an executive?"

"I don't, but it's possible he's a colleague. Next?"

She pulls up another photo. "Delivery."

"I have a separate folder of all deliveries."

"Does he get a lot of deliveries?"

"Almost every day."

I don't know if that's important or not, but it is something we can look into further.

"By the way, I reviewed her ReMarkable folders."

"ReMarkable? The device you can take notes on and save on a cloud?" I still use notebooks, but I'd been considering buying one of those.

"Right. But you can also save articles on it. Like things you find on the web. She had a folder labeled Geese. It was filled with articles on cheating, parents cheating, why people cheat, that kind of thing." Shiloh shrugs. "Thought it was worth mentioning."

"Can you show me that folder?" She clicks around and opens the folder. "Can we see the date she saved these articles?"

All of the dates are clustered over about a two-month period of time, right before Cassandra died.

"Interesting." Did Cassie divorce Jack because he cheated on her? But Cassie specifically said they grew apart. If he cheated, wouldn't she tell me? Of course, this folder was created ages after the separation. Maybe it has to do with another friend's parents. Or a school project.

"You're a professor, right?"

"I am."

"You know, this is all on the network. I don't know why they have us load everything if no one checks it. Same thing with this stupid project system they installed. Only the peons follow it."

I suppress a smile. "Let's get back to those photos."

Shiloh and I develop a system. She shows me a photo, and I tap the folder in her bottom corner of her screen if I deem it a businessperson. If it looks like a young friend, I'll point to the friend folder. Although there aren't many of those coming through the front door.

"Did you see any women?" I ask after the fourth middle-aged male visitor we place in the executive folder.

"No."

All the names of the board of directors for Sullivan Arms had been masculine. He's a weapons manufacturer. Perhaps it's simply a male-dominated industry. Or maybe he's not friendly enough with any female colleagues for them to stop by the house.

"Do you know how many kidnapping victims there are in the US each year? And runaways?" Shiloh's focus is on the monitor as she plays video and halts for an identifiable screenshot.

"Depends on the data source, but most estimates are around five thousand kids go missing each year." She smiles with approval at my answer.

"Yep. And forty-four hundred unidentified bodies found."

"You are just a ray of sunshine, aren't you? But, you know, those numbers don't align. They find most of those of the missing kids, and most of the unidentified bodies are adults."

"True. Do you know what percentage of abductions occur by strangers?"

"About point-one percent," I answer, wondering why she's asking these questions. "You're good with facts, aren't you?" She knows all the answers. She's quizzing me.

"Useless facts queen. If we ever do a team trivia night, stick with me." She smacks her lips. "Okay. That's it. By the way, we reviewed the photos in order of frequency. Those first two men came by the most."

"What about cleaning service? Or yard service?" I suppose the pool guy would never need to come up to the house. That might be true for the yard service, too.

"Cleaning service uses the side door. The only people who use the side door are Sophia, her friends, and her dad. There's no video inside the garage. If anyone arrived by car, parked in the garage, and came in the house that way, we wouldn't know. Erik confirmed that with the Wolf man yesterday."

"Right." I cross my arms and look at the last photo on her monitor. She said they are on the network, and she is texting me, but I like tangible material. "Can you print those for me?"

"Trees are crying all over the land," Shiloh says, but she hits print.

The typical kidnapping perpetrator profile doesn't fit this case. Unemployed with drug or alcohol problems doesn't fit anyone within Jack Sullivan's circle that we met so far, but we need background checks to confirm this. Male between the ages of eighteen and thirty-five is too broad to be helpful. Once we get the frequent visitors identified, we can confirm employment status and search records.

Someone went to a lot of effort to pull off this abduction. And according to Jack, his personal life comprises Sophia and work.

"Hey, Shiloh, can you also send me everything you find on Sullivan Arms? All the financial reports you gathered for Mr. Wolfgang?" I'll review those later.

"Yep." She rolls her chair back in front of her desk and types. "So, you doing the Wolf man?"

"What? No." I playfully shove her shoulder. She's as bad as Sabrina.

She giggles. I met her all of twenty minutes ago, and she's teasing me like we're mates.

"I met him two days ago."

Ryan steps out of his doorway and motions for me to join him.

"Got to go."

"Yeah, you do." Shiloh slips headphones over her ears. I tap her, not liking her tone, and give her a displeased face. The kind of jocular displeased expression I'd give Sophia during a FaceTime call. Shiloh smirks, and I roll my eyes. The familiar jesting pattern twists my insides. The reality that I might not see Sophia again filters through my conscience. It was one thing to believe she'd been rebellious. It is another thing to know she's been abducted.

Ice-blue eyes patiently track my route through the desks. I don't have to look to know he watches. His unreadable expression sends tingles across my skin. I stand straighter and push my shoulders back.

As I approach the wall of man, my oxygen supply dwindles. He easily stands half a foot taller than me, but his physical prowess isn't derived merely from height. It's his width and breadth, combined with the perma-scowl and those piercing light blue irises. His wavy dark hair and defined jaw round him out with a potent masculine beauty. My stomach knots, my pulse quickens, and I force my gaze to rise from the floor, up his strong legs, trim waist, and broad chest, to face the ice head on.

"This press release is going out Monday morning. Wayne Killington is stepping in as interim CEO."

I scan the one-page release.

"Did you know about this?" This feels big to me, but I don't get the same read from Ryan. He's acting like he always does, and he's simply updating me.

"I believe it's standard practice for a public company. He can't be expected to focus on work when his daughter is missing." I pull out my phone and do a quick search. A link from a financial news service appears with the headline "Sullivan Arms CEO Jackson Sullivan replaced by Wayne Killington." I click on the link. It takes seconds to skim the short article.

Comments are posted below the news article. I read a portion of one comment out loud. "Replacement due to personal reasons, but inside sources say the replacement is due to two years of subpar revenue growth." Ryan's shoulders lift slightly, and his blank gaze appears introspective. "The public is aware his daughter is missing. You'd think they'd lead with that."

"Did you know Wayne is his replacement?" When I first met man, I'd assumed he was Jack's driver, but probably because of the colorful Hawaiian shirt he wore.

"Jack said Wayne would be helping out. He didn't use the phrase 'interim CEO.' But Jack depends on him. He made that clear. That's not why I called you over. My FBI contact is here. Agent Liam Ryland. He texted about ten minutes ago. The FBI is assembling a team for this case. He's going to meet with us as planned, but the San Diego office is in the process of assigning a team to this case."

CHAPTER 14

114 Hours Missing

Ryan

Special Agent Liam Ryland enters our floor in a Saturday casual outfit of starched khakis and a button-down short-sleeve shirt. Based out of the Los Angeles field office, I met Liam once before. A contact in cybercrime provided his information when I originally spoke to them about the Sophia Sullivan case. After a brief conversation on the phone yesterday, Liam agreed to meet unofficially since it worked for his personal schedule.

My plan had been to run the case by him and see if anything stood out. The FBI gets involved in missing persons cases under specific situations. If Sophia had been under twelve, they'd be more than involved; they'd be leading the case. At under eighteen, they would assist with the case if the local police department asked. At the time of my conversation with Liam yesterday, they hadn't asked.

The spliced video proved foul play. And Jack brought the case before the public eye. If, for any reason, we suspected they had removed Sophia from the country, then the FBI would lead the case. Liam didn't say it on the phone, but given the increasingly high-profile nature of the case, I fully expect as soon as the FBI has a team in place, they will take the lead. Arrow's involvement will continue only so long as Jack Sullivan wants us involved.

Several heads in the cubicles watch as Agent Ryland crosses the room. I stand in the doorway to the conference room, arms crossed. I appreciate the agent offering his Saturday morning to meet, and I want his perspective, especially considering recent findings, but I also need him to understand ground rules. If Arrow is involved, we play my way. Some agents think they own the world, thanks to the three-letter acronym in their job title.

"Special Agent Ryland." I offer my hand. "Thank you for coming out."

His grip is firm, solid, and he looks me straight in the eyes. He's about six feet. Not too far off Alex's height.

"I'm Ryan Wolfgang."

His hands rest on his colorful blue-and-green belt buckle. White golf balls decorate the band.

"Did I hear correctly? You're working with Dr. Rolfe?"

"She's right here." I guide him inside the conference room. Alex rises from her seat and holds out her hand. Ryland blatantly scans her up and down, and I don't like it at all. As quickly as the rush of anger floods me, it dissipates when I observe surprise is Liam's dominant response.

"You were expecting my father, right?" The green in her eyes is stronger. Is it the room's light, or is that defiance?

"I've met Dr. Rolfe before." Ryland grins. "He's your father? He's given lectures at Quantico."

"He's my dad." She smiles good-naturedly, and her shoulders lift slightly. "But I'm also Dr. Rolfe."

"Well, your dad is a legend. Is he here?"

"No, lives in Edinburgh. I live here in Santa Barbara."

"She's assisting us on the Sophia Sullivan case," I put in.

"Got it." He points at a chair. "Can I sit?"

"Of course. Can I get you something to drink?"

"No. Thanks. I'm hoping to make this stop quick. I have brunch plans. I know yesterday you said you wanted my perspective, but as I told you on my way in this morning, it sounds like you are about to have the full services of the FBI at your disposal. We're pulling together a child abduction response team as we speak."

"That's good. I suppose you heard about the spliced video?"

"Agent Makowzki mentioned it. He's the one out of the San Diego office who called me. My supervisor knew I planned to come talk to you. Hear you out. But I doubt I'll be assigned to the case. It'll run out of the San Diego office."

He scratches his jaw. His gaze travels back to Alex. She is admittedly an attractive woman. Even on a Saturday morning with her dark hair pulled back into a braid. But his extended gaze has me wanting to rip him out of his seat and send him on his way. The irrational desire is a new one for me. I've never considered myself the jealous type.

"Are you assisting from a criminal profile perspective? Like your dad?" Ryland asks Alex.

"I believe the person who took Sophia knew her. The spliced video and the cleaned home do not speak to a random kidnapping. We can apply the standard profile of a kidnapper, but it's not highly relevant at this juncture. To answer your question, Agent

Ryland, about why I am involved?" He gives a perfunctory nod. "I am a family friend of the Sullivans."

"So, he knows your dad, too?" This time she gives a curt nod. "That makes sense. If I were him, I'd call you, too."

Alex's back straightens, and she grows taller in her chair. The top of her head is now higher than Agent Ryland's, and she faces him head on.

Ryland crosses one leg over his knee, seemingly unaffected. He taps his thigh with his hand. This isn't his case. He doesn't care.

"We're researching frequent visitors to Jackson Sullivan's San Diego home. We're also looking into anyone high within the organization. Can the FBI help us with background checks? Or any information you might have on them?"

"Sullivan Arms is a weapons manufacturer. The ATF might have more information than we do. But we can definitely assist you. You're thinking it's someone with his company? Not someone from her school?"

"We've reviewed all of her social media. There's nothing suspicious. We met with the students in her class and the faculty."

"Nothing?" he asks.

"Nothing caught our attention as suspicious," I answer.

It is quite possible an interview with an FBI agent might deliver different reactions in an interview setting. But I can be an intimidating person, and I didn't pick up on anything other than genuine concern.

"Send your list to research over. They're gathering the team today, but I can send it over to have someone work on it. It'll give you and the team a head-start tomorrow morning." He looks at us both, sets his phone down, and hits record. "Why don't you give me a rundown of where you are in the case? I'll send the audio over to the team lead, whoever that's going to be." Agent Ryland slings an arm over an adjacent chair. "Once I get this, I'll head out."

Alex turns those green eyes to me, tentative.

"Take it," I say.

She places one hand over the other on the table and begins speaking with an air of confidence. "Sophia Sullivan was last seen at four thirty p.m. on Monday. The video splice removed the bulk of that day from the side camera view. We have no record of what time she actually went missing. Jack Sullivan came home at around nine p.m. and couldn't locate her. None of her friends heard from her, but she did like several TikTok posts from six thirty to seven p.m. Her phone, an iPad, and her laptop were all found in her bedroom. Her laptop was charging, the other devices were not. There was no sign of struggle in the house, but the cleaning service cleaned the morning before we arrived at the scene. I spoke to the cleaning service, and they didn't observe any sign of struggle or anything out of place. We have no suspicious persons. We have no leads. Jack Sullivan procured Arrow Security's services Tuesday morning, as well as mine. He expressed concern at that point in time about the media. I've known Jack Sullivan for over fifteen years and can attest that his concern for the media is within character. The spliced video shows foul play. Jack Sullivan did not initially want to go to the media, but as of last night, with no other leads, he did. He has hired a PR firm, which is helping him. Arrow has a team that will go through Sullivan's contacts, searching for any more connections, this afternoon. Did I miss anything?"

"I think you got it all." Her concise summary laid it out well.

"And once the FBI is involved, Sullivan plans to continue paying you both?" Ryland asks, moving on to address the business at hand.

"Ultimately, that's up to Jack Sullivan, but it's my understanding he wants as many resources as possible working to bring his daughter home."

"What are you doing?" He directs his question to Alex. "Are you a profiler, like your pops?"

"I'm a criminal and behavioral psychologist. And, as I said, I am a family friend of the Sullivans. Sophia's mother was a close friend of mine. I'll be involved, paid or unpaid, until she's found."

"Dr. Rolfe is a value to the team. Do you have a specific concern we need to address?" Agent Ryland is making me regret ever asking him up here.

"No. Nepotism is interesting to me." Alex opens her mouth at the insult.

"There's no nepotism. I don't give a damn about her father, and I'd hire her on her own merit."

Ryland holds his hand up as if I have a gun pointed at him. I don't, but I'd halfway like to. His behavior is bizarre to me. Why does he care so much about her father?

"Didn't mean to step out of line." He pulls out his phone and checks it. "I need to head out. I'll look for your text with those names." He stands. I push my chair back and face him. "How well do you know Jack Sullivan?"

"We went to the Naval Academy together," I answer. I do not offer that I hadn't seen him in over a decade.

He nods. It is a thoughtful nod, one that says he is thinking things he doesn't intend to share. But his question implies his haze of suspicion is directed Sullivan's way. I don't blame him. The San Diego Police Department met with Sullivan multiple times. He's the father and bound to fall under scrutiny.

After saying our goodbyes to Ryland, I tap on Erik's office door.

"If Sullivan Arms were doing something illegal, like selling guns in some illegal manner, how would you go about finding that out?"

Erik wheels his chair away from the five monitors across his desk, and his head appears to the side of the last monitor.

"You mean, other than asking him? Are we not trusting Sullivan?"

"I'd trust him with my life. Doesn't mean he, or his company, hasn't broken federal laws."

"Well, pull up chairs. Let's brainstorm what data we need. I'll make sure I have resources gathering it. How'd that meeting go with the FBI?"

I pull out a chair and shake my head at my friend and business partner. "Fine."

"I'll reach out to one of the forensic accountants we use. Would Sullivan give us access to his books, or do we need to hack in?"

Alex's eyes widen.

"We probably won't find anything. It's a public company," I say. Of course, public companies get caught in illegal transactions all the time. But there is no need for my slender law-abiding sleuth to worry at this stage. Right now, this is pure speculation. A broad hunt.

A text from Jack comes through.

Jack Sullivan: FBI offered resources for an additional search.

My hired crew searched every single street in San Diego and the beach, but another sweep wouldn't hurt, so I responded with a quick "Great."

Five days in on a missing persons case with no lead, we'll take every bit of help we can get.

Through our office windows, the morning sky radiates crystal blue sprinkled with scattered fluffy white clouds. Skateboard wheels rolling down the sidewalk, laughter, a squeal, and the hum of music all filter in through the glass, a reminder that, outside, the world at large enjoys a Saturday. From my desk, I can see Alex in a temporary cube. When I approach, she's reading an article on ghost guns.

Ghost guns is a term used to describe guns built from parts without serial codes. It's a significant issue. There is no legitimate reason to want a gun without a serial number. No serial number means the gun can't be traced. Yet around forty thousand ghost guns a year are collected in crimes across that country.

"A little light reading?" I ask.

She rubs her eyes and shrugs. "It's like a rabbit hole. I search for articles about gun sales and find articles about gun laws, most of which seem to be aimed at protecting gun manufacturers. Nothing, though, with relevance to the case." She rubs her eyes. "I'm driving myself mad."

"Let's head out. Take a break."

"A break?" she wails, aghast at the notion.

"Yes, a break. We've got a full staff working. The FBI response team is still being formed, so we don't have a contact point. It's Saturday. Jack has to return from another visit at the SDPD to review the photos we sent him and respond with names. Let's get outside. Fresh air will do us good."

"Oh, Trace," she says, and those eyes close as she tilts her head back. "I need to walk my dog."

"Well, let's go."

"You're going with me?" she whispers. She glances several

cubicles back toward Shiloh. *Oh, yes. She's worried about image. Right.*

"I drove you here. I'll drive you back. We can get lunch. And we can discuss what you've learned." My response is louder than necessary. One or two heads glance our way. No one on Arrow's staff gives a damn. But I'll play it Alex's way.

CHAPTER 15

119 Hours Missing

Ryan

The garish yellow brick on her Craftsman glistens under the California noon sun.

As if reading my mind, Alex says, "I'm going to paint it."

"I didn't say anything." The car door slams, and the house emits a shrill, high-pitched, repetitive bark.

"You didn't say it, but I could see it. You are quite critical."

Is she serious?

"I have said nothing critical at all."

"It's in your face." Her index finger circles her own face. Unbelievable. "And your eyes. You are quite negative."

She opens her arched front door, and Trace bounds out, jumping up and down on her legs, most likely scratching her the same way he scratched me earlier. He trots over to a bush, lifts his leg, then trots back to Alex.

"I am not negative." She lifts the dog and carries him into the house. She sets him down, and the back of his body twists with the movement of his tail.

"I'm not so sure about that." She lifts her chin, disputing my statement.

"I assure you I harbor no negative thoughts of you." She lifts those challenging green eyes of hers, and my chest clenches. I slide an errant loose strand behind her ear. I should keep my hands off her, but my thumb caresses her cheek. "Quite the opposite, actually. When it comes to you, I would say I am quite positive."

"Positive?" One eyebrow lifts as she pronounces the singular word in a charming lilt.

"Positive I want to get to know you better." I shove my wayward hand in my shorts pocket, but those green eyes remain locked on me.

Her tongue licks across her lower lip. Her lashes flutter. There's a flirty tilt to her head that I register as an invitation and close the gap between us.

"Positive I want to do lewd things with you." Her breasts, encapsulated in that tight fitting tee, rise. She lifts a dark, shapely eyebrow.

"Lewd? As in illegal? A promiscuous indulgence of lust?" Her upper tooth sinks into her lower lip, teasing and tempting.

"Lascivious." I press my lips to her forehead and inhale, picking up on subtle scents with an underlying aroma of sweetness. "Erotic." My palm cups her ass, and I squeeze. Her muscle clenches beneath my touch. "Dirty."

She closes the distance between us, and I suspect she can feel exactly how turned on I am. We discussed dinner, but I'm not sure I have it in me to wait. Judging from the color in her cheeks and the rapid rise and fall of her chest, she's as turned on right now as I am. Those long fingers trace my chest, above my pecs.

She gazes up at me, and I detect a hint of uncertainty. But she doesn't back away. No, her hips flex against my groin. The sensation disrupts any logical thought processes.

"I thought you wanted to get some fresh air?" Her thumb roams over my nipple. The fabric of my shirt dulls the sensation, but it's kindling on a needy flame.

"It's Saturday," I say as my fingers slip beneath the hem of her tee.

"Yeah?" Her hips buck up, rubbing my groin, intensifying the pressure.

"We have time." I situate my thigh between her legs and taste those lips. Sweet, sugary. She slowly grinds her pelvis against my thigh. Like me, she's getting off on the pressure.

My head dips to meet those lips. I've been with women who were so much shorter that kissing felt awkward. But not Alex. She's just the right height. My fingers cup the back of her head as I deepen the kiss.

She grips my erection through my shorts. The unexpected pressure has me searching between us to confirm she's grasping me. She slowly smiles. It's a sensuous smile. An inviting smile. Her fingers squeeze my shaft, and my knees quake.

"You keep doing that, and I won't be taking it slow."

She rubs her palm flat, up and down. The pressure elicits a groan. *Fuck.*

"I warned you."

I lift her, and both her legs wrap around my hips. I walk through the sun-filled bungalow of open windows until I reach her bedroom and kick the door closed.

Her hips flex, and her center presses hard against the tip of my engorged erection. I pause, holding her, while I gather control.

Her arms wrap around my shoulders and her fingers tousle my hair.

"Are you sure?" I'll only ask once, but I will confirm consent.

"Yes." Her chin tilts up. "Don't let me think too much about it."

She's second-guessing this. But she doesn't need to. Sex is healthy.

"Shall I tie your hands?" I would like to tie her hands. Complete control. Freedom to roam her body and explore. To tease her with my mouth and fingers until she begs.

Those eyes cut to the narrow windows above her bed. The wooden shutters are open. The windows face the side of the street, high enough up that no one should be able to see in. Two large windows on the adjacent wall face the back yard.

"Close the shutters."

I set her down on the bed and lean into her, grinding against her center as I plunder her mouth. I squeeze her breast through her shirt and pinch her nipple. She doesn't react, so I pinch harder, and she squirms, her thigh rubbing against my hard-on. Her hands reach for me, but I step away. I want her just like that...eager and needy.

The shutters click closed with one bat of my hand. Sunlight filters through small cracks. I grip my shirt at my waist and tug, lifting it over my head. My shorts do nothing to hide my arousal.

Those green eyes hesitate. Is she rethinking this? We both need a release. Meaningless sex is all I do. Can she handle it?

I reach behind her head and tug, pulling at the band at the base of her braid, freeing the strands. Her dark hair cascades down her back and along her shoulders.

I'm going to see her again. Will that be a problem?

She mimics my earlier actions and holds on to the end of that tiny shirt. She pulls it up, over her head, exposing a sheer white bra and two perfect breasts. She reaches behind her, and the bra straps slide down her smooth shoulders, and she sends the scrap of material flying. Her nipples are every bit as sexy as I've imagined ever since seeing them through sheer fabric. Those perky, dark, aroused nipples beg to be sucked. Her long stomach is smooth, and it curves to her rounded hips. She's fucking gorgeous.

What we're doing might be unwise. Sex might cause problems. But I don't give a damn.

The dim room hides the shade of those forest eyes. Her arms are behind her. She supports her weight on her palms and, by doing so, thrusts her delectable chest out, those tempting, luscious nipples visibly turned on. I toe off my shoes. She rises, and her fingers cover the band on her skirt.

I cover her fingers with mine and give a slight shake of my head.

"You want to undress me?"

She shouldn't have to ask.

"Are you not speaking now? The way you're looking at me...it's the same way you looked at me when you barged in the bedroom before. I wasn't sure...but I think you like what you see."

I find it hard to swallow. The skirt glides easily over her hips and over those never-ending legs, exposing a matching sheer thong.

My throat tightens, and I force my swallow as I take her in and finally find my voice. "You like lingerie."

"I think you do, too."

The sheer thong bordered by white silk renders an alluring glow.

"You think?" I never really paid attention to lingerie. But she might be right. Last night I stroked myself with visions of her in red lace. What I really want is to get her out of it. To explore her. To sink inside her.

"Do you have a scarf? Or a tie?"

"I don't want you to tie me up. I'm not..." Her words trail, and she shakes her head. She doesn't trust me enough for that. I read her loud and clear.

I grip her hips and tug her to the edge of the bed. I get down on my knees. My thumbs loop under the thin straps. I gaze up into her dark eyes as I slowly drag her panties down her thighs, the hard pads of my fingers brushing her soft silky skin, over her knees, and down her calves. I let the slip of fabric fall to the floor.

My lips trail whisper-light kisses up her thighs to her trimmed apex. I press directly above her slit. With her gaze fixed on me, watching, I taste her. My tongue slips inside, and she inhales. Her feet rest on my shoulders, and I pull her closer to the edge of the bed and feast. Each moan, each mewl, each twist of her hips fuels me on. Her coming from my tongue becomes my one desire, my singular afternoon aim. My teeth graze over her sensitive nub as I force two fingers inside, and she lurches forward. Her feet slam against my back as her first orgasm escapes.

I rise off my knees, and she uses her feet to push my shorts down.

"I want you."

I lean over the bed and crash my mouth over hers, wanting her tongue, needing the same hungry, passionate kiss from earlier. Her breasts fill my palm, and I knead and stroke, then take her nipple in my mouth and tease the sensitive flesh. I shift her toward the middle of the bed, grab a condom from the wallet in my shorts, and climb to her, hovering over her, supported by my forearms and knees.

Those long legs wrap around me, her feet on my ass and thighs. I position my tip at her entrance. Her fingers wrap around my erection. I watch, mesmerized, as she strokes me and her thumb circles the pre-cum on the end.

"Now. I want you now." She traces my tip up and down through her lips. Warm and soft. My cock pulses with need. I roll a condom on and position myself at her entrance. My eyes flutter closed as I slip into her heat.

"So tight," I grunt, and then surge forward, balls deep. I still, frozen, my head resting in the crook of her neck. "Fuck, you feel good."

Her hips buck up, wanting movement, but I need a minute to regain control. When my eyes open, I gaze into forest green and hidden gold as we find our rhythm. I lift her hips, searching for that one spot, the spot that will send her head tilting backward and her back lurching forward.

I lift one long, slender leg and place it over my shoulder, raising her higher, sending me deeper. I bite the inside of her thigh, right above her knee. Her fingers roam my chest and my abs and around to my back. Her nails grate my skin.

She tenses around me, muscles quivering, eyes closed. She's close. I pull out and spin her on her side. I lie down behind her, lift her thigh, and slide back inside. God, she's soaked and tight and feels like heaven. My fingers match the rhythm of my thrusts, working her clit, as her pants and moans and noises grow frantic.

"Rye," she chants over and over.

"That's it, baby. One more time."

"I've already come. I don't know..."

"You can do it." Her muscles tighten, as if they have a mind of their own and can respond to my commands. "That last one was tiny. Give it to me."

I press hard on her clit, then slap my hand over her and vibrate my fingers rapidly, just like I imagine she works herself. Her head falls back against my shoulder.

"Ryan," she breathes out. My name so soft out of her lips catches me off guard, grabs my focus, and ends it for me. I pulse into her, spilling in burst after burst as the room goes dark. I gasp for oxygen. Her body quivers around me. She whimpers, and I place tender kisses along the side of her face. I cup her breast as my hips surge forward, not wanting to leave her.

When I collapse onto my back, my dick slips out. A slight haze of sweat chills my skin.

"Fuck. You're really good at that."

I chuckle. The sound feels foreign. Rusty from lack of use.

"You sound surprised."

"No." She is still on her side, her back to me. We both lie crossways over her comforter, and our feet hang off the bed. I trail a finger along her arm, down the curve of her waist, and up the arch of her hip. "Well, maybe. I didn't have high expectations."

I bite down, letting my teeth sink into her shoulder playfully. She squirms.

"Hey." She rolls her shoulder toward me, so her back falls partially against me and the bed. She reaches up to stroke my jaw, and I bend over her to take her mouth once again.

My heartrate normalizes, and as it does, the frenetic energy buzzing between us calms, replaced by a sense of tranquility. Our kisses slow.

Scratch. Scratch.

The sound comes from the direction of the closed door.

"Trace. Buddy. I'll be right there," she calls to her dog as if he's fluent in English.

Her head falls back against my shoulder. I loop a long strand of hair around a finger. A desire to pull a blanket over us and snuggle overwhelms me, so much so, I push off the bed. Soft kisses and post-coital cuddling aren't things I do.

There's an abducted girl we need to find. Now that we have that out of the way, we can focus.

CHAPTER 16

121 Hours Missing

Alex

In front of the mirror, I critique my body. My hip bones jut out too harshly, but I do like my smooth belly and the elongated shape of my belly button. The sheer fabric lifts my small breasts, breasts that have always felt inadequate. My nipples are raw from the sucking and tongue-lashing Ryan administered. He didn't seem to have any issues with their size.

The dim light conceals the stretch marks that cross my inner thighs. Those stretch marks appeared at age eleven after a continuous growth spurt of close to ten inches. My mum died two years before, and Dad hadn't been great about stocking clothes before my spurt. But that year, all my pants were high waters and skirts inappropriately short, until he gave up and bought several sizes too large. Belts kept the gathered fabric up on my narrow hips.

Dad would never in a million years approve of what I just did. He's no saint, but as a matter of principal, he doesn't date colleagues. But shagging's not quite the same thing as dating. Definitely not the same thing as a relationship. It's a physical act. A release. It's not a big deal. We have chemistry, and we acted on it. There's no reason for anyone to ever know what happened between us. I can only hope this doesn't sabotage future career opportunities with Arrow.

Heavy footsteps outside the door let me know he's done with the bathroom and he went to the kitchen. He leaped up and gathered his clothes and headed down the hall to the half bath. A considerate move, leaving me with my bedroom bathroom, but it also left me feeling dirty.

Conceptually, I fully support a woman's right to enjoy sex when the opportunity arises. But perhaps I'm not built for casual sex. Likely, that is the case. At university, sure, casual sex happened. Only most of the time mine happened with friends who grew to be more. Sometime in the future, when I have time, I'll do a more thorough self-examination to better understand what exactly about this situation is leaving me so unsettled.

With one last glance at my toothpick legs, I throw on my clothes and pull up my rumpled sex hair into a band. Having sex with a man I work with isn't an intelligent course of action. But Ryan is a professional. And he already agreed that anything that happened between us will be kept under wraps. If we're discrete, theoretically, there will be no downside to an occasional romp. And it was indeed great. A memory of his reflection thrusting into me from behind while working my clit has me squeezing my thighs together.

I check my t-shirt for dirt smudges and recall the feel of his hard muscles. How his massive body covered me. He's the biggest man I've ever been with, and I liked the novel sensation of feeling dainty. I am the Amazon woman. A different species from the petite girls at school and university. My dad says height doesn't matter. One friend back home claimed that when it comes to sex, the only thing that matters is the length of the torso. Still, at university, I never relished being climbed like a beanstalk. Something that is a non-issue with a man Ryan's size.

"You okay in there?" Ryan asks through the closed door.

"Yeah," I answer with one last glance at the mirror.

"Trace is scratching the kitchen door. Should I just let him out into the back yard?"

"Yeah. You can let him out."

I step into the bathroom and close the door. As I flip the lid on the toilet, I grab my phone and type out a text to Sabrina.

Me: You won't believe my nooner

But then I delete it. *How pathetic am I*? Desiring to tell a friend I just had sex. I mean, I will tell her. I hear about her sex life all the time. Now I finally have something to contribute to the conversation. But texting her right after...that is low class behavior.

I wash my hands, dry them, and wipe beneath my eyes. *All right. Go out there and be normal. Carry on like an adult.*

Ryan is in the back yard. The storm door creaks as I open it, and he glances up from his phone for one brief second. Trace raises his leg and wets the fence.

Ryan doesn't say a word as I approach. He's glued to the phone in his hand. Is it the sex? Did I muck up everything? Will a nooner prove to be the ultimate mistake?

I slide my hands into my shorts pockets and waffle back and forth from my toe to my heel. Waiting. He's engrossed in his phone. Maybe he's avoiding me. Maybe I should just query about diseases then send him on his way.

"The meeting with the FBI team in San Diego has been confirmed. Eight a.m. tomorrow. Can you make it?"

"Do you think they'd want me there?" Agent Ryland hadn't been exactly welcoming. The FBI has its own Behavioral Analysis Unit, or BAU. They don't need me.

"You're on my team. In my experience, FBI agents are accustomed to working with multiple parties. It comes with crossing jurisdictions. And in a case like this, additional manpower is a good thing."

"I'm available." It's a phenomenal opportunity for me. I will absolutely be available.

"We can fly down in the morning. Jack said Wayne will pick us up from the helipad."

Ryan drops his phone into his pocket and looks off in the sun's direction. His shades provide cover. He's unreadable. Which isn't an issue for me. I do not need to read him. He is a colleague with benefits. Possibly one-time benefits.

"Should we go back to the office?" I ask.

"Erik didn't have any updates. Let's go on that walk." Trace trots to the far fence and sniffs the air.

"Good idea. Especially if I'm gone all day tomorrow. I wonder if my neighbor will be okay watching him. Do you think we'll spend the night?"

"Doubtful. But you never know. One of the good things about the FBI taking up the case is that they have resources. Boots on the ground means we don't have to do it all." He looks beyond my tiny yard, into my neighbors' yards. "I bet Stella would take care of him."

"Stella? From your office?"

"She has a fenced-in back yard for her dog. Well, it's Trevor's dog, but basically hers. And she has a teenage son you can hire. Want me to call her? She'll be understanding if our plans change."

Given I barely know my neighbor Jenny, and I have already leaned on her, I say, "Sure."

He dials Stella while I get the leash. When I return, his back is to me, arms stretched across the fence, surveying land that isn't mine. His shorts curve over his rounded butt cheeks and end above his knee. Dark, curly hair covers his legs, except along the smooth inner curve of his muscular calves. I flush, remembering the flex of all those hard muscles as he pounded into me. Those thoughts are quite unnecessary, so I blink and shake them away.

"Ready?" Trace's body vibrates with happiness at the sight of the leash in my hand.

"Yep."

"How much time do you have?"

"Same as you."

"What do you mean?"

I lead him left onto Hailey Street. Cars buzz by. Trace happily trots along, pausing to sniff each parking meter post.

"You're my plans for the afternoon."

"Until we get the background reports?" I hope one of the executives at Sullivan Arms stands out. The longer we go without leads, our chances of locating Sophia dim.

"Are you happy in this neighborhood?" Ryan asks.

"I like State Street." There are plenty of bungalows throughout the area that I couldn't afford. The only reason I'd been able to snag this one is because it is so tiny, and the minuscule lot size prevented a developer from coming in, knocking it down, and putting in something larger. "How'd you pick your area?"

"Real estate agent." He scans the street as we walk. He is always scanning his surroundings. "Do you do this walk at night?"

"Yeah. Why?"

"I'm not sure it's a good idea."

"It's really a good neighborhood," I assure him. "Mostly families. Young families. And a lot of dog walkers."

"Have you met many people?"

"I've met a lot of dogs." I smile up into my reflection in his shades.

He doesn't return my smile. His hands are in his pockets, hinting at casual, but his upright posture and attentive stance says alert, borderline formal. Even in shorts and trainers, he carries a professional air.

"I suppose I should trust you've not got any diseases? We didn't really talk about it back there..."

The corners of his lips lift into an almost-smile, the first sign of real life since we'd headed out into the neighborhood. A woman pushing a stroller approaches, and he waits until she's passed before answering.

"I'm clean. I always use a condom." He exhales and tilts his head my way. "I did really enjoy that."

"I really enjoyed that, too," I say, entertained by his formal choice of words.

"So, college life. What's that like?"

"What do you mean?"

"Do you hang with other professors? Students? Are the students hot for teacher?" He grins. I rather like how his face softens when he relaxes.

"It would be scandalous if a professor dated a student. I mean, I think decades ago no one batted much of an eye as long as, you know, the professor wasn't attached. But, nowadays, no, the university is quite serious about sexual misconduct. When they hired me, I had to sit through a training."

"Well, that's about your behavior. I'm asking about the students. I think about what it would be like to have you as a professor."

Gods, that smile. I want to reach up and plant a kiss smack dab on those lips. Or grab his hand and link our fingers.

"Did you have the hots for one of your professors?"

"At the Naval Academy? Absolutely not."

A girlish giggle erupts, not at his words, but his exaggerated expression. "What was the Naval Academy like?"

"I think different from the typical college experience. But good. Not many women around, at least in my class. That might be changing. Like I said, it did not inspire me to continue my academic career."

"No. They inspired you to go save the world."

"Something like that."

"What made you leave the military?"

"Things happened right about the time my term was up." His jaw muscles flex and he looks straight ahead. He visibly stiffens. Whatever happened wasn't good, and he doesn't want to talk about it. "I considered reenlisting, but... You remember Erik, from the office?"

"Erik Lai." The man introduced himself as Erik, but his full name is on a plaque beside his office door.

"Met him at a bar. Trevor and I. We'd been on the same team. We were both weighing reenlistment. On leave. Traveling through Asia without much of an agenda. And this sauced American is sitting at the bar. He picked up pretty quickly we too were American. Bought us drinks. By morning, we'd agreed to work for Erik as his private security."

"Security?"

"He was in a bad place. He needed it." We round another corner. "One thing led to another."

"It's funny how that happens, isn't it?" I feel like that's how I ended up with my doctorate. One thing led to another. Of course, that wasn't exactly how it happened. Each step took a lot of work. It's the rearview illusion. During the course of it, it seemed the drudgery would never end. In the rearview, it's like it flew by in a nanosecond.

"Yes, it is."

"Do you have any regrets?" I ask, peering over at him. His lips flatline, the stiffness returns, and I hate I asked the question. "Not liking Santa Barbara?" I ask in a lighter tone.

"No. I like it here. Seventy-two and sunny, what's not to like?" The muscles along his jaw soften once again. "I like what we're doing at Arrow. No two days are the same. I make my own decisions. I don't go into situations knowing half the story." He swallows and glances down at me. "I get plenty of outdoor time. We're near the ocean. Live next door to my best friend."

"Erik?"

"No, Erik lives in Napa. He's a close friend. As is our other partner, Kairi. She also lives up north. But Trevor, he's like a brother." And he just sent him off on a dangerous assignment.

"Is everything okay in Damascus?"

Ryan's eye twitches, and his chest heaves upward. The muscles along his jaw tense. "Trevor texted earlier. Our buddy is going to lose his leg."

"Shit."

His bottom lip shifts, and his chin juts up. "Yeah. Shit." We turn back into my driveway. "Shrapnel from an explosion. But we'll make sure he gets the best medical care. And everything he needs when he gets home."

"That's important to you, isn't it?"

"Hell yeah, it is. Military doesn't always do that. Supposed to, but..." He looks away. I have heard stories about healthcare in the US. Back home, healthcare is available for all. I haven't gotten sick yet, so I don't know what it is like over here. But those stories do concern me. I have health insurance with my job, so I should be okay.

It is hard for me to understand how a country as wealthy as the United States doesn't offer healthcare to its citizens. Seems to me all the money dumped into insurance should go to actual health-care, and that would solve the problem. Whenever you bring in a middleman, issues are going to arise. Of course, I suppose, the other side, the foreign side, always seems odd, no matter which side of the border you're on.

I unlock my front door, and Ryan's hand covers the doorknob. He pushes the door wide, his arm held out, holding the door for Trace and me to pass.

Ryan sits down on my sofa as I bend to detach Trace's leash and give him a good scratch behind his ears.

"Ryland sent over some background information." His thumb scrolls on his screen. "He says Larry Reyes has been on the ATF's radar for years."

"Who is he?"

"One of the men who visited Jack Sullivan's house regularly. He's an executive at Sullivan Arms."

The photograph he shows me is of a relatively young Hispanic businessman with black hair, thick black eyebrows, and tan skin. My stomach curls in on itself. I've studied all the American acronyms, but I want to be certain.

"And ATF is...?"

"Bureau of Alcohol, Tobacco, Firearms, and Explosives."

CHAPTER 17

122 Hours Missing

Alex

The portrait photo on Sullivan Arms' website of Larry Reyes reveals more than the grainy black-and-white screenshot. Thick eyelashes frame dark brown eyes, and a charismatic smile rounds out the image of a consummate professional. Jack said he's a rising star within Sullivan Arms and currently serves as the youngest senior executive. When asked how his company defines senior executive, he said anyone with an SVP title. Larry recently divorced and doesn't have any children.

The same style portrait of Cliff Hartman shows a balding older man with heavily salted hair and a paisley bow tie. The business executive serves as Chief Compliance Officer for the organization. He and his wife have a second home in San Diego, and when they are in town, he comes to visit Jack.

When asked why his wife never visited, Jack said the pair are separated. Apparently, once their oldest went off to college, Mrs. Wheatley expressed her dissatisfaction with the marriage.

"Explain to me the ATF connection," I say to Ryan as I study these photographs.

"I can only assume it has to do with his role in sales within the company. It's possible the ATF watches all executives at arms manufacturers. But I doubt it. US law is written to expressly protect gun manufacturers' privacy and rights. We'll learn more in tomorrow's meeting. What do you think?"

"Do you think it's odd Jack is divorced, and these men are, too?"

"Last I heard, the divorce rate is at fifty-two percent."

Ryan takes a phone call and leaves into another room.

He's right. A divorce by itself is meaningless. And these men are colleagues. Visiting Jack's house doesn't mean anything either. We're grasping at straws searching for a proper theory.

On a whim, I call Jack. He answers on the first ring.

"Alex. Do you have something?"

"No, I'm sorry." I should've realized he'd get hopeful when my name flashed on his phone. "How are you holding up?"

He exhales, and it comes across like a wind tunnel.

"How can I help you?" He mutters, and it sounds like profanity strung together. "I don't mean to be rude. I'm sure this is hard on you, too."

"I am concerned. And frustrated. But I can't begin to grasp what you're going through."

A shorter exhale relays more static.

"There's something we learned about in Sophia's folders. It could be nothing. At all. But I meant to ask you about it."

"I thought you said you didn't find anything."

"I didn't. At your house. But Arrow's team went through her

electronic files."

"What'd they find?"

"She had one folder. It's full of articles on affairs. What it means when someone cheats. The impact to a family. That kind of thing. I mean, this is probably grasping—"

"Fuck." He mutters the expletive so low I barely hear it. "I didn't know Sophia knew."

I close my eyes, overwhelmed with gratitude we didn't discover the Geese folder until after we knew she'd been abducted. Otherwise, I would have taken it as a probable motivation for leaving her father.

"I can't believe Cassie told her." He sounds absolutely broken. My heart aches, and I so wish I hadn't dredged up this piece of history.

"Cassie never told me. She always said that the two of you had grown apart. It's probably not relevant. It was just a loose end. I probably should never've asked." It would have been over three years ago that he cheated. I shouldn't have brought it up.

"I don't know who it was. If you're looking for probable suspects, I can't help you."

Wait, what?

"Fuck. I hate Sophia found out. She never once said anything to make me think she knew."

"Cassie cheated on *you*?"

"She came clean when I returned from a business trip early."

"Did you walk in—"

"No. Nothing like that. She could've gotten away with it. I think guilt was eating at her. She told me. We separated. At some point after the divorce, we started having family dinners on weekends when I was in town. We began growing closer. She asked if I could ever give her another chance."

"What did you say?"

"I had a lot of travel coming up. I told her I'd think about it. That was three days before she died. She never said anything to me about Sophia knowing."

"Were you at Cassie's house when she asked about getting back together?"

"Yes. Why?"

"Because I bet Sophia overheard you. That's around the time she started collecting articles."

He huffs. I wait, expecting him to say something more, but there's only silence.

"And she never told you who she had the affair with?"

"No. But, whoever it was...she wasn't in love with him. She was just... This isn't the lead you're looking for."

His words trail off, and I don't push for more. It's a loose, interesting end, but the timing isn't right. A jilted lover would have no reason to kidnap Cassie's daughter three years after Cassie's death.

Ryan enters the room. I put my index finger up to my lips.

"Well, I'm sorry for dredging up old memories. And, Jack, for what it's worth, I know Cassie loved you."

"Thanks. Keep asking questions. We've got to find her."

"We will. Try to get some sleep."

The line clicks. Jack isn't in a good place at all.

"Was that Jack?"

"Yeah. I called him. I wanted to ask... I didn't think it was anything. And it wasn't."

"What?"

Cassie and Jack's marriage feels private, and I am awash in guilt for digging where I shouldn't have.

"I was asking about something that might possibly lead to a motive...but no dice." It's close to the truth without airing their dirty laundry.

"Motive." The word rolls off Ryan's tongue as if he's weighing it. "Theoretically, if someone wanted him out of the CEO role, that could be a motive."

"By chance, have you asked Jack if that might be the case?"

"I did. He understands our logic but says there's no way. Wayne fought him on stepping aside. His uncle didn't want it to happen. His uncle's concern was the fiduciary responsibility to the board. He doesn't want to be sued by investors. Once this is over, Jack will resume as CEO."

"And we encouraged him to go to the press. No one else did."

"Wayne is furious he went to the press. He's worried about the impact to the Sullivan brand."

"I don't get that." If anything, I'd expect sympathy from customers.

"Sullivan Arms' marketing campaign stresses self-defense. Wayne apparently blew a gasket that the PR team allowed this to happen. Says if the owner's daughter is kidnapped, then that goes against their positioning that guns keep your family safe."

"What does Jack say?"

"He doesn't give a damn. Only reason I know about it is he had me on speaker phone when Wayne charged into the office. But he backed down pretty quick. Said he'd go do damage control."

"It's hard to imagine this negatively impacting sales, but if it does, then does that give a competitor motive?"

Ryan concentrates on a far corner, his expression a nearly blank slate. His lips scrunch, and he gives a quick shake of his head. "No. I can understand Wayne's concern, but he's too close to his marketing campaign. Maybe a touch possessive over the PR agency. In recent history, fear serves to drive gun sales, not hamper them. And the fear the ads strive to create drives sales for all gun manufacturers, not just one brand."

"So where does that leave us?"

"Other than Reyes, no other executive was in the FBI database. They'll still pull together background reports, but no one has a criminal history, and there are no red flags."

"And Reyes did sales?"

"He has a lot of international accounts. My bet is that's what put him on the ATF watch list."

"I keep thinking that it could be random. But then I remember the spliced tape. It's not random. I hate to say it, but I assume you've checked insurance policies..." I let the words trail off. It sucks to vocalize it, but the reality is, tomorrow we'll be with a new team, and they won't leave any stone unturned.

"Sullivan doesn't need money. He doesn't give a damn about his reputation in the press. This trail isn't going to lead back to Sullivan." Ryan speaks with the conviction of someone who has given the matter thought and studied it from all sides. I agree with him. "If it leads back to Jack Sullivan, it's going to be related to his role as a dominant player as a gun manufacturer. At least sixty percent of their product is exported. It's going to be a deal gone bad. An SOB angry that a deal didn't happen. We aren't looking in the right places yet."

"Did you ask him about any deals?"

"He says he doesn't negotiate any of the wholesale deals. It's all in the sales department."

"So, a deal could have gone badly, and he's unaware? But the slighted party goes after the CEO's daughter?" That doesn't make sense.

Ryan's lips contort, and his eyes squint. He's not buying too heavily into this line of reasoning. His eyes widen and he shakes his head. "Anything is possible at this juncture. I called Wayne. Asked him if he'll have time to talk with us. Gave him the heads up we'd like to go over any deals that didn't end with happy customers."

"What did he say?"

"Happy to do anything he can once he's finished with damage control." Ryan pauses, and a hint of amusement dances across his lips. "He colored his statement with some descriptive words I haven't heard since my Navy days. Said he couldn't think of any soured deals, but he'll bring whatever he can find tomorrow."

Ryan squints, looking off to his left once again. When he's thinking, he has a tendency to look off to the corner. Something clicks in that brain of his, and he dials his phone. He sets it on speaker so I can hear.

"Wolf!" The woman answering sounds happy and excited.

"Hey, Kairi. I'm here with a colleague, Dr. Rolfe. We're working the Sophia Sullivan case."

"Nice to meet you, Dr. Rolfe." Ryan rolls his eyes. I assume it's at his partner's exuberance.

"Can you check out or reach out to some regulars on gun marketplaces?"

"You mean places like Black Market Reloaded and Agora?"

"Exactly. This is a longshot, but we've only got longshots right now. Can you see if you see any transactions with Sullivan Arms product?"

"Sure. Not a prob. Does it matter the product? Assault? Silencer? Parts?"

"No." He pulls on his chin, contemplative. "Parts? You mean for ghost guns, right?"

"Yep."

"People care about manufacturer for those?"

"I've never been in the market for parts myself. But I've read that ghost guns are a big issue. If forty thousand ghost guns are apprehended in a given year, that means a ton of parts are being sold by someone. My guess is it's a big market."

"See what you can learn. Thanks, Kairi."

When the call ends, Ryan leans back against the sofa and rests his head against the wall. "Stella hired a forensic accountant, but we should ask the FBI if they have resources. If there is anything to be found."

I sit down on the sofa beside him. There's nothing to say. His assessment of our situation to Kairi is absolutely correct. We're limited to long-range shots in the dark at the moment. It reminds me of fox hunting when you've lost the scent. You ride the trail based on knowledge of the land and foxes, but it's all a guess. Sometimes you get lucky, and the hounds pick up the scent. Sometimes you don't.

He reaches over and slides the tie down my ponytail, letting my hair free. He lifts several strands and loops the pieces around his fingers. Light flutters scurry down my spine.

"Erik's wrapping up and hitting the road." His gaze is off to the far corner once again. I'm the only one in the room, yet my sense is he's talking to himself more than me.

"Why?" I ask, more to prompt conversation than for any other reason.

"He doesn't like to be away from his woman for too long." His deep introspection breaks, and a hint of smile softens his somber expression. "It's better for all of us if he heads home. He can be one grumpy SOB without her." The tips of his fingers massage the base of my scalp, and I inch back, giving him better access. "He's got Shiloh running the research."

"It seems like the FBI would already have a lot of the information you're asking Kairi and Erik to find."

"Maybe. But the FBI follows rules. Arrow's objective is to find Sophia."

"I thought Jack gave you complete access to everything."

"He gave us some top-level stuff. But Erik's behind the firewall. He's digging in places Jack probably doesn't know exist. We'll see if he finds anything. My theory is Jack has been playing in the sandbox with the wrong unsavory character. We've just got to pick up a trail." He checks his wrist. "Now I'm hungry. And if I remember correctly, you promised me a dinner date."

Sophia has been missing for five days. In the world of missing persons cases, that's not a good thing at all. Her blonde hair and happy sapphire eyes haunt me, because those eyes were so happy, and now I can only imagine how terrified she must be. And we're in essentially the same place as we were on Tuesday. Without a single proper lead.

Getting dressed and going out for a night on the town feels wrong. I mean, there isn't much more we can do until the meeting tomorrow. But there's a heavy weight holding me down.

Picking up on my reluctance, Ryan says, "We can order in? Four a.m. is going to come around early."

"You're getting up at four?" The man's workout schedule is bonkers.

"I'll want to get a run in before we head out. When are you planning to drop off your dog?"

"I'm not sure."

Ryan picks up his phone and texts. Waits. Reads a response and sets it down.

"Stella and her son Ethan are spending nights at Trevor's condo. He likes for them to stay there when he's out of town. His condo is right beside me. Why don't you come back to my place tonight? Stella and Ethan can easily take care of Trace. Even if we end up staying the night."

"You're just assuming we're spending the night together?" I pull back, twisting on the sofa to get a better look at him. He tugs gently on the hair still tangled in his fingers.

"Yeah, I am." He lifts me like I weigh nothing and positions me on his lap, one of my thighs beside each of his. "This is a shit case.

It's one of those that brings you down." His thumb caresses my cheek. "A little comfort is a good thing."

His eyes don't feel so icy from this angle, with me straddling his lap, gazing down at him from above. My thumb traces his thick eyebrow. The contrast of his black hair, thick eyebrows, and jet-black eyelashes against those light blue irises stuns. The pad of my thumb continues down to his sharply defined jaw, the stubble sprouting below his cheekbone, the dip in the center of his chin, hovering over the location of the smallest dimple that evades detection most of the time. He's so gorgeous, his manly beauty hurts. He only softens at specific angles. When he feels safe and when he can drop his guard. It's ironic that a man so physically powerful builds walls to guard himself.

I bend to his soft lips, pressing my own against his without thinking. Warmth stirs as he kisses me, and I rock against his growing desire. His large palms circle my ass, guiding me. Then with one grunt, my body is airborne. His fingers dig in, holding me up, and my legs wrap around his sides.

"Woman, you don't have any coverings on any of these windows. And they open onto the street. What are you thinking?"

His heavy footfalls resonate through the apartment.

"They're expensive. That's what I'm thinking. Have you priced window treatments? Each month, I tackle a house project on my list." He reaches my bedroom and kicks the door closed. "At least I have them in my bedroom."

I bounce on the bed when he drops me unceremoniously on the mattress. With one hand, he lifts the bottom of his shirt and pulls it over his head. Bloody hell. He'd be so damn popular on Instagram. I reach forward, fingering the ridges of his stomach and the swirl of black curly hair while gazing at the curves of his pecs. His body qualifies as a postmodern work of art.

"Didn't you say you're hungry?"

"I am." He smiles again, and the serious, stern man dissipates. Both his hands grip the sides of my shorts. With one fluid movement, my shorts and panties are over my ass, down my thighs and calves, and over my feet.

"No, sir." I shake my head to emphasize my point. "If we're doing this, this time I get my way with you."

"Is that so?" He full-on grins.

"Yes. Do you know how many military men I've been with?"

His eyes narrow.

"You don't want to guess, do you?" I can't help but grin right back at him.

"Not something I want to think about." I crawl forward, my bottom completely bare. My hand clutches his waistband.

"Off." I raise my eyebrows for emphasis. "I've been with no man with your build. Most grad students don't look like this." I wave my hand over him, then let it rest lightly on his abs and glide down his happy trail. His stomach muscles flex in response, and I grin up at him, then point at my headboard. "On the bed. Now."

He drops his shorts to the ground. My gaze falls to one impressive erection. Sweet lord, the man is smoking. Lust pools between my legs. I sit back on my ankles as he climbs up on the bed, his back on the pillows. The temptation to grab my phone and snap photos is high because he is quite simply unbelievable.

"You're going to like my bed," he tells me.

"Why is that?" My hands flatten on his thighs, my mouth inches above his groin.

"I have a big—" I raise a singular eyebrow once more in question. He smirks. "Bed."

He chuckles, but any trace of humor evaporates when my thumb smears the pre-cum pooling on his tip. My tongue laps up from his base, over a thick vein, and his eyelids flutter. My lips cover him, taking him in, and he sucks in air. He tastes salty. I lick up his shaft once more, take him in my mouth, and suck. He tilts his head back and closes his eyes.

"I bet your legs hang off the edge of this one at night."

"That's not exactly what I want you to be thinking about right now," I tell him, then swirl my tongue over the soft skin of his tip. "I sleep diagonal." Then I take him again, bobbing up and down, sucking hard, and pull off with a pop. "Do you really want to talk about how I sleep?"

He grips a chunk of comforter in his fist and shakes his head. I drop my head and find a rhythm, our gazes locked on one another. I can't take him all the way, so I grip his base. The width of his cock expands in my mouth, and he groans. His leg muscles twitch.

Those watery blue eyes watch my every move. Hungry. Needy. The man has enough muscular power to bulldoze through other men, but at this moment, I hold the power. This strong beast of a man is at my mercy.

I dip my head lower and suck in one of his balls. His ass comes an inch off the bed.

"Holy fuck," he gasps. "Oh, fuck yes, keep doing that."

And I do, loving how he squirms, and his muscles cord, flexing in reaction to me. I return my tongue to his cock, and he grips my arms and lifts, pulling me over him.

"No. Ride me."

Through his gaze, he pleads, and I acquiesce. I position myself over him. He reaches for my breast, pushes the bra cup down, and teases the nipple as I let his tip slide between my lips. Back and forth in a hypnotic natural movement. When he's at the perfect juncture, I let my hips fall. Taking him. I am so wet with desire, but also tight. Those big hands cover my hips and guide me. As I stretch around him and he fills me, I never lose sight of those animalistic, ice-blue eyes.

I lean forward, and he kisses me with a hunger that fuels my need. My legs slide down the sides of his thighs, and I ride him low, my clit rubbing against him with every grind of my hips. He thrust his hips up. My body tenses, on edge, so close, trembling, seconds from release.

He flips me over on my back and pounds into me. All control lost. My hands cover his ass and his back as he hits that spot just right, over and over, and my body releases hard. I scream out as my back arches forward, only to slam into a wall of hard, sweaty muscle.

He chases his release through my orgasm, pressing sloppy kisses to my forehead, my neck, my chest, until his back arches as he jerks. The vein in his neck bulges, his facial muscles tense, and those eyes lock on mine as he pulses out his release. That raw gaze sucks the oxygen from my lungs.

He collapses onto me, and we cling to each other, straddling the bed, our entwined legs at the bottom corner of the bed and heads closer to the headboard. His chest heaves and his heartbeat thunders. A noticeable wetness pools between my legs, but I don't mind.

As our breathing calms, he shifts his weight onto his side. He caresses my neck and shoulder, and I hum my approval of his soft touch.

"I like it when you take charge," he says. I reach up and run my fingers through his short hair, ruffling the longer pieces along his crown. "Maybe you'll like it when you finally let me take control."

"You mean, tie me up?"

A borderline evil grin flashes. He chuckles and slaps the side of my ass. "Get up. Get packed. Now I'm starving."

"Packed?"

"Remember? My house. Early morning."

"I didn't agree..." There's a flirty smile plastered on my face, but inside alarm bells ring. Sleeping together implies more, and we aren't doing that, are we? Packing to spend the night at his house?

"Dog," he says as he lumbers into the bathroom.

"I can be ready early in the morning," I tell him through the bathroom door.

"Don't you need someone to take care of the yapper?"

"Trace has been my dog for fourteen years. He is not a yapper." I snatch my clothes off the floor and sidestep him as he exits the bathroom. He loops an arm around my waist, catching me.

"Pack extra clothes in case we need to stay the night in San Diego. I don't know what will happen tomorrow."

I do need Stella to watch my dog. And we have a very early morning. So I say, "Fine."

We shagged. I can stay the night and it won't mean anything. But there is one thing he needs to remember.

"Don't forget. No one is to know that anything happened here." I wag my finger over the bed. It wouldn't reflect well.

"I remember. Is Trace's food in the kitchen?"

"Yeah."

"I'll pack it." Barefoot, he exits my bedroom, looking far too comfortable in my home.

Ryan did not lie when he said I'd like his bed. Larger than a California king, it is custom made. He has to get custom sheets made for it. I asked. My feet haven't had that much room at the end of a bed since elementary school. Trace stretched out at the bottom as if even he found the extra space to be luxurious.

As expected, Ryan woke at an ungodly hour. I slept a little later and have now showered, packed, and have poured myself a cup of the coffee Ryan made before leaving. Black leather and dark furniture dominate Ryan's apartment. Pre-programmed automated shades opened early this morning, letting sunlight brighten the monotone space.

A knocking sound on the door alerts Trace from his spot stretched out on the sofa, but he doesn't bark. This isn't his space, therefore he's not territorial.

When I open the door, Stella from the Arrow offices stands before me in a robe, her auburn hair twisted on top of her head in a messy bun.

"Hi. I thought I'd try to catch you before you guys leave so I can meet Trace. Sorry I couldn't come over last night. My son had a game."

"Oh, no. Thank you for taking care of my dog." Trace wags his tail. "I really need to get him associated with a doggie daycare."

"Hello, Trace," Stella says, greeting my canine like he's a human. "It's not a big deal. We're right next door. And my son loves all animals. You know, we have a German shepherd. Does Trace like other dogs?"

"Sometimes," I answer honestly. Trace is a small-sized dog, but he has the ego of a lion.

I've already written out his care instructions, which really aren't extensive, but writing them out prevents confusion. As I take her through it all, she gives me the most curious smile.

"What?" I ask.

"So, you and Wolf?"

"Oh, no. It's not like that. We're strictly professional."

She still smiles.

"Seriously."

"But you stayed over?"

"Just because of the early hours." There was another reason, too... "And the dog. You were...are...going to take care of my dog.

He thought it was easiest. I slept in the guest room." That's a total lie, but it's the lie we shall both tell. Technically, when we got back here, other than our shower time, we just slept. And lord, he is just the right height for me in the shower.

"What do you think of sleeping over, buddy?" Trace wags his tail. "Well, you can stay with us any time, but don't get too used to staying here. This is what we call a bachelor pad," she says as she scratches Trace's head. That's an odd comment to make. She's clearly warning me and not my dog.

"Is he that much of a player?" I could totally see that.

"From what I've seen, more of a loner. There was this girl he was dating, but that ended up being completely fake."

"Fake?"

"Yeah. He suspected she wanted to spy on him, so he played along."

"They spied on each other?"

"Among other things." Stella stands and glances around the condo. "And then, Trevor is convinced he's seeing someone in San Diego. I'm not so sure." My ribs contract, but I focus on relaxing my facial muscles. "When you're down there, if you get any scoop, you'll have to give us the skinny. But of course, I'm the curious one. Trevor couldn't care less." That smile remains on her face, and I do my absolute best to mimic it. Stella claps her hands. "Okay, well, I'm gonna head back home. I'll bring my son back later in the morning. He'll be the one walking Trace."

The door swings open, and a sweaty Ryan fills the doorway. His wet t-shirt clings to his pecs, and his skin is flushed. His presence sucks the oxygen from my constricted lungs, my belly goes on the fritz, and when his eyes scan me, I swear, unruly sensations course over my skin.

"He got ransom instructions. Twenty-five million to an offshore account. I'll be ready in five."

CHAPTER 18

137 Hours Missing

Ryan

Alex spent the drive to the helicopter on her phone. Texting someone nonstop. I can't read the screen on her phone at the angle she's holding it, but before she angled the phone, I catch the name Timothy.

She has every right to talk to other men. The fevered back and forth of her texts implies to me he is a friend. What bothers me the most is how much the idea of him being more than a friend bothers me. I don't do relationships. And my muscles shouldn't tense. I shouldn't have a desire to go alpha over her flirting with another guy. But I do.

After liftoff, I glance her way. She's still on her phone.

"So, yesterday, and last night. We didn't use a condom." On her bed, I just didn't want to stop her. In the shower, I figured why bother. But in the light of day, questions arise. "Don't get me wrong, I liked it." Bright green eyes flicker my way. "Hell, liked might be an extreme understatement, but, ah, we're all good, right?"

"I have an IUD. We're good." She returns to her blasted phone.

I have no idea if I pissed her off or if she's just more enthralled with Timothy. I fall into a meditative trance following along our coordinates.

When we arrive in San Diego, the same Range Rover from before awaits us near Helipad 3. Wayne Killington once again leans against the SUV, holding a phone, texting. The man must be a former smoker because once again he's sucking on a sucker. As I shut the helicopter down, Alex continues to type away.

"Almost done?" I ask.

"Yes." No smile, no warmth. If I didn't know better, I'd say she's pissed. But she can't be angry at me. I've said nothing this entire trip. And if it's about the damn condom, she could have said something either damn time.

After disembarking the helicopter, she approaches Wayne with a smile and a professional handshake. In his loud, Hawaiian-print shirt, khaki shorts, loafers, and sunglasses, Wayne looks like he should hang out in a cabana with a cigar and Magellan. The lollipop stick dangling from the corner of his mouth augments the laidback vibe.

The parking lot is empty other than Wayne's Range Rover. A helicopter with the Sullivan Arms logo occupies one of the other helipad spaces. I point to the vacant pad.

"Jack out somewhere today?"

"Nah, he's back at the house. He's got SDPD and FBI with him. You guys making any progress?"

"Maybe." The newly assembled FBI team might make fast work of this case.

"What's the next step?" Wayne asks as soon as the car doors slam shut.

"We're going to let the FBI tell us. They'll be taking the lead on the case." That's the official stance. If the FBI and Jack disagree on how to handle the ransom, he'll cut the FBI out and tell me to do whatever I need to do. It's his daughter. He wants her back alive, and he doesn't give a damn about the money or putting someone in jail. The FBI will want a prosecutable case.

The turn signal blinks, and he scans the road, looking both ways.

"Which FBI team is involved? Missing persons?" Wayne asks as if he's making conversation, but I sense he's interested. It's understandable. Most people go their entire lives without coming across an FBI case. Plus, Jack and Sophia are like family to Wayne.

"That's not exactly what they call themselves, but yes, missing persons." I withhold the ATF mention. I expect that word of ATF involvement inside a gun and ammunition company will cause concern.

"Is all this hoopla normal for a missing persons case?"

"I'd expect so. But this is a kidnapping."

Wayne's fingers grip the steering wheel at the noon location. The angle of his head looks like he's checking his rearview, but I suspect he is checking out Alex, not the road behind us.

Alex has finally put away her phone. She's gazing out the window, but she is listening to every word between Wayne and me.

"Why is it now a kidnapping?" Wayne asks as he merges onto the freeway.

"Ransom." I watch him closely.

Wayne's eyes widen, and his mouth opens. He turns his head to me, and a car horn blares as Wayne veers into the next lane. "No shit?" he asks. Unless he's a very good actor, he didn't know this.

"How's Jack holding up?" Alex asks.

"Haven't seen much of him. Which is fine. Everyone at the company understands. It's a small company. He's had a tough go of it." I suppose that explains why Wayne is out of the loop.

A John Denver song plays on the radio. I don't know the name, but I recognize the voice.

"I heard ATF is getting involved," Wayne says as he turns off the freeway. Alex and I exchange a glance. "Is that normal?"

Alex's dark eyes look to me, silently telling me to take the lead on this.

"Where'd you hear that?" I ask him. It's interesting that he doesn't know there's a ransom, but he knows we're looping in ATF.

"Jack mentioned it."

Alex picks up her phone and types. The Timothy guy seems to be more interesting than our case.

"My wife's worried sick about Sophia. She's convinced we aren't going to find her, seeing as so much time's passed."

The vehicle turns from a standard San Diego neighborhood, with small yards and houses from the eighties and nineties, into the gated community. Media vans line up along the road leading to the grand waterfall gated entrance. Judging from the bored expressions of the men and women sitting in the front seats of the van, they've been parked here for a while, blocked from getting any closer to Jackson Sullivan's home. Wayne slows at the gate, gives a two-finger salute to the person at the guard station, and the gate slowly opens.

Other than a few gardeners and yard crews, no one stands outside in the front yards of the immaculate homes. The grass in this gated community is lush and green, especially compared to the yards we passed on the way in. The lots are easily three to four times the size of the neighborhood we just drove through. Yet more people were on the sidewalks enjoying the blue sky San Diego day than in this ritzy area.

Black SUVs pack the front circle at Jack's home. Wayne pulls to a stop on the street.

"Guess you'll need to get out here," he says. "You good with your luggage?"

"Are you not coming in?"

"Nah. Someone's gotta show up for work. Especially with this shit show." He grins, but he does so in a way my fingers itch to grip my Glock. "Nah, you've got enough cooks in that kitchen and I'd be nothing but a lookey-loo. I can do far more for Jack back at the office. Is he gonna go public with this ransom?"

"Haven't spoken to him yet about his strategy."

"Eh. I pulled our ads for right now. What a fucking nightmare." He twists his head back and forth and exhales. "You guys have a good day. Bring Sophia home, you hear?"

"Right." I tap the roof of the car and wave as he drives away. I'm too on edge. Overly reactive to everyone and everything.

Alex and I approach Jack's front doors side by side. Through the glass, I count six different suits. The video camera on the far right overhang swivels in our direction. The glass globes around the vegetation in the courtyard remain stagnant. The front door opens before we reach it.

Agent Liam Ryland, my FBI contact, watches us approach.

"Turns out I'm on the team. Meeting starts in five. Any trouble getting here?"

"No. We've been here before."

"You staying?" He pointedly looks at the bag across my shoulder and the small black suitcase Alex wheels behind her.

"Only if needed."

"I can take our bags up to the rooms," Alex offers. "I'll be right back."

I should let her go. I should greet all the agents. But I follow her. She's acting strange. Whatever's going on needs to be resolved. I need her to have my six if we're going to be outnumbered by a swarm of territorial agents.

She pushes open the guest suite door. Fresh flowers are out on the table, just as before. Alex rolls her suitcase into the room she stayed in last week. I drop my bag on the bed in her room. She raises one solitary eyebrow.

"No one's coming in here," I say, knowing she is thinking of our little keeping-it-secret game.

She crosses her arms, and one toe taps the ground. I don't know what the hell is going on, but I want to pull her up against me and interrogate her.

"If there's..." She huffs and brushes past me. "Come on. We're going to be late."

Confused, I follow her down the stairs. She has something she wants to say, but damn if I know what it is, and with the strides those long legs make, there's no time to find out.

Alex and I gather in the back of Sullivan's home office.

He's lost weight in the last few days. There's a greasy film over his unkempt hair. Dark circles shadow the skin below bloodshot eyes, and he sports the beginning of a beard. When we enter, he acknowledges us with a nod, but not much more.

Liam and another agent, Agent Mokowski, lead the discussion, recapping everything we know. I would grow antsy, except they complete the recap in under five minutes. Easily done with no evidence. Everyone in the room already knows the gist. Wealthy girl missing, initially a suspected runaway, then evidence of tampering with the security camera feed provided evidence of foul play. Anonymous ransom received.

A projector on the wall lists the ransom demands.

Twenty-five million dollars to be paid via cryptocurrency.

Once the funds are received, they will provide an address for where to locate Sophia.

No option to negotiate. If funds aren't received within forty-eight hours, they kill her.

The slide flips to a video.

I have not seen this video, so I surge closer.

Sophia is bound to a bed, sprawled out flat. Each wrist and ankle is tied to a bedpost. The skin below the binding on each wrist is rubbed raw, and there appears to be some blood. She tugs on the bindings. She's not wearing a blindfold, nor is her mouth covered. Her face is red and splotchy, and she whimpers. Her blonde hair appears matted and dirty.

The lack of blindfold means they aren't worried about her outing them when this is over. And wherever they have her tied up, they aren't worried about her being heard.

The dress she is wearing is floral. The cut of the dress isn't something I see regularly, and I doubt it's something Sophia would own.

Agent Mokowski speaks up. "This video is the only proof of life provided. We have a team reviewing it closely. There are no windows. No artwork. The walls are cinderblock. The iron bedframe isn't manufactured in the US. The dress is not a dress from Sophia Sullivan's wardrobe. Which means they put her in this dress. Possibly because the outfit she was wearing was damaged or soiled. Reasons they waited to make the video and the ransom could be because they needed to transport her. Or because this wasn't the original plan."

Jack speaks up. His hands rest on his hips, and his wrinkled shirt is unbuttoned at the collar, with the sleeves rolled up nearly to his elbows. "I don't care about the money. I've already requested the funds be collected."

Agent Ryland and I exchange a glance. We both understand his desire to pay the ransom. But doing so almost guarantees Sophia's life will end.

We need a lucky break. Something that can lead us to her captors.

Another agent stands, introducing himself as Drake Williams from ATF. He points at a photo of Larry Reyes and another man.

"We've been watching Larry Reyes for two years. This man he's with is Carlos Morales. He's a reseller, meaning he buys legal arms and equipment and delivers it to countries on our watch list. Specifically, he's the biggest source of weapons to two of the cartels in Mexico. He's good at what he does. If he wasn't, he'd already be locked up."

He clicks, and a photo of Larry Reyes in an outdoor setting by a pool with the other man flashes.

"This is a photo of Reyes and Luis Sanchez, head of the Jalisco cartel, taken last summer." He flashes another photo of the two men in a restaurant in Mexico City. Another photo flashes of Reyes and a group of men on a city sidewalk. "There's no financial evidence of wrongdoing. At least not by Larry Reyes. But we know he has connections."

Agent Ryland adds, "To be clear, we have no reason to connect this kidnapping to Larry Reyes. But, of the board of directors and executives, he's the only man with a compelling background."

"It's guilt by association," Jack says. "Larry's a young guy who likes to party in Miami. He's successful for his age." Jack turns to me, addressing me as if he and I are the only two people in the room. "I've already told them I don't think he's involved."

"Is he based out of here or Texas?" Sullivan Arms is headquartered in Houston, Texas. But the security camera footage showed he visits Jack in San Diego regularly.

"He's a frequent business traveler." Jack sounds resigned.

"Where's he live?"

"He has an apartment here." He exhales loudly. "He likes it here. Look, I'm tired of you guys coming up with theories and being wrong. You are wrong on this one. We're going to pay and get her back."

"If we're wrong, you won't mind us talking to him, right?" Jack's eyes flick to mine. He's listening to me. "You've talked to the cops for extensive periods of time since this began. If he's innocent, like you say, he won't mind talking to the FBI. If he's your friend, he'll do anything he can to help you get your daughter back."

Jack rubs his jaw. He's considering it.

"We've reached out to him already. Sent agents by his addresses both here in San Diego and Houston. No one home."

"Just because he wasn't home doesn't mean he's guilty." Jack heads over to his desk, head bent down, jaw muscles flexed. "Let me call him." He turns his head to Ryland. "You didn't tell me you sent agents by."

"Didn't need to tell you. In this investigation, we can talk to anyone we like. The goal is to find your daughter. Remember?"

Jack dials a number. With the phone pressed to his ear, he sinks into his desk chair. His gaze flickers over the room and settles on the frozen screenshot of his daughter. Her legs and arms are thin and underscore her youth. Her expression is one of terror. She's afraid of the person filming her.

Every single agent in the room watches Jack. Quiet prevails. We all want to hear this conversation.

Jack purses his lips and ends the call. "Voicemail," he announces.

He dials another number.

"Linda. Can you tell me where Larry Reyes is? I can't seem to get him on his cell, and I need to speak to him."

There's a pause.

"And when did he go on vacation?"

Another brief pause.

"And where did he go?"

Pause.

"Right. Can you see if you can get him on the phone for me? Yes, my work cell. Thank you."

I text Erik.

Any update on those financials? Also, have you accessed sales by sales rep?

Jack tells the room, "He's on vacation. She doesn't know where. Has been out of the office this week."

Agent Ryland turns to a member of his team. "Locate Larry Reyes. Access his credit card transactions. Process the paperwork to see if we can get his number run through Phantom."

Phantom is a powerful program that provides access to someone's phone without having any interaction. All you need is a phone number. It's designed to help fight enemies abroad. But in rare instances, the US government will use it to fight homeland crime.

"This is guilt by association," Jack utters, almost to himself.

"Jack, you have to recognize there are too many coincidences here."

He purses his lips once more. "And we don't believe in coincidences?" he asks, but he knows the answer.

"No, we don't," I confirm.

The agents break into separate groups. Jack has his hands templed, and his head rests against them as if in prayer. He'll send payment as soon as it's available. It takes a while to prepare twenty-five million to be paid via cryptocurrency. No one has that kind of money sitting in a cash account. But once it's available, Jack will pay.

I'll feel better once we have an idea who we are dealing with. If there is an opportunity to negotiate, I'll step in. If we can determine her location before the ransom deadline, then many more options open up.

I motion to Alex to join me outside. We could use some fresh air.

"Do you think he should pay?"

The door clicks closed behind us.

"Depends. If these are professionals, then they will return her. Their business model depends on being trusted. But that's more what we see internationally. If these aren't professionals, if this isn't something they do regularly, then they are more likely to want to dispose of a witness."

"You keep saying they, but inside they are talking about one man."

"They have a person of interest. Even if he is upgraded to suspect, he didn't do this alone."

I pull out a chair at a round table and motion to Alex to take it, then I take the seat beside it.

"What are you thinking?" She pins me with her gaze, studying me like I am a suspect.

"It doesn't make sense. The timing. My gut tells me this wasn't originally designed for a ransom. If that's your plan, you don't wait six days. I think there was a different plan, and then all the press broke. Something that happened changed the original plans."

She leans forward, her elbows on her thighs. The tip of her shoes rubs against mine. I caress her knee, and she looks away.

"Is something wrong? You didn't say anything the whole way here. Are you seeing someone else?" If she's cheating on me with someone, this ends right here.

Her irises transition from forest green to a bright, vivid green. The transformation is fascinating to observe. Those lips open, and she sits up straight, reaching her full height.

"On the flight here, I was talking about work with my TA."

"On a Sunday?"

"Preparing for class tomorrow." She tilts her head and swallows. She's not telling me the whole truth. "But what about you? Stella told me she thinks you're seeing someone in San Diego." Her hands flatten on her thighs, and her elbows splay out to the sides.

I sit back. *Damn.* I was right. Alex was mad at me the whole ride down here.

"Why are you looking like that? Do you think this is funny?" She's agitated. That's not my goal.

"No." Movement behind one of the windows catches my attention. We may not have much time. "I'm not dating anyone. I'm from here."

"Why did Stella—"

"I didn't know she thought that. I visit San Diego a lot."

Those dark, arched eyebrows seem to fuse above her nose. She analyzes everything. She's too smart to buy I visit the city because I like it.

"She also mentioned you dated a woman for a case."

"And?" Is that judgement? We were tracking a fucking terrorist.

"She said you don't usually date."

"She's right."

"Why me? Because we're working a case together?"

I blink away rising frustration. This is one of the reasons I don't do relationships. I hate bullshit crap like this, but I am smart enough to know stating that out loud won't win any points with Alex.

"I've never dated a woman I worked with before. And to clear up things, I never cared for the woman I dated that Stella told you about. If anything, that was similar to an undercover gig."

"So, you slept with her for the job?"

"If you want to put it like that, yes. Where is this coming from?" She narrows her eyes. "Are you jealous?"

"I guess Stella's warning bothered me."

"Stella is relatively new to the team. She doesn't know me well."

"I can see how that would be the case. You're difficult to get to know."

"Do you think?"

"Yes. You don't open up easily, do you?" I grit my teeth, not liking at all where she's headed. "I don't know where I was going with all of this. I probably shouldn't have said anything."

"If it bothered you, if anything bothers you, you should tell me. Otherwise, I'm in the dark. And I don't like being in the dark."

"No. You like being in control, don't you?" I nod with caution, sensing an impending attack. "You handle not being in control better than I thought you would."

"How do you figure?"

"You haven't fought the FBI joining this case."

"My ego isn't attached to it. I want Sophia home. Only in the movies are cases solved by one person. Nowadays it takes an army. At the right juncture, I'll get involved."

"I get it." She shrugs. She looks happier. Lighter. Her eyes are once more a deeper shade of green. "I was wrong." She doesn't make any fucking sense.

"How were you wrong?"

"I pegged you as someone who demanded control."

She's not wrong. I left the military because, at the end of the day, I refused to put my life, or the lives of my team, in the hands of a nameless person up above me ever again. I started my own company for control. My greatest frustration is my inability to fix my sister.

"Do you like control?" I counter her observation with a question. She moved to another country to get away from her father. It appears she doesn't like being controlled.

"I've never had it. I wouldn't know." Her chin lifts, and there is an unmistakable challenge.

I can't help but think about how she's had me at her mercy, twice now, in the last twenty-four hours.

The door out onto the deck opens. An agent sets one foot onto the deck.

"We've got an update on Larry Reyes."

CHAPTER 19

138 Hours Missing

Alex

"Agents visited Larry Reyes' home in Texas. He's not there. Neighbors said he hasn't been home since last week. We don't have a search warrant. There was nothing notable in his yard. Here in San Diego, his super said he hasn't been home this week. All of this could mean he is on vacation somewhere. Given the timing of his vacation, he remains a person of interest."

Agent Ryland addresses the room from beside the whiteboard that hangs on one wall of Jack's home office. Ryan, six other FBI agents, and I listen. Jack sits behind his massive office desk, looking pale. His eyes are glazed.

"Any updates on the source of the ransom request email? Or the account seeking funds?" I ask.

All of the agents in the room turn their attention to me.

Normally, I would shrink from so many more experienced law officers staring me down, but I've been mulling an idea over in my head.

"No. Whoever is doing this is tech savvy. And they know the identities of crypto accounts are protected. They also are aware enough to know that even a billionaire doesn't have twenty-five million easily available. They gave Jack time to pull the funds together." Excitement percolates. Ryan's gaze centers on me. He gives a short nod, urging me to continue. "When she was first missing, our first thought was that she might have gone off with a friend or someone who convinced her to leave. We were also worried that someone may have abducted her and didn't know who she was."

Agent Ryland looks at his watch. I ignore him.

"Jack's PR company has blanketed the news with Sophia's case. You can't go anywhere without seeing something about the Texan billionaire's missing daughter. And then we get a ransom." I hold up an index finger and move to the middle of the room. "Work with me," I say, letting my gaze travel from man to man to man. "A team of individuals did this. This is not one person working alone. Even if Larry Reyes is in on it, he couldn't do it by himself. Nothing in his educational profile would give the expertise to pull it off without help." I look to Ryan. "Our bet is that a ransom was not the original plan. We went six days without a ransom. If a team kidnapped her with ransom in mind, they would have reached out. Going to the media makes it more difficult to pull off a successful kidnapping. Someone within that team changed the plan after the media hit and the reward was placed."

"That's one theory," Agent Ryland says. "How does that help us?"

"I bet there's dissension within the group. We don't have any solid leads right now. We have a deadline approaching on a ransom that Jack Sullivan would pay only out of desperation, because once he pays it, there's no way to ensure those kidnappers return her."

I spin around and look to Ryan to back me up.

"In countries where K&R is standard business, you can rely to some degree on kidnappers keeping their word. Those kidnappers are professionals, and they rely on their word being good for ransoms to continue being paid. Right?"

He nods. He gets where I'm going. It's evident in his softened lips and relaxed jaw muscles.

"This is the United States. Nothing about this is standard. We don't know who kidnapped her. We can guess it's somehow related to Sullivan Arms, but we don't know why. I can write up half a dozen different possible motives and theories, but none of those get us to Sophia."

"Where are you going with this?" Agent Ryland's crossed arms and direct-facing posture tell me he's about to cut me off.

"Let's turn the tables." I catch Jack's attention and approach him. "Use the media. Offer a reward to anyone who comes forward with information about her location. Double the ransom if she's returned to you safely."

"I thought businesses like Arrow made money from negotiating down the ransom, not raising it," Agent Ryland mocks me.

"They aren't letting us negotiate. They didn't offer two-way communication. We have a deadline and no options. A video with no way of knowing how old it is. We suspect there's dissension. We know there's no way this is an individual. Chances are multiple people know what's going on here. A sophisticated crime like this doesn't happen in the dark. This isn't a lone madman."

I press my palms down on Jack's desk and face him. The FBI can't stop Jack from paying a ransom. They can't stop him from doing this either. And they, like us, are fresh out of leads.

"Put the heat on. Get a phone number out there for leads. Set up people to take calls, because we'll get inundated."

"You offer a million dollars, and you'd better have fifty people manning those phones." Agent Ryland's annoyance comes out in his mocking tone.

"You don't care about the money, right?" I ask Jack.

He shakes his head. "I just want my daughter back."

"Let's put heat on them. Even if they don't dissent, offer more and say once she's in your home, you pay. You set the rules. They want to be paid without any guarantee she'll be returned. You tell them you'll pay more once she's delivered home. Or you'll pay for information leading to her."

"Fifty million? To the person that delivers her to me? You think that would do it?" Jack asks.

I look to Ryan for confirmation. His lips are pursed, and his eyes are hooded. He's thinking it over.

"You go before the press. You tell the press that there's a ransom. But they aren't offering the option to negotiate. And there's no reason to believe they won't kill her. Say that's unacceptable. You'll double the ransom to anyone who delivers her safely to your home or delivers information that allows you to find her and bring her home."

Light blue eyes look to me, and they crinkle with his slight smile. "Alex is right. This is a good idea. There's more than one person involved in this. If greed is the underlying motivator, let greed draw them out. And if greed isn't the underlying motivator for the architect of this plan, then it'll be a motivator for someone on that team."

Agent Ryland's hands rest on his hips. He carries on a private conversation with one of the agents near him. The two men break apart, and Ryland addresses the room.

"We can set up the number for you to use and monitor it. And it goes without saying, but we don't recommend any ransom being paid."

Color returns to Jack's face as he dials the PR agency he's been using to get them working. The FBI agents get on their phones, presumably because they each have their own tasks to prepare for this change in tactic.

Ryan sidles up to me.

"Solid tactical plan. Low risk. Potentially high reward." He's standing close to me. Possibly too close, but all of the agents scattered to give themselves relative privacy for their calls. Jack isn't paying attention to us as he's engaged on the phone.

"Thank you." Praise from Ryan is akin to acing the boards.

Ryan's phone vibrates. He checks it and gestures for me to join him back out on the deck.

"Erik," he says as the sliding glass door closes behind me. "Right. Interesting. Thanks."

He disconnects the call.

"That was Erik," he says. "Our forensic accountant says there's nothing unscrupulous on the books. The only thing that stands out from the annual reports is that three years ago sales exceeded forecast by thirty percent. Stock price was gangbusters. But March 2020 was the best gun sales month on record. The last two years, they've hovered near earnings forecasts, but are still hugely profitable. There are analysts who are saying that Wayne Killington returning as Interim CEO makes Sullivan Arms stock price a buy. Those analysts are crediting aggressive marketing led by Wayne's team for Sullivan Arms' recent success."

"Why?"

"Three years ago, when Wayne was interim CEO, they launched a new marketing campaign. We'd need to look at the ads, but it appears they shifted from a hunting focus to a personal safety strategy. They followed the market, and it paid off."

"Three years ago. When Cassandra died? Jack stepped down?"

"Apparently so."

"Do you know who he was at dinner with Monday night when his daughter was kidnapped?"

"That gives Wayne Killington a potential motive. Is that what you're thinking?"

"Motive doesn't equal guilt. But yes. It's also probably worth researching to see who else did well with Wayne Killington as CEO. My guess is Larry Reyes also did well. He moved into Wayne's role as head of sales when Wayne moved up."

This case has been particularly frustrating because it's easy to create theories. But accumulating evidence is difficult if not impossible. I hope our game plan works. We need whoever is behind this to make a mistake.

"Do you want to stay here tonight, or do you want to go home?" He looks out over the balcony. I glance over my shoulder. I can see others near various windows, phones pressed to their ears.

"Jack will hold a press conference within an hour, don't you think?"

"I do. The only reason they aren't parked outside his house is because this is a gated community. But every major news station is parked outside those gates."

"Let's stay. If this works, I think it's gonna go down fast."

CHAPTER 20

145 Hours Missing

Ryan

A replay of Jack Sullivan's announcement plays on the muted television screen. The caption below the replay reads "Billionaire Jackson Sullivan Offers $100 Million for Safe Return of His Daughter."

Two FBI agents remain in the house, conversing in the kitchen. Jack leans his head back against his office chair. His hair holds a greasy sheen, and his closed eyelids highlight dark circles. Gray whiskers mix with black ones all along his unshaven jaw.

"By doing this, I just ensured a degree of danger to every single billionaire's family in the world."

Alex's downturned lips and sad, forest green eyes convey the weight of guilt. She must agree with him.

While it's hard to harbor sympathy for someone who has

amassed an obscene amount of money, no one should fear for their loved ones every single day. Regardless, Alex's idea to turn the tables is a solid one. Later, when the case is dissected, many will argue that her recommendation represents out-of-the-box thinking that could save a life.

She didn't recommend the one hundred million bounty. That's a figure Jack came up with all on his own. To him, fifty million felt like too small of an amount. We'd all watched from the sidelines as he pleaded for his daughter to come home safely. His tearful, heartfelt message rang clear—he wants his daughter back, at any cost. The high dollar amount offered pissed the hell out of Ryland.

Jack's phone rings. The ring tone is set to the loudest setting, and the shrill sound spills out of the open office doors and echoes in the open marble foyer. Alarmed, he stares at me, and I nod. *Pick it up*. He glances down at the phone, then shakes his head.

"It's my uncle."

The phone number he gave to call is being answered by employees at his PR agency. The other FBI agents left to sit with those employees to track any calls that come in. The chances that a phone call related to Sophia will go directly to Jack's personal cell are low. But it doesn't mean each time his phone rings his heart doesn't jump start. Or that we aren't dealing with someone who has his personal cell number.

Alex stands, and my hand goes to her lower back. It's a natural movement, leading her out of Jack's office to give him time to speak with his family. Both his brother and his uncle have been in regular communication with Jack since this began. His uncle is Chairman of the Board of Sullivan Arms but is otherwise retired. His brother left the family business years ago. From what I can tell, their interest is one hundred percent centered on Jack and Sophia.

When I close the doors to his study behind me, I follow Alex out onto the deck. Two hours have passed since the announcement. In a few hours more, Alex and I will go upstairs to bed, hoping to be alerted to a call.

This plan of hers is a solid one. But the wait is excruciating.

"Do you know Jack's uncle? Anyone else in his family?"

She leans over the balcony. Her dark hair is wrapped up in and over itself, and as I step up behind her, my fingers tangle in the loops of hair, searching for the binding to undo it.

"I might have seen them at the funeral. But I don't recall being introduced to them. Cassie and Jack eloped, so there wasn't a wedding. Those are the only two places I would have come into contact with Jack's extended family. Cassandra's parents came out and visited us years ago."

"Are her parents still alive?"

"No, they passed away years ago. Her mom had cancer, and her dad died of a stroke a few years later."

Alex's hair falls free. I should stop touching her. But the deck is dark. Jack turned off all the outside lights and drew down the shades, lest any photographer have a telephoto lens. It's just the two of us outside on the deck.

The muscles along her neck and shoulders are tight. I knead the tight cords with my thumbs, eliciting a moan. She raises up, off the balcony, and I close the distance between us, holding her close against me. The curves of her ass tease my groin. One arm wraps around her, below her soft breasts. The other holds her hips. Her back to my front. Close enough her heartbeat reverberates through me. I brush my lips across her temple.

"If someone comes out, they'll see us," she says, but she doesn't pull away. I don't lift my arms. If anything, I hold her tighter.

The moonlight reflects over the ocean. A dark form passes on the beach near where the ocean laps on the sand. Golden lights flicker in homes all along the curve of the coastline. There's a peacefulness to this paradise. A peace that has stood in direct contrast to current events. A dichotomy that is impossible to ignore. And this woman in my arms offers a comfort from the disjointed scenery.

Her hands cover mine, the back of her head against my shoulder, resting in the crook of my neck.

"When we're done with this case, I still want to date you."

"Is that what we're doing?" I don't miss the humor in her tone.

I could tell her I hope so. Or I think so. Or something soft and unassuming. But I have no desire to give her an out. "Yes." It's all I say and leave it at that.

Heavy footfalls approach from behind us. The swoosh of the automatic sliding door has her pushing away. I let my arms fall to my side.

One of the FBI agents addresses us. "A phone call came in. We have an address. It's about an hour away. Teams are loading up now."

I drive Jack's Range Rover closely behind Agent Ryland's sedan. Jack sits in the passenger seat beside me. He's still, but easy to read. He's both exhausted and desperate. There's a thin veil of control binding him together. Alex sits in the back seat. From time to time, she texts on her phone. Her left knee rises and falls, tapping much the way it did on our first helicopter ride to San Diego. Her hair is bound up once again in a complicated twist.

Temecula is about an hour outside of San Diego. The FBI agent riding in the back seat with Alex gets updates along the way. A team of agents have arrived and are scouting the area. The address the caller provided is off Temecula Parkway on Anza

Road. Google Maps shows the address provided is an abandoned storage facility.

The agents call in to say the fence around the facility has been damaged. The area is overgrown, but there are fresh tracks along the dusty dirt and gravel path.

Five minutes after the update call, we park behind a couple of other vehicles about half a mile from the address. The FBI has contacted the local police department. Two police cars are parked across the road with blue and red lights flashing.

Agent Ryland gets out and approaches them. A minute later, the flashing lights are turned off. The call came in from a man who chose to remain anonymous. If we find Sophia, they provided him a number to call to claim his reward money.

Whether or not any charges are levied against him remains to be seen. That piece of the operation isn't a piece I particularly care about. My only concern is locating Sophia and getting my friend's daughter home safely.

"The SWAT team is going to approach from the back. There's always a risk this is a setup. You all stay here."

Agent Ryland's command is firm, and he charges off with the two police officers following him.

"You've got better skills than any of those agents." I glance back to my friend. The corner of his lip lifts. He's going through hell, and he's trying to make me feel better.

"This is their show. They've got a wealth of information they haven't shared with us. Perfectly happy to hang back and keep you safe."

"You think these bastards might come after me?"

"You never know. We've got a wild card."

In any mission, there are unknown variables. Risks. In this situation, a man called in a tip. He didn't provide information for payment, but he did ensure he had a way of claiming his reward. We sit in the car beneath a cloudy night sky, waiting.

Agent Ryland didn't leave us with a way of monitoring the SWAT team progress. I have my phone on the dash, ready and waiting for a call. Jack lays his head down on the dash. His hands come up below his face. He looks like he might be praying. I happen to know Jack isn't a particularly religious man, but there's not a person on the planet who won't pray to a higher power when faced with no other options.

"I can't sit here. I'm going to go." Jack's hand rests on the door handle.

"You go, and you run the risk of alerting them. You go, and you run the risk of the FBI mistaking us for one of them. It sucks. But wait. It's the smartest play. Let the experts do their job."

I catch Alex's eyes from the back seat. She blinks her agreement. Sitting and waiting is torturous. It's hard to fucking do. But, in this scenario, it's the best play.

Forty-five minutes pass in silence. It's not the time for small talk. I have the window down so I can hear any footsteps. Every few minutes, I get out and circle the vehicle. A couple of cars whiz by. Each time, my hand falls on my gun at my waist.

The phone lights up with a shrill ring.

"We've got her. Ambulance is on the way. Location is secure. Drive up and onto the property. Sophia wants her father."

End of Part 2

CHAPTER 21

Alex

Red flashing lights cast shadows over sandy ground and stucco walls. Overgrown weeds sprout in pockets along the buildings. Agents swarm the ground, many in full tactical gear. An armed agent approaches our SUV and visually checks the interior, shining a flashlight over each of us and the floorboards.

Ryan flashes identification and says, "Agent Liam Ryland requested we approach."

"Just up ahead. He's waiting for you down the road, past the two buildings."

The Range Rover's wheels crunch the rock-strewn ground. We bypass an old building with broken windows and a crooked, rusted sign that reads "Temecula Storage."

Jack cracks the door open. The dashboard lights up, and the car emits a high-pitched warning sound.

"Not yet." Ryan's tone brokers no room for negotiation.

From the back seat, I reach forward, covering Jack's shoulder, holding him in place.

We round the building, passing a cluster of four agents in tactical gear. All four scan the area in high-alert mode.

The whir of an ambulance's sirens filters through the car windows.

The storage building to our left is two stories high with countless doors, the kind you roll up and down. Judging from the vines and rust, the facility has been out of use for years. Beyond the storage facility, the narrow dirt road continues, leading to a stucco home with a tile roof. Light pours out of the windows, and the front door is wide open. A black SUV is parked out front. A red light flashes on the dashboard. There's a man in handcuffs beside the SUV.

"Larry," Jack grits out.

We'd suspected Larry Reyes. But he didn't do this by himself. He's simply the one who got caught holding the bag. Someone on his team fell for our reward scheme and turned him in. Agent Ryland stands to the side of the SUV. Jack jumps out of the car, taking off at a brisk run, and Ryan slows the car to a stop. I hop out and close Jack's door.

"You ready?" Ryan asks me. He sounds concerned, but the worst is over. We've found Sophia.

I click my phone to camera mode. "Let's go."

Two agents in full gear chat off to the side. Ryland hovers behind Jack, who is holding a barely recognizable Sophia. Skinny, pale legs with knobby knees sprawl out across the dirt. She's barefoot, and there are open red cuts and welts around both ankles. Her hair is matted. Her face is pressed into Jack's chest. Her shoulders shake as she sobs. The one thin, waif-like arm clutching her father bears bruises, and her wrist is red and raw.

The ambulance sirens grow louder.

Larry Reyes' head is down. He's wearing a crisp white button-down, business slacks, and dress shoes. An agent shoves him into the back seat of the SUV, and the flashing lights reflect off moisture on his cheeks. His eyes are glassy, his lips pursed. The former business executive is crying. He's already mourning the life he knew.

Meanwhile, twenty feet away, the young girl in her daddy's arms unleashes her own torrent of emotion. Relief from being saved, no doubt, and god knows what else. It's the god knows what else that tears at me. She spent nine days in captivity. Based on the dirt smudges, it doesn't appear she's bathed in nine days. The stench of urine has me wondering if they gave her access to a bathroom, or if they simply tied her up and let her lie in her own filth.

I want to approach her, but the scene before me holds me back. Jack clutches his daughter, tears flowing. My palm flattens against my sternum, pressing hard to keep the roiling emotions in check.

The ambulance comes into view, spins past us, and stops. In a flurry of activity, paramedics surround Sophia. A female paramedic bends over her, taking her pulse and listening to her heart.

Ryland talks to Jack's back. "She's going to be okay. She might be dehydrated, but she'll be okay. They'll want to do a rape kit analysis. She's been drugged. There are track marks on her arms."

Firm, warm pressure on my lower back pulls me out of the scene. Ryan's presence grounds me.

"Want to go inside?" As he asks the question, the pressure on my lower back increases, directing me away from the unfolding drama.

The paramedics have everything under control. Sophia needs her privacy. She needs her father.

Agent Ryland approaches us, blocking our entrance into the home. "We're still processing the scene. They held her in a back bedroom. Someone was staying here with her. When we approached, Reyes ran out the front door. There could be others on the loose. One man drove away before we stormed the house."

"Did you get a look at him?" Ryan asks Ryland.

"Similar in height and build to Reyes. Hispanic. Wasn't dressed as nicely as Reyes. It's possible he was hired help to keep Sophia alive."

"You think they planned on returning Sophia? In exchange for the ransom?" The uncertainty of their intent is the primary reason we offered the counter-reward.

"No way to tell. They could have been keeping her alive until payment was received. This place has been deserted for a while. Records show electricity was reconnected to this building three weeks ago. The plan could have been to disconnect service and leave her here to be found years from now."

"Who owns the property?" Ryan asks.

"Tax deeds are to a Raymond Eardley. He died six months ago. His will is held up in probate. Looks like the suspects searched for property that wouldn't have an owner coming around. This is far off the road. No neighbors nearby."

"No one around to hear her scream," I say. I take in the rundown house, and with all the noise and lights, I swear I can hear her screams.

"Or to see her struggle as they got her into the house," Ryan adds.

"Any thoughts on motive?" I ask. Why would an up-and-coming business executive do this?

"Track marks could have been to subdue her. Or it's possible it's part of a larger human trafficking ring. But she's not your typical trafficking victim." Ryland states what we've been saying all along.

"I feel like at every turn in this case we have more questions than answers." Ryan's hand remains on my back, reassuring me he's here.

At least now Sophia is safe. I won't go so far as to say she's secure. I don't doubt nightmares will haunt her for years. Unfortunately, depending on what they were shooting into her veins, she might also have to overcome a drug addiction.

Abductors love to foster a drug addiction. The need for the drug becomes so great they quickly instill obedience. The captives will do anything for their next hit, for their next reward.

Jack climbs into the ambulance beside Sophia. He'll get her the best care money can buy. He'll see to all of her medical needs. He'll do everything he can to give her back as much as possible of the life she had, although undoubtedly her innocence is no more. The girl she was died in these shambles. The woman we rescued is the survivor.

The ambulance leaves the scene, taking father and daughter off to fight the next set of battles awaiting the two of them. The FBI will find the man who drove away. With luck, he'll talk, or Reyes will talk, and all questions will be answered.

Ryan and I hover on the outskirts of the house. I snap a few photographs before Agent Ryland observes me and asks that we clear the scene so as not to risk contamination.

The sedan holding Larry Reyes drives off, transporting him for processing.

Agent Ryland approaches us as the taillights of the unmarked sedan fall out of view.

"Did he say anything?" I ask Ryland. My curiosity is high.

"Requested a lawyer the second his rights were read."

"Did he seem surprised? When the FBI showed up?" I wish we could have been here to see it all go down.

"Not particularly. For a split second, it looked like he might run, but he was surrounded in the front, and he held his hands up. We've got it on a head cam. You can check the video later."

"One man got away?" Ryan asks. "You think he knew the place was being surrounded?"

"No." Ryland's hands rest on his waist, his elbows out to the side. "I think it was dumb luck he left when he did. We got the tags, though. Debated pulling him over, but we opted to not spook the occupants inside the house. We'll find him." Ryland oozes confidence. "Also have men inside Larry Reyes' house in Texas."

"Did they find anything?" I ask.

"Photos of Sophia on the walls. Her school schedule. Security footage from her home address on his hard drive. He's going to need that lawyer he requested."

Agent Liam Ryland looks pleased with himself and the case. He looks like he's ready to crack open beer and celebrate. Ryan has a more cautious expression. He's surveying the scene with a grim expression.

My phone rings and flashes my dad's name. I excuse myself and step away from the activity. For once, I'm thankful for my dad's call.

"Hey, Dad."

"News flashed. You've got her? Sophia's okay?"

"Yes." My dad does care. He can come across like he's all work, but there's much more to him. "They took her away to the hospital."

"What'd they...is she okay?" My dad has been working with law enforcement for decades. He has a vast firsthand knowledge of the bad things that can happen.

"She's okay. She was bound, captive. Possibly raped. Drugged. We don't know everything yet."

"Human trafficking?" he asks.

The drugs and possible rape would fall in line with standard human trafficking. Get them addicted, then they become compliant, desperate for the next fix, willing to do anything. But Sophia is an odd target for human trafficking. Typically, human traffickers target young girls from broken families, the kinds of girls who won't be missed. Or whose families won't have the means to conduct a thorough search.

"I don't think so. It doesn't fit." Dad understands me. He knows what I'm saying.

"Tell me about the man who took her."

"Business executive. Hispanic. Mid-thirties. Divorced. Frequent business traveler."

"Mmmm." Dad mulls it over.

"They did find evidence he's been tracking her."

"You think it was all for a ransom?"

"Maybe. But why hold on to her for so long if it's all for a ransom? Wouldn't you want to relay the ransom before the feds were called in? Before there's national media attention?"

"Are you going to get some time with him?"

"I doubt it. He lawyered up immediately."

"Well, when things calm down. After a few days have passed. See if you can get in to meet with him. You aren't affiliated with the FBI. If he's got a high-powered attorney, he might not let you in. But, if you play your cards right, he might. If you get some time with him, he might want to talk about what he did and why. Could be an excellent opportunity to publish a study on him. And on the case. Turning the ransom around, it's a strong-arm tactic. And clearly it caused someone he hired to rat him out. Whose idea was that? FBI?"

"It was my idea."

A familiar deep chuckle crosses the line. I'm smiling, because my dad's laugh is one of the best sounds in the world. He's practically halfway around the world, but his familiar belly roll wraps around me. I wish I could bury my face into his neck, just like Sophia did with her dad.

"That's my lass. Good work."

"I don't know, Dad. It doesn't feel right to me." I've heard my dad say things like that before when working a case. There's an instinctual element to cases as you piece together the details.

"Well, like I've told you before, you're dealing with a mind that works differently than your own. You are going to need to find a way to spend some time with him. To understand his thought process. What he ultimately wanted to get out of this. If he's ever done anything like this before, and if not, what was his trigger event."

Ryan's light blue eyes flash across the courtyard. His head is bent, in a continued discussion with Agent Ryland, but he's watching out for me.

CHAPTER 22

Ryan

"The missing persons aspect of the case is resolved. But the case will remain open." Agent Ryland answers my question as I keep Alex in my field of vision. "The District Attorney prosecuting Larry Reyes is going to need more information on who his accomplices were and what happened. The DEA has also expressed interest. You can't involve a couple of known Cartel affiliates and not stir up multiple federal agencies."

"Understand."

"Will you still be involved?"

"Jack asked for my help finding Sophia. And when he asked, the FBI wasn't yet involved. I assume he won't need additional assistance. Arrow will be taking over his personal security."

"Smart. After that reward he paid, he and his daughter will need security for the rest of their lives."

"He needed better security before this happened." Jack

Sullivan attempted to fly under the radar and out of the public eye, but he didn't succeed.

"Are you heading home tomorrow?"

It's almost two in the morning. I'll get some shuteye before I contemplate flying a helicopter home. Alex is still on the phone, off to the side, away from the commotion. There's a softness to her expression that has me suspecting her call is a personal one.

"It will depend on Alex," I answer Ryland. "Alex didn't get to see Sophia this evening. I don't know what she's going to want to do. How long do you think they'll keep her at the hospital?"

"If they drugged her with heroin, which is what I suspect, they may need to keep her under supervised withdrawal."

"We're staying at Jack's tonight. Tomorrow, after we speak with him, we'll decide what our plans are. If you need me at any point, you've got my number."

"Same."

Alex ends her call and joins us.

"You about ready to head out of here?" I ask her.

The FBI forensics team will have this area taped off potentially for the next couple of days. They are wrapping up the work they need to complete tonight.

Alex looks to Ryland. Is she seeking his permission?

"As you know, I'm a professor at UCSB. I'd be very interested in doing a case analysis. Studying it from a criminal behavior perspective."

"I can understand why. The counterproposal to the ransom produced positive results. It will be interesting to learn how that altered the kidnapping team's plans." Alex nods, enthused he understands. "I'll need to clear it with my supervisors. The biggest concern they will have is sharing any information before trial."

"I was going to ask to meet with Reyes on my own. If his lawyer allows it. Spend some time with him. A criminal mind isn't as different from a healthy one as people would like to think. And often they are more than willing to share their thought processes."

"You'll need to get in line. There's a host of people wanting to meet with Reyes. We'll be tracking the cryptocurrency payment on the ransom as well."

"To reclaim the payment?"

"Not necessarily," Ryland says. Alex's brow wrinkles. "It's all part of the case. Figuring out how the pieces fit together."

I speak up to provide additional explanation. "The kidnappers assumed cryptocurrency is the ultimate cloak. But the FBI has a group that specializes in tracing crypto payments. Eventually, there's a good chance they'll slip up and they'll find out who received the payment. They may have provided the information that led us to Sophia, but there's a good chance that the same person has ties to the cartel."

As we walk back to the car, it takes a tremendous amount of restraint to refrain from reaching for Alex's hand or to place a hand on her lower back. I'm tired. We were never in any danger, but having Alex on the outskirts of an FBI raid had me on alert all the same. As my adrenaline crashes, I fight an unfamiliar desire to pull Alex into my arms, to reassure myself that this whole thing ended and she's okay.

On the car ride back to Jack's, Alex and I are quiet. I park Jack's vehicle in the front circle. Lights are on in the house, and we push open the front door. A male voice calls out, "Hello?"

Instinctively, I hold a protective arm against Alex and counter with a cautious, "Hello?"

Wayne comes around the corner. He's wearing sheep-lined bedroom slippers, plaid pajama pants, and a maroon robe.

"Alex. Wolfgang. Good to see ya." Seeing that it's Wayne, I lower my arm, allowing Alex to pass. "Jack called. Updated me.

My wife wanted me to come over, double-check everything is ready and okay for them to come home."

"Will she be released from the hospital soon?"

"If Jack has anything to do with it." Wayne rubs his forehead. He's in pajamas, but his hair is brushed and in place. "You guys staying here?"

"For tonight."

"You'll be heading back tomorrow?"

"Possibly. I'm going to connect with Jack tomorrow and see what he needs."

"Right." Wayne steps past us, head down, shaking side to side slightly. "Can't believe it was Larry."

"Did you know him well?"

"Larry?" Wayne asks with a swell of incredulity. "Absolutely. He's been on my team for, well, we were his first job out of college. Rose through the ranks pretty fast. Good kid. I'm blown away."

"Would you mind if I took some time to talk with you about your experience with him?" Alex asks Wayne.

"Are you working with the FBI on the case?" he asks her.

"No." Alex dips her head in a way that makes her look demure even as her height surpasses Wayne's. "I'm hoping to do an analysis on this case. It could help criminal profilers in future cases. A case review and analysis, if you will."

"Huh." Wayne's hand rests on his belly and he rubs up and down. "Sure. I'm a little swamped these days. What with doing everything for Jack and, well, he's my first priority, but once things calm down, I should be able to work you in."

"That would be wonderful. Thank you."

"You must be relieved for Sophia to be found," Alex says. The hand on Wayne's belly stills. "I mean, you'll have Jack back in the office."

"Oh." He smiles and steps to the door. "Eventually. He'll need to be there for Sophia for quite a bit. And that's fine." His back is to me now, and his slippered feet slide as he shuffles to the front door. "I'll cover as long as he needs me to. He's like family. That's what you do for family." He pauses at the front door and looks over his shoulder. "Thanks. For everything. For finding Sophia. Being a good friend to Jack. All of it." He taps the front door handle. "Lock this up behind me, okay?"

"Goodnight, Wayne," I say.

After locking the door, I follow Alex up the side staircase that leads to the guest rooms. Our bags are in the center of the living area. In a few hours, morning light will break.

She pauses at the doors to the bedrooms with a questioning expression. She's unsure, but I'm not. I place my hand on her hip and guide her into the bedroom.

"Let's go to sleep."

I remove my shirt and pants and pull back the comforter and sheets. She pauses, then opens her overnight bag, grabs a few toiletries, and steps into the bathroom. We are quiet and methodical, moving through the motions of preparing for bed.

I close my burning eyes. The bed shifts with her weight as she climbs in. She covers her legs with the comforter and lies down beside me. There's a foot of space between us, and we're both lying stiff on our backs, looking up to the ceiling. It's awkward, and there's no reason for uneasiness.

I reach for her and tug her to me. The smooth silk of her nightdress glides against my side, and one of her long legs covers mine. I press a kiss to the top of her head.

We're both exhausted, but this position feels natural and right. It's been an exhausting, emotional day. We both need sleep. We'll regroup in the morning. Check on Sophia and determine our next steps.

"Sleep," I tell her. Through her chest pressed up against my side, I can feel the soft thud of her heartbeat. My muscles relax into her warmth, and I ease into sleep.

I sense someone watching me. My eyes are closed, and my hand flattens against a cool surface. My fingers clench down into a surface that gives. A mattress. My eyelids bat open. Shadowed white walls, rays of light piercing through unfamiliar dark curtains. The ornate bedpost triggers my memory. I'm in Jack's guest room.

My slow train of thought reflects back over yesterday's events. I rub a hand over my eyes and remove heavy kernels of sleep. The bed dips, and I breathe in coffee.

Alex peers down at me, a white porcelain coffee cup in hand. She's wearing the silk chemise I curled into last night. The same one that curves around her breasts and rises high on her thighs. But those dark forest eyes drill into me. She's not here to tempt me. She's got something on her mind, and the way her focus is on me, it feels personal.

"Morning," I say cautiously.

"Morning." She sips her coffee without lifting her gaze.

"Everything okay?" I don't have a wealth of relationship experience, but I'm not a schmuck. I recognize a woman who wants to talk. Unease in my gut rises because I'm fairly certain talks aren't good and I thought we settled everything yesterday.

"Are you seeing someone else?" Her tone is light. Steady. Her gaze doesn't lift from me, because she's studying me. She's watching my reactions. She wants the truth.

"I told you, I am not," I say, but my gaze falls to the lumps of my feet beneath the gold-swirled comforter. I push up and slide back until my back hits the bedframe. It feels a bit like I'm being interrogated, and my defenses rise. "Why?" I practically growl.

Her head snaps back as if my question slapped her. My cotton-mouth is heavy, and I push the comforter off my lap and head to the restroom. I close the door, relieve myself, brush my teeth, splash water on my face, and take stock in the mirror. There's a day's rough growth covering my jaw, and my eyes are hooded. The skin on the right side of my face is a blustery red from where I was sleeping so hard. Before she positioned herself to wake me by staring at me.

This is bullshit. I brought her into a room with me, and we slept together without having sex. Can't say I've done that before with a woman. Isn't that a relationship litmus? But the fact is, whenever she's texting on that phone of hers, I'm always wondering who's got her in a conversation frenzy. Maybe she's right. Maybe revisiting to clarify any outstanding questions isn't the worst idea. I'm not interested in anyone else. She spends her days around single college students.

With one last glance in the mirror, I swing the bathroom door open, prepared to have the talk. But she's no longer in the bedroom.

I step onto the narrow balcony and find her sipping that little cup of coffee while she leans against the window frame, looking out at the swaying palms. With two long strides, I stand behind her. I brush a loose strand of hair off her cheek and gently tuck it behind her ear. I caress her hip, loving the smooth feel of silk beneath my fingers.

"I'm not interested in dating anyone else." Her thick eyelashes flutter, and she tilts her head, angling it so she can fix me with her forest gaze again.

"What I stumble on is that Trevor is your close friend, and he believes you are."

There's no reason for me to keep my sister a secret. I simply keep family shit close to the vest. Always have, for as long as I can remember. Besides, mental illness isn't something to flaunt in the military. My mother has never been officially diagnosed, and that probably helped my military career. And a sister with a drug addiction isn't light conversation. Trevor might be like a brother, but we've never had a moment where it felt like the right time to unload something so heavy. Sure, Trevor has hinted that he thought I was dating someone in San Diego. In all fairness, Trevor suspects I'm sleeping with any woman who knows my name. Have never seen a reason to correct him. Those green eyes study me.

"Get dressed. There's someone you need to meet."

She does as I say, and it's not until our shoes click against the marble foyer that she speaks.

"Have you heard from Jack? Is he back from the hospital with Sophia yet?"

"He's moving her to a private care facility this morning. Flying in some specialists to review her bloodwork. Also a therapist with experience with kidnap victims." He's throwing his money at the problem. Not that I can blame him. If I were in his shoes, I'd spend money like crazy getting her the best medical care.

We step out into the bright California sun and are met with a sweet scent in the air and light chirps. It's not until we're in the car, driving out of the neighborhood, that she asks where we're going.

"I'm taking you to meet someone."

As we drive down the street that leads out of the neighborhood, Alex points at a white stucco mansion with a tile roof. It's a gorgeous home, comparable to Jack's, only from its position in the neighborhood, it's clear it doesn't back up to the ocean. That may be so, but given the size of the house and lot, it's a safe bet the back yard features a stunning pool and resort-like atmosphere.

"I think that's Wayne's house."

"He still has a home in Texas too, right?"

"He does. So does Jack."

A couple of news vehicles are parked outside the community entrance. The occupants in the news vans barely give us a second glance as we drive by. They are waiting for Jack and Sophia to return home.

We drive past the luxury gated community and into the portion of San Diego where most people live. The houses are smaller, the yards not quite so green and lush or manicured.

"Can you imagine owning two homes that grand?"

"I can imagine it," I answer honestly. "But that's not my dream."

"What's your dream?"

"I want to make a difference." I tap the steering wheel. Her knee bounces, and I place my free hand on her thigh. Her leg stills, and I catch her gazing at me. I focus on the road ahead, but I want her to get to know me. The real me. "As a kid, I wanted to catch the bad guys. After 9/11, those bad guys became real."

"Why'd you leave the military?"

That's a more difficult question to answer, mainly because I can't get into details. We aren't allowed to talk about our missions. National security requires discretion. Her hand falls over my hand, the one on her thigh. My thumb brushes up and down.

"Don't you find in life, often there are multiple factors that play into any one decision?" I angle my gaze away from the road and back to her. "Especially big decisions?"

She nods and licks her top lip. Smiles. She's got a great smile. Her cheeks rise, and her smile reaches her eyes.

"I suppose that's true. What factors played into your decision to leave the military?"

"Well, one, my sister." I turn off the freeway. There's a green directional sign with the words New Rise Rehabilitation Center, along with signs for gas stations, hotels, and fast food. But she zeroes in on the relevant sign.

"Is your sister not well?" No one knows about my sister. Therefore, I don't get questions about her. I give myself a second to weigh a respectful answer.

"She has good days and bad days. She's fighting some powerful demons. I personally don't think she's been accurately diagnosed yet. I'm working on it." I pause, glancing over at her. Bringing her to meet Indie might be a bad idea. But I want to share this part of my life with Alex. I don't want her to doubt me. Seeing is believing. "I should warn you, my sister isn't my biggest fan. As a matter of fact, right now, she's pretty angry at me."

"Why?"

"I strongly encouraged her to go back into a rehabilitation facility."

"And by strongly...?"

"I threatened to cut her off. She's living in an apartment I own. Driving a car I own."

"How old is she?"

"She's my half-sister. She's twelve years younger. Twenty-five." She's closer to Alex's age than mine, but there's no comparison between the two women. Indie is stuck in a rut, trying to figure her way out of a dark place and find her independence. Alex is financially independent and successful in her own right. "She'd probably be in jail, but I hired a lawyer for her after her last DUI. Part of the agreement my attorney secured required her to spend time in a rehabilitation facility."

"Doesn't sound like she has anything to be angry at you about."

"She thinks I conspired to have her arrested so she'd have to agree to rehab to avoid jail."

The pads of her fingers trace my knuckles and run along the veins on the back of my hand. The sensation soothes.

"Did you?" she asks gently.

"No. Although I can't deny it would've been a solid plan. But I can't control her. Our mother says I'm her crutch, that by keeping her off the streets I'm enabling her. She might be right. If she relapses again, my next plan is to let her end up on the streets. I don't know what else to do."

"That must be incredibly difficult for you." I give her a questioning glance, uncertain where she's coming from. "You possess complete control over every aspect of your life. Except her."

She hit the nail on the head on that one.

"Were you guys close?"

"No." I shake my head and flick the turn signal. "I left for college, knowing I wasn't leaving her in a great place. Our house, it wasn't as bad as it could have been. But it wasn't a great environment. When I left, I went years without seeing her. Military life."

"You feel guilty." She says it as a statement, not a question.

I am self-aware enough to know she's absolutely correct. When my mother called and said she was kicking Indigo out of the house, a sense of responsibility overcame me. Indie and I might not be close, but she's my blood.

After showing identification at the gate, we drive through. Indigo might refuse to meet with us. They won't force her to visit with anyone.

"And her name is Indigo?"

"My mom was in a hippy phase."

"Ryan is a nice name," she says. There's a small smile on her face, but I think she's sincere.

"My personal theory is that my mom adapts to the man in her life. My father was conservative. Second-generation American. From what I can tell, he never intended to stay with my mother, but she did love him. Over the years, she dated different men. Indigo's father was the opposite of mine. Bass player for a band. Polar opposite to my dad. He did stick around for quite a while. Until he died of an overdose."

"You know, addiction can be hereditary." She's not the first person to mention this to me. But bipolar personality disorder can also be hereditary. And carries a tendency to gravitate to alcohol.

We pull into a parking spot. On the sidewalk, I take her hand. Reaching for it is as natural as walking, and there are no officers or agents around. But I second guess the move when she glances at me. But the green in her eyes is warm, and her fingers intertwine with mine. I relax as our strides sync. Her long legs easily match my stride.

At the reception desk, a woman I recognize with curled yellow-blonde hair, a pearl necklace, and a name tag that reads Priscilla greets us. She smiles, and I tell her I'm here to see Indigo Wolfgang.

"You have the same last name?" Alex asks quietly while the receptionist places a call.

"Our mom never changed her name after she and my dad split."

"Mr. Wolfgang?" the receptionist says.

"Yes?"

"I'm sorry, but your sister isn't available to meet at the moment. Do you have a schedule of our visiting times?"

"Yes. Of course. I'm from out of town." I let the phrase hang there, on the off chance being an out-of-town visitor bears weight. In truth, most of my visits occur at the request of my sister's therapist. But, of course, she's not simply sitting in a prison cell. She has an active, full schedule here. "I'll come back."

"The weekends are a good time," Priscilla offers. Of course, I know this.

Once we're outside, I tell Alex, "Sorry. Shouldn't have driven you out here. But I wanted you to see that she's real." There's no better way to build trust than to provide evidence.

My phone vibrates in my pocket. I pull it out and see Liam Ryland's name.

"Agent Ryland," I say as greeting.

"Are you back home?"

"Still in San Diego. Planning to head back later today. Do you need something?"

"Only for you to keep your eyes open. Larry Reyes hung himself. Was discovered in his cell this morning. We suspect it's homicide. Well-constructed homicide. Someone out there is tying up loose ends."

CHAPTER 23

ALEX

"How does that happen?" I voice out loud the question that has been bandying about in my head nonstop since we learned about Larry Reyes. "Shouldn't he have been on suicide watch? Isn't that customary with new arrests?"

"He was in a holding cell. If they prove foul play, it happened fast."

The muscles in Ryan's jaw flex. His head adjusts slightly as he alternates his view between the side mirrors, the road, and his rearview. He repeatedly checks the rearview.

I turn in the seat, looking behind us. We're on the freeway, and it's San Diego. There are a lot of cars on the road with us, but nothing stands out to me.

"Do you think we're being followed?"

"No."

I sit back in my seat, studying the man beside me. He's tense and on edge. I haven't seen him like this. Yes, he's always been no-

nonsense. He maintains exemplary posture, which on his frame intimidates others. He's wearing sunglasses, and I can't see those light blue eyes, but his body posture indicates a high alert level.

Silence prevails until we enter Jack's home. A man in dark gray slacks, a button-down short sleeve shirt, and a gun holster greets us at the door.

Ryan holds out a hand to the man as he approaches.

"Kirk Baxter?" Ryan says.

"Mr. Wolfgang," he responds with a brief nod.

"This is Alex Rolfe. She's with me. Is the updated security system installed?"

"Yes. With the exception of a couple of locations on the property near the beach and along the south side of the property. An electrician is coming out to wire electrical out to those areas."

"For the next week, I'm going to increase security. Two people on site, twenty-four-seven."

"Three shifts?" Kirk asks.

"Yes."

"If Arrow doesn't have the manpower, I have some buddies."

"We're always looking for good people. Tell Stella. She can handle the interview and onboarding."

I step past the two men, into the house. There's a vacuum cleaner running in a room in the back part of the house. I head back to Jack's office.

The whiteboard the FBI had used has been cleaned. The bulletin board someone brought in has been removed. Out the back window, the ocean sparkles beneath the golden sun. The squawk of a seagull penetrates the glass.

On the oversized formal desk sits a stack of manilla folders. I flip one open. Inside are printed copies of the Sullivan Arms Board of Directors and executive team. This is the material the FBI requested to review the higher-ups.

Ryan enters the office. I glance up at him but continue flipping through the pages.

"Jack hired additional security?" I ask.

"He agreed we need to overhaul his current system. After hearing about Reyes, I decided to post the additional on-site security. And I'm sending security over to the facility for Jack and Sophia."

"Do you think they'll come after Sophia?"

"We don't know what she witnessed. Chances are neither do they."

"Whoever 'they' is," I say, flipping through the photographs of the men. All men with the exception of the head of human resources, a surly older woman.

"You ready to go?"

"I'm going to take these files. Do you think Jack will mind?"

"Jack's attention is one hundred percent on his daughter. What are you thinking?" He jerks his head to the stack of folders I have scooped up into my arms.

"These are copies of the material provided to the FBI. I just...I mean, we clearly missed something. I want to go through it all."

"Is this for the case review and analysis?"

"It's for the case," I say.

"The FBI won't need our assistance. They're fully aware this case isn't closed. This is a priority for the San Diego field office."

"And probably one of the Texas offices too, right?"

"They're probably looped in."

It's not until I'm seated in the helicopter, reading through the files, that Ryan's deep tenor breaks into the headset.

"What are your next steps?"

I want to get all of these different pieces out on a wall again. Go through phone records, which are in one of the files. Thankfully, the FBI doesn't have an aversion to printed documents. I want to go through and color code calls between executives. Explore each person's ties. It's the kind of work my father did in his study when working a case. It might not lead to anything other than a clear way to present the case in my review, but I can't shake the feeling we're missing something. We originally focused on connections to Sophia. But now I want to go through and look at connections to Larry Reyes. Because as far as I can see, there is no connection between Reyes and Sophia. And as a successful young businessman, kidnapping for ransom doesn't fit.

"You don't want to tell me?" If I hadn't spent so much time with him, I might miss the amused expression partially concealed by his headset and sunglasses.

"I want to talk to Wayne more."

"You suspect him?"

"What? No. He has about as much reason as Reyes. Neither of those men needed money. They had good jobs with fat bonuses practically guaranteed until retirement. But he knew Reyes well. All I have on Reyes is the information in this file. I'd like to get a sense for his state of mind and his personality."

"It's rather clear Reyes was working for someone. Someone with enough power and influence to arrange his murder in a holding cell."

"Right. So, who? I'm curious who his biggest clients were."

"Why?"

"Well, what if this was supposed to be a diversion? Like it has more to do with a shady gun deal, and they just wanted the executive team distracted?"

"I've thought about that. But Erik had an investigative accountant review the books. He didn't find anything below board."

"Well, who knows when Wayne will have time to talk with me, anyway? But..."

"You can't let it go?"

"It's a puzzle. I don't like unsolved puzzles."

"Puzzle lover?" he asks. The farther away from San Diego we go, the more he relaxes.

"I'd stay up all night. Never understood how people could just have it out on a table for days."

He laughs. It's low and deep. I have this stirring desire to reach out and cover his hand with mine, like I did on the way to meet his sister. But instead, I focus on the reams of paper in my lap.

When we land, we swing by to pick up Trace from his apartment, and he drops me off at my house.

"Busy afternoon?" he asks from the driver's seat. Trace tugs on his leash, ready to leap out of the car.

"I need to catch up with my TA. He's really gone above and beyond for me this past week. What about you?"

"Busy," he confirms. "I'm behind. BAU office work."

I nod, open the door, and grip the leash. Trace bounds forward, eager to get into his house.

Ryan carries my luggage to the front door.

"Thanks," I say.

There's uncertainty in the air, or in me. We never really finished our conversation. We're only seeing each other, but I'm not sure what he expects or wants.

"Alex." He breathes out my name, long and slow. His touch on my hand calms the jitters that came out of nowhere. "I'll see you later?"

"Yeah. Later." He places a quick peck on my cheek, his foot hits the grass, and he stops. "Wait. Let me check your house."

"What?"

"Just..." He holds up a hand. "Work with me. I'll feel better."

I unlock my front door and swing it wide for him. Sixty seconds later, he returns to the front door.

"All clear. Thanks for that."

"Any time."

Again, he stops the moment his foot hits the grass. He turns around.

"What—" His lips silence me. His tongue delves into my mouth, and his hand palms the back of my neck. The unexpected kiss steals my breath. This kiss speaks volumes. He wants me. He is my protector. And he will be back. This thing between us is something I don't need to question.

CHAPTER 24

ALEX

"Why don't you sound more excited?" Sabrina's question is reasonable.

I should be thrilled. The prominent headline of the day is "Sophia Sullivan Home Safe." The news is abuzz with the record one-hundred-million-dollar reward paid for the information that led to her safe recovery.

More questions have been placed on who won the reward and the long-term ramifications of such a high reward than on the specifics of the case, but my guess is Jack hasn't authorized much information to be released to the public. His goal will be for the media buzz to die down. The media doesn't seem aware that the person arrested in connection with her kidnapping committed suicide or was potentially murdered while awaiting arraignment.

"Sophia is safe, but she's still going to have so much to go through. This ordeal is hardly over for her." I limit my response with Sabrina out of respect for Jack's wishes. He'll control the narrative as long as he can.

"The article I read said that the FBI is still investigating persons of interest related to the case. It's still considered an open investigation."

"That's true." I had a very similar conversation with Timothy earlier, only our conversation also included reviewing the upcoming exam and double-checking he reviewed all the concepts while covering for me.

Trace lifts his head, then bounds off the bed, letting out a series of shrill barks as he runs through the house. It's late in the evening, but I've already put on my pajamas and prepared for bed.

Trace's incessant barking doesn't stop. Someone is probably walking their dog by my house. As I stretch an arm out, it strikes me that's nonsensical. Trace leaped off the bed. He doesn't have a view of the front of the house from my bed. Is someone at the door?

I end the call with Sabrina, promising to meet her for coffee in the morning, and shuffle through the den. A deeper knock mixes with the shrill rapid-fire barks. Trace's tail wags back and forth frantically, and his front paws rest on the wood.

I unlock the front door, leaving the chain latch on, and crack the door open the few inches the chain allows. A hulking dark form shifts and blocks my view of the late evening dusk. Trace ceases barking and sits, his little tail wagging.

My gaze travels up a wide, familiar chest, to an unshaven, grizzled jaw, to Wayfarer sunglasses. My heart cinches. Breath escapes.

"Ryan?"

He lifts the sunglasses, and those light blue irises take me in.

"You gonna let me in?" His question snaps me out of my daze.

I push the door closed, slide the chain off, and open the door wide. Ryan's wearing the same outfit from earlier today. His eyes are slightly bloodshot, and there's an air of weariness about him. I step back to let him in. His trousers fit tightly over his shapely, firm ass. His broad shoulders exhibit perfect posture as always.

"What are you doing here?" I close the door behind me with one quick glance out onto the street. Ryan's vehicle is parked in my drive.

Trace jumps up against his legs. The little dog's paws barely strike above his calf. Ryan bends and picks him up, maybe to prevent stepping on him. He holds Trace easily in the crook of his arm and lifts his chin up, out of the way of Trace's lapping tongue. Trace calms and sets to sniffing all along his chest.

"Do you mind if I sit?"

In three strides, I'm on the sofa, my legs up under me, and I point at the other end. "Have you eaten?"

"There were some leftover sandwiches from a meeting at the office. You?"

"Yeah." I look down at my outfit. Heathered gray pajama pants and midriff tank. "Has the FBI learned anything more? Did you get updates from Ryland?"

"Spoke to Ryland on my way over. They don't have any new leads. Still searching for the man who drove away last night. No headway on tracking the reward payment."

"Great. We don't know anything."

"We don't. But whoever orchestrated Reyes' death may not know that."

"Is that why you're here?"

He lifts his gaze from the floor to me.

"You know, you don't need an excuse to come over. You are more than welcome anytime."

"Good to hear. Would you mind if I stay over tonight?" I study him. He's a difficult person to read because he restricts his movements. But regardless of the toe-curling kiss earlier today, he strikes me as the kind of guy who would take things slow in a new relationship. Which means he's here for a different reason than simply wanting to spend time with me.

"You're nervous, aren't you?"

He lets out a loud exhale. "My gut tells me this is unsettled. We're working blind. Too many unknown factors and players. You asked about my reasons for leaving the military. One of the factors, a big factor, is that I felt responsible for taking my team into an ambush. If I had listened to my gut, those men would still be alive."

"But in the military, you have to follow orders."

"You do. That's why I didn't re-up. I promised myself I'd listen to my instincts moving forward. I wouldn't put myself in a position where I couldn't."

"So you started your own company?"

"Exactly. I call the shots at Arrow. And right now, I don't like this. I'll sleep better if I'm with you."

"And you only want to sleep?"

Last night we only slept, but we crawled into bed at three a.m. Within minutes, sleep took us both. I inch forward on the sofa. My heart thuds a million beats a minute as his gaze wraps around me. His dark strands are combed in place, his broad shoulders erect, his shirt and pants wrinkle-free. He could walk out of this house and address a crowd or lead a meeting. He's so put together at all times that I feel this need to run my fingers through his hair and mess it up, to loosen him up.

My cheeks burn, a reminder that I am not an aggressor by nature. Our relationship is tender and new, which breeds uncertainty, but I know I want him. He once told me he doesn't do relationships. But he also told me he doesn't want anyone else. At least right now.

My thighs straddle him, and large hands press against my hips. His touch singes. Feral eyes observe my every moment. I place my palms against his chest.

Like a mind reader, he asks, “What do you want?”

But I need to finish our talk from earlier.

“I don’t want to date anyone else.” His stoic expression gives nothing away. But those hungry eyes give me confidence. “Either,” I add, reminding him he said it first. “I want you.”

The warmth and pressure of his touch progresses up my spine, to the nape of my neck, and his fingers grip my hair. Gently, with the lightest of pressure, he brings my lips to his.

This kiss is tender and slow. My fingers venture to his scalp, twisting the short ends. His hands roam my ass and hips. We kiss until I am out of breath. And then he places his lips below my ear and down my throat.

“I want you.” My words are wispy.

“Do you, now?”

He rises off the sofa, lifting me with him. My legs wrap around his waist as we sail through my small home. He kicks the bedroom door behind him. Seconds later, there’s a scratch of indignation. Trace never likes closed doors. But neither of us cares.

“I think I need you.”

Those light blue eyes are warm. Any ice has melted. The door is closed, his hair in a disarray, and he doesn’t look nearly so controlled.

It’s my turn to caress his cheek. The rough stubble presses the pad of my thumb like a million tiny pinpricks.

He’s a bastion of strength that brings out a confusion of impulses and reactions. But the overarching one I feel is need. Desire. My lips press against the dip in his clavicle. I feel his chest expand with the intake of air. His hands cup my ass, and he brings me up hard against him, lifting my heels off the ground.

The tip of my nose brushes along the side of his neck. He smells of Jack's shower soap, a mixture of rosemary and mint. He most likely shaved this morning, but coarse, dark growth covers his jaw. I stand higher, on the tips of my toes, and brush up against the soft curve of his ear. I lean forward, my hands captured, pressed against his chest, and I take the tender skin in my teeth.

"Are you trying to drive me crazy?" he asks.

"No." I inch back, enough that our eyes can meet. "I think I need you, too."

"You have on too many clothes."

I press my lips to his while I reach down to his waist. As if reaching downward is an incendiary action, his kiss deepens and his hand slips beneath my pajama pants to my bare ass. He backs me up until my thighs hit the bed. He breaks the kiss, and I'm panting, but there's a heaviness in the air that slows his movements. He tugs on my shirt, and I raise my arms. It's gone. I'm not wearing a bra, and the rough pad of his thumb rubs my nipple. I close my eyes, absorbing his heat against my cool, tender skin. He kisses along my neck, his rough growth digging against my throat, burning, while his hands grip my waistband and push down, sending my sweats and panties to my ankles.

He centers his hot gaze on me as he unbuttons his shirt and lets it fall to the floor. His pants and briefs quickly follow. With our clothes removed, he steps closer until we are skin to skin. His erection presses against my belly. The skin is smooth, but he's oh so hard.

He pushes the comforter and sheets back from where I'd already turned the covers for him, making room for us both.

"Lay down."

I do as I'm told.

"Spread your legs."

Again, I do as asked, knowing full well he can see every bit of me. He lifts my arms, placing them over my head.

"Keep them there."

He can see my need, my desire. He gets up onto the bed, and the whole frame creaks with his weight. The mattress sinks. He takes my nipple into his mouth, and his tongue swirls and sucks, pulling to the threshold of pain. My back arches as he positions himself between my legs.

He swipes his tip through my center. A low growl escapes. The savage noise elicits a sense of urgency.

"Please."

He raises his head, his attention diverted from watching his tease, and pushes in as I hold his gaze. He fills me, stretching me, slowly. I tilt my head back as my body takes all of him, my mouth open, sucking in air, but never letting those light blue irises out of sight.

He rocks into me, and my hips rise to meet him. He braces against one arm, and the muscle bulges, while he cups my jaw with his other hand, his hips ever so slowly lifting and plunging.

"God, I needed this." His drops his head, and his pace quickens. "Do you have any idea how good you feel?"

"I want to touch you."

"Do it."

My nails scratch against the firm planes of his back, over his smooth, muscular ass, pulling him into me, as if I can take more of him, as if we can somehow be closer than we are.

The bed creaks, and with each shove of his hips, the headboard slams against the wall.

Bang. Bang.

He slows, backing off, a slow smile spreading on his lips.

"It's okay," I assure him. My hips rise to meet his, urging him on.

Bang. Bang. Bang.

The fleeting thought that I'm going to need to repaint my wall leaves as quickly as it arrives.

Perspiration coats his chest and neck. Our skin slaps, and the aroma of sex encapsulates the room. He reaches between us and presses hard against my mound, his hips never slowing. He moves his hand and gives a garbled, "You do it. Touch yourself."

The veins along his throat bulge, his skin flushed, his thrusts erratic. My skin is slippery, my muscles tight and on edge. I'm close. My thumb presses against my clit, in jerky movements thanks to the rocking of the bed.

"Fuuuck," he groans. He pulses hard, his control lost. "Alex," he adds as his head falls over mine. And that's when I go over the edge. Seeing this strong, formidable man lose control sends me into the abyss where body supplants mind.

We hold each other, my legs and arms wrapped around him, his massive body collapsed over mine, our breathing heavy and rapid. I don't want to let him go, but he heaves and falls to his side, pulling me against him. I clutch the edge of the comforter and pull it around us.

"Damn, Alex. I think I love you."

CHAPTER 25

Alex

"I about flipped out when I read your billionaire friend offered one hundred million dollars in ransom," Sabrina says. "I wish I'd known something. Anything. That's like lottery money, right there." We're in line at Common Grounds, our favorite coffee shop.

"He didn't offer the money *in ransom*." The person standing in line in front of us glances over her shoulder. I offer her a small smile, then notice the white earbuds in her ear. She turns her attention back to the menu board. "The kidnappers refused to provide proof of life. They refused to negotiate. We didn't have any reason to believe they'd turn her over, but we did know there was more than one person involved. We bet that if we offered twice the ransom in the form of a reward for information that led to her recovery, and we made her recovery a requirement for the reward being paid, there would be dissension."

"Huh," she says as we take a step forward. "You bet that honor among thieves would break down with enough financial incentive."

"We bet greed would win out, yeah."

She cocks her head to the side and zeroes in on me. She brings her index finger up to her cheek, and her thumb goes below her chin. It's her version of the Hillary-Clinton-I'm-gonna-figure-you-out pose.

"There was no *we*. That was your idea."

I roll my eyes and look away from her, but I can feel my smile erupting.

"Look at you." She taps my arm. "How cool is that?"

I scrunch my nose and agree, "It is pretty rad."

"So, will you be working with the FBI from now on?" she asks, her excitement clear in her smile and the bounce on her heels.

"I doubt it. I could potentially apply for a position. They also hire outside resources. But..." My preference would be to stay here in Santa Barbara and continue helping Arrow when and how I can. But, given I'm sleeping with the founder, I pretty much squandered that option. My dad's disappointed expression comes out of nowhere, wordlessly telling me he told me so.

"I don't want you to leave. Would you have to move to, like, Virginia or somewhere?" She's thinking of Quantico, the infamous FBI training ground.

"Don't worry. It's not going to happen."

It's our turn to order, effectively ending that line of conversation. Coffee in hand, we find a tall round table and place our items on it.

"How are things with you and that SEAL?"

I side-eye my friend. She's not paying attention to me, though, as she's busy attempting to smoothly spread cream cheese onto half of her muffin. In the helicopter ride the other day, I dished a lot. I needed to get things off my chest.

"It's good, I think."

She halts the knife, and her eyes widen. "Did he stay over last night?"

"Yes." Again with the scrunchy nose. Of course, I'm a good six inches taller than Sabrina, so I'm probably just giving her an inside look at my nostrils.

"And the sex? Still good?"

The question has me thinking back to last night, and a low-level heat flash strikes.

"It's..." Amazing. Orgasmic. I settle on, "Fantastic."

"Ooohhhh," She does a little dance on her toes. "Well, you did say his muscles are to die for." His body is insane. All parts of him are bonkers. So often, tall men have chicken legs, like mine, but his are solid and muscular. "But did you find out...did you ask him about—"

"He's not seeing anyone else." She tilts her head, silently questioning. She's being a good girlfriend because I unloaded a ton of doubt the other day. "I confirmed it."

"Yay." She grins. "This is like...I don't know, what? A week. And you're still liking him."

"Ryan is... He's... You know, at first, I said he was all business? Hard to read?" She nods. "He's not as hard to read as you get to know him. He's quite the big softy. He's loyal. Intelligent." I think about his sister, his complex relationship with her, and how much he cares about her. "He's a good guy."

Sabrina grins like a lunatic.

"What?"

"You like him."

"Yeah, I do."

Admitting it to Sabrina isn't so hard at all. I mean, sure, last night he said he thought he might love me, but he said it in a post-sex grateful way. The way you say you love someone's pudding.

He loves having sex, and I have to say I do, too. Obviously, I like him. You can't love having sex with someone you don't like.

But he's not normally a relationship guy. I'll need to be realistic. He is a protective guy. And right now, he is feeling all kinds of protective. I can roll with this as long as I keep my head above water and my heart guarded. We've agreed to not date other people, and that's something. Hell, technically, it's a relationship. I'm in a relationship with cautious guardrails.

"Does he have friends?" Sabrina nudges me, hope written all across her bright, happy face.

"I'll definitely ask." She does a little jig, more than satisfied with my answer.

Back in my office, I lay out the files I procured from Jack's home. On the bulletin board, I post photographs of the key players. Jack Sullivan. Sophia Sullivan. Wayne Killington. Larry Reyes. Carlos Morales. For good measure, I write the word "affair" in the center of the board.

I draw a dotted line between Larry Reyes and Carlos Morales, because we have photographs connecting them. I add Cliff Hartman's name because he's an executive, the compliance officer, and he visits the house frequently.

We have no idea who Cassandra had an affair with, but it's an open-ended item, and one I still can't wrap my head around. I never probed her on why her marriage ended. It's not in my nature. But I keep thinking back to her saying, "We grew apart." It doesn't particularly matter as related to this case, but when searching for motivation, a jilted lover would qualify as a person of interest.

I am thumbing through the list of the board of directors and senior executives, searching for anyone else of relevance, or this time, someone I could see Cassie messing around with, but then I get another thought. They mentioned only someone with connections could arrange a swift execution of someone in a holding cell. Should we look for government connections? Should I look at who these men donate money to? Their political affiliations? I lift my pen to the whiteboard when a tap at the door stops me from unloading my rambling thoughts.

A young man with thick dark hair and deep brown eyes enters. He's wearing black jeans, dress shoes, a gray button down shirt and a black blazer.

"Professor Rolfe?"

"Yes, hi." He glances over my shoulder at the bulletin board. He blinks rapidly, and I interpret his reaction as recognition to at least one of the photographs. I haven't been closely watching the news, but based on his response, I assume news coverage has expanded to include Larry Reyes. "May I help you?"

"Oh, yes. Hi. I'm a grad student in the foreign language department. But I heard you were doing some consulting with the FBI. I thought I'd stop by and introduce myself. I know you have a TA, but if you find yourself needing any additional resources, I want to volunteer."

"Oh. Do you have an interest in criminal justice?"

"Absolutely." He looks away, and his hand partially covers his mouth. Interesting.

"You're back," Timothy says, entering the small office behind the grad student.

"I am. Timothy is my TA," I say to the young man. "And this is..." I gesture to him, letting the movement of my hand ask for his name.

"Raphael Hendrickson." He shoves his hands into his front pockets and backs out of my office. "I'll let you two get to it. I know it's not your office time right now. I just wanted to introduce myself."

"Thanks, Raphael. If you send me an email, I'll keep you in mind."

He disappears down the hallway. His dress shoes click on the linoleum floor at a rapid pace.

"I thought the case was closed." Timothy steps closer to the whiteboard to study the photos.

"It's my understanding the FBI isn't considering the case closed."

"So, are you still working on it?"

"I'm assessing it. I can't shake the feeling we missed something."

"But Sophia's safe, right?"

"She is. And K&R cases are generally considered closed when the abductee is rescued. But that's the case in countries where K&R is an industry. Here in the US, there is a desire to catch the people responsible. So, the case will remain open. And I'm going to write a review of the case."

"The work you are doing is amazing." Timothy's pupils increase in size. He stands before me, his right foot pointed directly at me, and then he adjusts himself.

I have to be reading those signals wrong. I raise my shoulder, rotating to the board, showing him my back.

"Ahm, Alex. I was wondering, would you like to go to dinner with me?"

Oh, no.

"I mean, I'd love to hear more about the Sullivan case and what happened in San Diego. It'll be my treat."

I could be reading him wrong. I could be, but I might not be. *You have to evaluate behaviors in cluster patterns.* Dad's voice speaks loudly in my head. Cluster or not...

"Timothy, I'm your boss. We could both get in a lot of trouble."

His cheeks redden, and he shoves his hands in his pockets.

Much the way the earlier grad student did. It's the universal sign for not wanting to talk.

"I didn't mean like as a date."

"Of course." I give him a tight-lipped smile. Submissive, non-aggressive. And with that expression, it's clear I'm not going to pursue this line of conversation. "I can't go out tonight, but I'd be happy to go to lunch tomorrow. Actually, did you take accounting?"

"Freshman year."

"Any chance you'd understand these financial statements?"

He laughs. Full-on laughs. His laughter clears the air of any tension.

"I am not an accountant."

"Yeah, I'm not much on it either. We did have a forensic accountant review everything. If he couldn't find it..." I trail off, thinking that I have no chance. The forensic accounting world requires a level of expertise I do not possess.

"I won't figure it out," Tim says, saying exactly what I was thinking about myself.

"It is interesting, though," I tell him. "You know, I had always thought that gun and weapons manufacturers had their best years when a Democrat is in office."

"Because there's fear they'll lose the right to own guns?" Timothy asks.

"Yeah. I mean, from what I can tell, completely unfounded fear. But I've read a number of reviews over the last several decades, and it was a consistent trend. Gun sales slumped when Republicans were in office. But they did well the last year under Trump. I suppose the pandemic helped."

"I've read about that. Fear drives gun sales."

I drop the file folder with all of the financial information onto my desk with a thud. The company is profitable, but I'm not going to decipher more than that from a financial statement.

"Are these people on your board suspects?"

"Persons of interest." I point to Larry. "He was definitely involved. But he didn't do it alone."

"Is the FBI tracing the reward?"

"Trying." I shrug. "Jack played it straight up. True to his word. Paid into an account as directed."

"Is that who you are trying to find?" He backs up against the wall, arms crossed. His foot still angles in my direction.

"Not necessarily. I suspect the recipient is a low-level person. He, or she, is probably in hiding because he double-crossed his team. And he teamed up with dangerous criminals. What I want to know is who recruited Larry Reyes." I am careful not to mention any specifics regarding Reyes, because to my knowledge, specifics on the case haven't yet been released.

"Right." He jerks his thumb in the direction of the open door behind him. "I'm gonna head on."

"Sure. Have a good night," I tell him.

I spend the next few hours mapping out what I know about each person on the board and their relation to each other and noting any affiliations I can find through online searches. Then I call Erik from Arrow Communications.

"Hey, Erik. This is Alex Rolfe."

"Yep," he says. *Am I out of line calling him directly?*

"When you were looking into the executives and board members, did you by chance look at their communication logs?"

"To see who talked to who the most? Nothing stood out. Communication patterns followed chain of command."

"Would you mind emailing me what you found?"

"It's posted in the network."

"I'm not sure I have access."

"I'll send. Anything else?"

"Your forensic accountant. Did he understand the drive behind sales fluctuations?"

"We'd need to see the marketing plans to fully understand fluctuations. But share of international sales increases year over year. Those are to wholesale distributor accounts and probably have the biggest impact to the bottom line."

"Huh. How can I tell what sales are international versus domestic?"

"The way they have it set up, you need to know the vendor. I'll send you the file."

"Thanks, Erik."

A dial tone crosses the line. He hung up.

I stare at the board. I don't see anything new. Temptation to call my dad and review the case with him brews, but there's no point. Not right now. We will be getting new information. Any day now, Sophia will spend time with someone from the FBI. She may have seen or heard something. The FBI could have already met with her. They could already know so much more.

A text comes through.

Ryan: Dinner?

Me: Sure.

My phone rings. It's Ryan.

I answer with a simple, "Hi."

"We received confirmation the prison security tapes were tampered with."

"What do you mean by tampered?"

"Like what they did with Sullivan's home security. Deleted actual footage and replaced with earlier footage. Only, because it was a prison cell, it was more readily apparent what had occurred."

"Wow." It's the only response that comes to mind. Sullivan's security company had apparently been relatively amateur, but one would expect the government to be high tech.

"Exactly. Why don't I come by and pick you up? You can leave your car—"

"Don't be silly."

"Are people still in your building?" It's after seven, and the building has mostly cleared out, but the patter of feet in the hall and hushed voices assure me I'm not alone.

"There are people here. I'll be fine. Where do you want to meet?"

"What are you in the mood for?"

"I really don't care," I say as I begin stacking the file folders and putting them away in my tote bag.

"We could also order take out."

"Take away works." He wants to eat dinner with me. That's all I care about.

"And you're ready to go?"

"Packing up while we're on the phone."

"I'll meet you back at your place."

I pull my office door closed and lock the door. The hall is empty. As I walk down the hallway, I pass one professor's open door. She and I make eye contact and both nod.

When I reach the elevator bank, the word "elevator" is dark. *Huh.* I push the down arrow, but the arrow remains dark too.

"They went on the blink like thirty minutes ago," a male voice calls out. “I called, but I don't know when anyone will get here to take a look at them.”

“I’ll just take the stairwell.”

“Smart,” he says. I get a glimpse of the graduate student talking to me. He’s sitting in an open office in front of someone’s desk. I lift my hand in a wave.

The click of my shoes on the concrete steps echoes through the stairwell. The Life Sciences building is only four stories tall. The elevator being out of commission is hardly an emergency. I’ll be surprised if they have it fixed in the morning. I practically float down the stairs, because this thing between Ryan and me is feeling real. Once again, he called me, wanting to have dinner. Concerned about me.

A door on the lower floor opens. I move to the side and glance down the open center, still moving steadily down the stairs. The only sound remains the click of my shoes. I slow my footfalls, listening.

It’s possible someone exited the stairwell. The echo in the stairwell, combined with watching one too many crime dramas, pricks my nerves.

“Hello?” I’m on the second floor. I have one more floor to go.

I hear a step. And another. The shoe sound is of the front part of a shoe. Or a shoe with a soft pad, like trainers. I continue heading down.

A man’s hand grips the metal railing one floor below. My breath slows.

“Hello?” My question echoes.

I continue descending, but at a slower pace. I scan up the stairwell. I’m approaching the ground floor. I’m halfway between the second and first.

A hand glides up the rail.

Step. Step.

The person's gait is steady and produces an S sound across the concrete.

Slow.

Steady.

At the bend in the stairs, the hand slides around the turn.

Raphael, the graduate student from earlier, faces me. Eyes void of emotion. Lips in a flat line.

"Raphael," I say, artificially chipper. I am overly aware of my heart beating. Pounding.

I glance up the stairs, judging the distance to the stairwell door.

He steps closer.

"You on your way out?" he asks.

"Yes. Did you forget something?"

"I'll walk you out," he says.

The light in the stairwell is dim. If I scream, I doubt anyone will hear. He continues climbing. A stairwell light flickers. The electrical hiss holds a sinister flair.

"I forgot something. I need to go back up." My hand heats the cold metal stair rail.

He raises an arm. A pistol is tucked into his jeans. The butt shines.

I spin and run.

CHAPTER 26

Ryan

On the corner of State and Victoria Streets, flowers are set out in front of a market. Red, yellow, white, pink, and orange cluster together in tall aluminum buckets. I consider Alex's bright yellow bungalow. But she's mentioned twice that she plans to paint it a different color.

A woman with an apron wrapped around her waist comes out onto the sidewalk. She lifts one of the tall, narrow buckets. "Can I help you, sir?"

"Are any of these flowers representative of Ireland?" I don't have enough information to pick a color, and I know nothing about flowers, but something from her homeland might be appealing.

"Well, when I think of Ireland, I think of shamrocks."

"Do you have that?"

"Clovers?" The woman looks at me like I am a naive child. This is a stupid idea. "No. Here." She sets down the bucket she was holding and pulls out a phone from her back pocket. She looks through a list. "This says Easter lilies. I've never been to Ireland, but I've always associated those flowers with religion, and I think Ireland is religious? Irish or not, they smell great."

She lifts several white flowers with a pink interior and thrusts them close to my nose. I obediently bend and sniff. Alex would probably like the sweet scent.

"Do you think a woman would like these?"

"Definitely." She smiles up at me, again looking at me like I'm slow. A part of me wants to simply walk away, but I've already stopped. I should have never stopped.

"How many of these bunches should I get?" The flowers are tied into groups of three. She sells me on a dozen.

After being wrapped in pink paper and taped, the bouquet is enormous. On the bright side, the pale pink paper keeps it from feeling like someone died. But the bundle fills my passenger seat. There's no telling how Alex will react to this bulky gift. When I bring back take out, or take-away as she calls it, I can tell her the restaurant was running a special and giving out free bundles of flowers. Red dust from the flowers covers the side door, and I let out a curse.

Why the hell did I stop for flowers?

My phone vibrates against the holder in my car. Time slows. My peripheral vision darkens.

Breaking News: Shots Fired on UCSB campus. Updates to come.

I shift the car into drive and slam on the accelerator. A sharp horn blasts from the car I cut off. I shout at Siri, "Call Alex Rolfe."

The number dials as I tear through the streets of Santa Barbara, scanning for off guard pedestrians.

Ring. Ring.

My heartrate climbs.

Ring. Ring.

Sirens sound in the distance. The sound grows louder the closer I get to campus.

I have one handgun in the glove box. One rifle and two knives in the trunk. My vest is back at my apartment. *Fuck.*

"Hi. You've reached Alex Rolfe. I'm not the best at checking voicemail, so please send a text and I'll be sure to get back to you."

"Siri, hang up."

"Siri, call Alex Rolfe."

Ring. Ring.

"Ryan." Her voice floods me with a staggering sense of relief. The onslaught is stranger than the pile of flowers. *Thank god.*

"Where are you? Are you okay?" My tires squeal as I round the corner and accelerate, one block away from her building. Up ahead, police barricades block the street.

"Someone came after me."

"Where are you?"

"I'm outside. With the police."

"What happened?" I park in front of a fire hydrant, the only spot available, and jump out.

"A man met me in the stairwell. He had a gun." *Why the fuck were you in a stairwell?* "I took off running. I knew something was wrong. Another professor was still in his office. We barricaded ourselves in and called nine-one-one."

"Did they get the guy?" I speed past a police officer.

"Sir, you can't go there."

"I'm here for my wife." He won't gun me down for charging past him for my family.

"Sir, you can't—"

I push forward.

"Ryan? Where are you?"

On the northwest side of the parking lot, there's an ambulance and multiple cop cars.

"Did you get shot?" I break out into a run in a straight line for the ambulance.

"No. He shot at the door, but the bullet seemed to jam the lock. The police had to break the door down to get in. Campus police responded to our call first, and he shot at them, but he didn't hit anyone. I think he was trying to give himself clearance to get away."

"Did they catch him?" Alex's dark hair comes into view. She has a phone pressed to her ear. Three police officers are standing near her. She's leaning against the vehicle, her back to me. I end the call.

"Alex!" She turns, and within seconds she's in my arms. My hands roam her hair, her back, her arms. I grip her biceps and hold her away from me, scanning her body from top to bottom.

"I'm okay," she says. "Ryan, I'm okay. He didn't get to me."

A police officer steps up to us.

"Dr. Rolfe was smart. She ran the moment she saw his gun."

Alex's eyes are a bright shade of green, her cheeks flushed. She caresses my arm.

"It's okay, Ryan. It's okay."

I crush her to my chest and breathe her in. She smells like the pile of flowers in my seat. Her head comes to my shoulder. My fingers tangle with her hair as I hold the back of her head to me. I need this moment. He didn't harm her.

I close my eyes, breathe, and get control. Her fingers lightly caress my neck. My heartrate slows. I open my eyes and take stock.

Six patrol cars on this section of the parking lot, two ambulances. Crowds of students stand to the north side. News crews line the barricades.

"The man. Who was he?"

"I don't know." She blinks. "He introduced himself as a grad student and gave me a name, but I doubt it was a real name. The police are looking into it."

"He got away?" There's no one sitting in the police cars.

"He did. The campus police didn't follow him. The cops arrived after he'd left the building."

"There's security footage?"

"Yes. One of the officers mentioned they would be checking it. The moment I saw him in the stairwell, I knew I couldn't trust him. He had an aggressive stance." She exhales. "And I knew it couldn't be a coincidence that the elevators stopped working."

"The elevators stopped?"

One of the policer officers, a Black female, mid-thirties, about five foot five, answers my question. "Electrical to the elevators was cut. Campus police said it looked like an amateur job. Also, if someone had been in them, it would have been an immediate emergency."

"Do you have video of inside the elevators?"

"The university does," she says. "We'll be checking it."

"If these are the same guys we've been dealing with, they've already deleted any footage that will give anything away."

"You think you know who it is?" She positions herself directly in front of me, hands on her hips, elbows out to the side.

"I don't know who the individual is. But I think I know the group. If you don't find anything on the video, then we're dealing with the same people."

CHAPTER 27

Alex

"Yes, I'm okay. I promise."

"There's a flight out in the morning."

"Dad, it's not necessary. I'm okay. And I'm safe."

Ryan sits beside me, his gaze never leaving me, scanning me from head to foot, in the same way he's been doing since the incident at school. He insisted we pick up Trace and spend the night at his place. He says because of its location, it's more secure than my standalone house that can be approached from any angle. He also placed a security guard at the base of the steps to his condo, an action I disagreed with, but he refused to budge, so I dropped it.

"Do you know why someone would target you?"

"The only thing I can figure is they think I know something. But we really don't have any information the FBI doesn't possess."

"To your knowledge," my dad emphasizes. "You know, typically, if an investigator is attacked, it's at the crime scene. That's why police officers guard crime scenes. In case a perpetrator returns to remove evidence."

"I think they are trying to eliminate loose ends. Larry Reyes could clearly connect us to the persons involved, and they eliminated him."

"Did you meet with him?"

"No. We didn't get a chance. The FBI didn't get to meet with him either. He lawyered up immediately, and the lawyer he hired was from Texas. By the time his lawyer arrived in California, Larry was dead." The tea kettle whistles and Ryan heads into the kitchen.

"You realize this is someone with police connections. He had to have a connection on the inside."

"You mean, in order to get to Reyes within his holding cell?" Of course my father assumes we haven't thought of this. "The FBI is handling the investigation. And I believe internal affairs is involved."

"And Sophia will be a target," my dad adds.

Ryan delivers my tea to the coffee table, and the cushions sink as he sits beside me. He reaches around me and manhandles me, pulling me up against his side. He's been touching me constantly, as if reassuring himself that I am indeed okay.

"Arrow Security has a full detail set up for Sophia and Jack. They won't be able to reach her."

"And you?"

I exhale and pull a nearby throw over my lap.

"I'm not at my house. I'm staying with someone who will keep me safe. You don't need to worry."

"Jack should hire security for you. Or the police should."

"Dad, I'm with the head of Arrow Security. At his home. We're safe."

Silence descends on the line. Ryan brushes his lips against my hair.

"Are you in a romantic relationship with him?" The judgment is like a gavel on wood. I glance up at Ryan, wondering how much he can hear. He flattens his palm against my hip, and his fingers spread across my stomach. Possessive.

"I am."

"Well, I'm going to want to speak to this young man." I roll my eyes at the idea that my curmudgeonly old da is going to be stern with this late-thirties former SEAL. Ryan nudges me and gestures to the phone. As I suspected, he's heard everything.

"Fine, here he is. His name is Ryan Wolfgang."

Ryan takes my phone. He sits up.

"Hello, sir. How can I help you?"

"My daughter tells me she's in a romantic relationship with you." My dad's voice comes through crisp and clear, possibly because Ryan holds the phone about an inch away from his ear.

"Yes, sir." Those blue eyes flit to me, mirth evident in the wrinkles at the corners and the lift of his lips. "I care about her. I'll keep her safe."

"Yeah, then how did they get to her today?"

"It won't happen again, sir." I straighten, knowing full well that statement means Ryan thinks he can control my whereabouts.

"You got any training?"

"Yes, sir. Navy. Three tours. I own a security firm. They won't get another chance to get to her."

"Eh, we can't control everything. But I feel better knowing she has someone like you watching out for her."

"Yes, sir. But she's got a good head on her shoulders. She saved herself. I have every intention of doing my best with her, but you raised an astute daughter."

"I taught her to pay attention to human cues. She's a lot like her mother. Smart. Strong-willed. Stubborn as hell. But she'll always be my little girl. She is my heart. Do you hear me?"

"Loud and clear. Sir."

There is a beep, and Ryan holds the phone out. Jackson Sullivan is ringing through. I take the phone from Ryan.

"Dad, Jack is calling. I'll call you later, okay?"

"Keep me updated."

"Love you, Dad."

I click over and catch Jack before it goes to voicemail.

"Jack?"

"Alex? I heard what happened. Are you okay?"

"Yes."

"Where are you? Did Ryan set up security for you? The guy in charge at our house didn't know."

"I'm with Ryan."

"Oh. Good. But you're okay?"

"Yes."

"Any idea why they would go after you?"

"My best guess is that when we countered the ransom, we fractured the group. The remaining members aren't working cohesively and are working without all information at their disposal."

It's truly my best theory. The more I think about the man who came earlier, posing as a student, he wasn't a professional. If he had been a professional assassin, I would be dead. He seemed interested in the contents on my board. He might have been listening to me talk about the case with Tim.

"Jack, I noticed something earlier today. I don't know if it has any relevance or not. But sales at Sullivan Arms spiked the year after Cassandra died. Any idea why?"

"We had some big contracts come through. But that was the biggest sales year on record for the entire industry. When the pandemic hit that March, gun sales exploded. Are you still working with the FBI?"

"No. I'm just—"

"Alex, drop it. I don't want you getting hurt. Just let it go."

"Jack, you understand that they killed Larry Reyes, right?"

"It was suicide." His voice quivers, and his tone is low. He's uncertain.

"No, it wasn't. The investigation is ongoing, but the FBI doesn't believe it was suicide."

"I know. That's why Ryan beefed up security. Do you agree? You believe they're coming after Sophia?"

I catch concerned blue eyes watching. He hears everything. The volume setting on this phone is high.

"He told you that, right?" I ask, squinting at Ryan. Surely, he's been keeping Jack in the loop.

"I was told the extra security was out of an abundance of caution."

Everyone has been treating Jack with kid gloves. I angle my head, silently accusing Ryan of being overprotective. Hiding the truth is a poor strategy.

"Well, after today, we know it's quite necessary. You have to be careful. Has Sophia told you or the FBI anything? Did she see her captors?"

"She's given them descriptions of her captors. She never saw Larry Reyes, so he was staying out of her line of sight, knowing she'd recognize him."

"So, they really may have planned on returning her for the ransom."

"Possibly." A door clicks in the background. "She's told the FBI everything. She's been interviewed by three different agents and an FBI psychologist. Everything she knows, she's already told them. There is no reason for someone to take her. Coming after you does not make sense."

"I know. Jack, I feel like there's more here. And it has to do with something within your company."

"Alex. Listen to me. I don't want you working on this anymore. Let the FBI do their job. Leave it alone. It's not worth it. Besides, Sophia wants to see you. She's where our focus should be."

"I want to see her, too." He's correct. My primary concern should be Sophia. Cassie would want me to be there for her.

"Maybe next week? Can you come down?"

"I don't teach class on Thursday. Let me know if that works."

"Will do. And Alex? Just drop this case. It's not worth it. The FBI can pursue it, but I don't want any harm coming to you. Cassandra would not want that. Can you let it go? Just plan to be here for Sophia. She thinks of you as her aunt."

"Of course." The lie comes easily. I don't touch my mouth or scratch my nose. I would probably pass a polygraph. Because it's a partial truth. I will be there for Sophia.

"She's not ready for visitors yet. But her doctors think by next week, so Thursday could work."

"Is she still going through withdrawals?"

"Somewhat. But she's getting stronger."

When I end the call with Jack, I settle back into Ryan.

"I can only imagine what Sophia has gone through." He cups my elbow and caresses my arm.

"What about you? How are you doing? You had a dramatic day."

He's right. I did. And the spike in adrenaline followed by a slow, winding decline has misted my eyes at times as emotions welled up. But I'm okay. Perhaps growing up with a father who worked on cases and hearing about tragic situations steeled me for this. I can't say I don't feel it, that I don't tremble when the memory of my panicked climb up the stairs hits. But I'm okay. And when I think back on it, the man in the stairwell didn't have a well-thought-out plan. He didn't shoot at me as I ran. He followed me, attempted to catch me, but he was careless. It's almost like he lifted that arm so I would see his gun. To give me a head start running.

"Do you think it's possible that someone just wanted to scare me? That today wasn't about actually catching me?"

"If the FBI wasn't on the case, I might say yes. But scaring you off doesn't make sense. The FBI hasn't closed the case. There's a team of investigators still looking for the man who escaped. And now they're looking for this guy."

"Right. It just feels too easy. And now Jack is telling me to drop it."

"Jack doesn't want you hurt. And his focus is on his daughter." *As it should be.* "You feel like it was too easy because you escaped. You are observant. Your gut told you something was off about him. You noticed his eyes, his body posture. You froze long before you saw the gun. And then you reacted and ran. You survived. There's nothing easy about what you did. Some people would have remained frozen on the stairs. Some wouldn't have been able to comprehend the danger. You ran, protected yourself, and called for help. You're also lucky. If he had broken into that office before campus security scared him off, the results of today could have been very different. Nothing about today was too easy."

CHAPTER 28

Alex

Outside my house, a man sits inside a nondescript sedan. From the wall near my front window, I watch him. A mix of frustration and annoyance simmer. Agent Ryland contacted Ryan and informed him facial recognition of the man who held Sophia, based on her descriptions, has identified him as a person connected to the Morales cartel. The suspect has been on DEA's watch list and is part of a separate ongoing investigation. The man from the stairwell may also be connected to the cartel.

Agent Ryland didn't say the FBI was closing the investigation, but Ryan's take is that the DEA case will take precedence and priority. They will prosecute those entangled with the kidnapping, but attacking a woman in a stairwell is a low-priority crime. They know these men do bad things. They aren't out to arrest them for crimes that will land them in prison for a year or two. No, they are looking to bring down an operation. Between the DEA and ATF, Ryan suspects they have multiple deep undercover operatives in place. Given the ATF monitors arms sales, and Sullivan's company sells weapons, everyone suspects that ultimately there will be a connection between illegal arms sales and Sophia's disappearance.

But kidnapping for ransom isn't the cartel's modus operandi. And the DEA enforces controlled substances, or drugs, which has me wondering if the kidnappers were communicating with Jack and requesting something other than money. It's conceivable the counter-ransom broke up the criminal faction. Maybe some of the low-ranking employees weren't paid well enough to inspire staunch loyalty. Here's the problem with criminal investigations. You can theorize all day, but ultimately, you need evidence.

Five days have passed since the attack at my office. Twice I have driven to the office, parked, then put it in reverse and returned home. That first day, the police tape for the investigation turned my stomach. The university wasn't allowing employees in the office anyway. Now, the tape is gone. The dean notified our floor we can return to the building. That email led to my first fight with Ryan. I refused to have a security detail accompany me to the office.

I haven't fought harder on the topic because my preference is to work from home. Or it has been. I have taught my classes, but I haven't been up to my office. Both the elevator and the stairwell provoke uncomfortable nerves I can't quell.

This coming weekend, Ryan and I will return to San Diego. He'll visit his sister, and I'll get to finally see Sophia. I am very much looking forward to getting out of Santa Barbara.

The man in the sedan flicks his fingers in a half-wave. My position by the wall must not conceal me as much as I hoped. I lift my coffee mug to him. The Arrow employee is not trying to hide. Ryan wants anyone watching my house to know he's there. But

Ryan's also striving to give me privacy, hence the reason he's sitting in a vehicle and not in my home.

Ryan and I have spent every night at his place since the attack. I'm essentially using my home as an office. Each night, it's assumed we'll stay together. Last night, he unpacked my suitcase and hung up my belongings in his closet.

Against one wall in my den is the standing whiteboard from my office. Ryan brought it back to my house for me. I haven't touched it since the attack. I haven't had anything to add to it as the investigation has essentially concluded. But my hope is that I might uncover something more when I spend time with Sophia and Jack this weekend. Even if we never locate her abductors, the case will be an interesting one to review, given we countered a ransom with a reward.

The university would love for me to produce something publishable from this incident. A review of the case or a criminal profile. Larry Reyes is dead. We may never find out who he was working for, but it seems reasonable he may have been working for the cartel. As the head of sales, it would be logical for the cartel to be one of his clients. We already know he had been responsible for greatly increasing international sales.

Wayne Killington claimed to know the man well. He'd been a mentor and hired him right out of college. He'd said he would talk to me.

I pick up my phone and jot out a quick text. I haven't seen Wayne since we returned to Santa Barbara.

Me: Hi, Wayne. This is Alexandria Rolfe. I hope all is well. I'll be in San Diego this weekend, if by chance you have time to get together. If not, I completely understand.

. . .

I send it off before I can second guess it. All I really want is to ask questions about Larry Reyes, to gain a deeper understanding of his personality than the company bio provides.

Internal affairs will work to determine if someone within the police department was paid off. I'm certain the FBI will continue to work to identify the other players, either within Sullivan Arms or outside of it. The investigation is ongoing with multiple agencies at play, but things have quieted down. My role has concluded, and I believe that whoever perceived me as a threat has picked up that I am not a threat. If either Sophia or I had information that could lead to conviction, surely they realize the FBI would have already arrived at their doors.

The phone in my hand vibrates, startling me. It's an unidentified number.

"Hello?" It's probably a telemarketer, but there's always a chance it's a reporter or a student.

"Alex girl. Just got your text. You're in luck. I'm in your neighborhood."

"You are?" I peer down the street.

"Well, I'm in Santa Barbara. At the marina. My boat was getting some work done, and I'm here to bring her home. You feel like going for a boat ride? If you come on over, you can drill me with questions while we take her for a spin. We can make sure everything's working right before I drive her home."

The prospect of taking a break and spending a couple of hours bouncing over waves appeals to me. There's a cloudless sky, and it's a warm day. I've seen the boats traveling along the coast, but have yet to venture out in one.

"I'd quite love that. Where should I meet you?"

"Why don't you meet me at the marina? I'll meet you at the gate."

I latch a leash onto Trace's collar and lead him outside to the

Arrow employee's sedan. On the way, Trace lifts a leg and does his business.

"Hello," I say to the man. His automobile is off, and his windows are down. This job assignment must be dreadfully boring.

"Hi." He scans past me, to my house. I glance over my shoulder to see what he's looking at, but when I return my gaze to him, I notice he's glancing every which way. He's on lookout.

"I'm going out to meet a friend." Wayne Killington isn't exactly a friend, but after we spend time sailing around, he might truly qualify.

"Give me the address, and I can follow you. Or I can drive you."

I glance back at my house. Someone destroyed my office. It's not inconceivable they might come to my house. That's the whole reason we've got the equivalent of an officer stationed here.

"What about my house?" I bend and lift Trace into my arms. "Not sure this guy's going to keep anyone out."

"Where are going?"

"Just the marina. Going sailing with a friend. It's close enough I could walk it."

"You going out in a boat?"

"Yeah."

The man's brow crinkles.

"Why don't I drop you off at the marina? I'll come back to watch your house, and when you return, you can text us and someone on the team will pick you up."

"That sounds a bit unnecessary and over the top. I doubt anyone is watching me to know where I'm going. This would be..." I think about the chances of that guy from the school running into me at the marina. He knew I'd be at school, but I never visit the marina.

"Let me drive you." The man has sandy blond hair that's cut close to his scalp and brown eyes. He's also got a determined set to his jaw and the confidence to look me straight in the eye. I don't foresee me winning an argument with him.

"Okay. Let me deposit Trace back at the house and get my things."

Five minutes later, I'm in the passenger seat of his sedan, headed to the marina. I learn his name is Lucca and not much else. When he pulls along the busy street in front of the marina, there's no parking anywhere. As he slows in front of a pedestrian crosswalk, I see Wayne standing on the boardwalk. I jump out of the car and shout back to Lucca, "I'll text when I return."

"Do you see your friend?"

"Yeah. He's right there."

I'm several feet away when I hear him call, "What's his name?"

A horn beeps, urging Lucca to stop holding up traffic. I hold my phone up, indicating I'll text him.

Wayne smiles wide. He's wearing sunglasses and a gray shirt with the outline of palm fronds all over it. Compared to what he's worn in the past, this Hawaiian print is subtle. His shorts are a darker shade of the same color gray, and his brown leather shoes have a leather shoestring that ties. I've not seen shoes quite like those.

"Thanks for the offer. A boat ride sounds magnificent."

He gives me a quick hug and a kiss on one cheek.

"Yeah, I've been burning the candle on both ends. Needed to get outta the office. Away from the desk. You know what I mean?" He rubs his jaw as he smiles, and his gaze runs down my body.

"Am I dressed okay?" I'm in a loose, long skirt, a t-shirt, and flip-flops. A cloth tote bag hangs off one shoulder with a note pad and my phone that I'll use as a recorder if he lets me.

"Whatchu got in there?"

"Just stuff for work."

He shakes his head and turns his attention to the gate where he punches in a code. "You're as bad as me. Can't get away from it, can ya?"

"Well, I'm just an assistant professor. I've got to prove myself." My hope is this angle will help him to open up with me if he sees what he shares might help me produce a more impressive piece for publishing.

"Jack told me what happened to you." One of Wayne's funny shoes points in the direction we're headed. He's ready to go, but he's gracious enough to take this moment to address the event on campus. "I wish all of this mess could be behind us." His warm tenor is welcoming, and I find myself looking into his eyes, which are directed at my feet. "I can only imagine how scary that must have been for you."

He's uncomfortable talking to me about a potentially emotional situation. Many people are uncomfortable discussing tough topics. I put on a brave smile and shrug.

"It wasn't fun, but...I survived."

He brightens and cocks his head to the side. He can tell I'm not on the verge of breaking down into tears or asking to rehash it.

"Yes, you did. You're a trouper." He's got such a personable smile. It's easy to see how he rose to the top in a corporation. "Let's take the captain for a spin." He sets the pace along the boardwalk, seemingly relieved to have that uncomfortable bit behind us. "Sunshine does wonders, especially in crazy times."

Wayne waves to a man on the dock and gestures for me to follow along.

"So, are you still working on the case? Is that why you came on out to chat with me?"

A seagull swoops down nearby, disappears in the murky depths, then pops up with a flapping fish.

"Whoa, did you see that?" I point, but Wayne doesn't appear amused. His pace slows, and one hand falls on his hip. "Ah, no, I'm not really working the case. Since we countered the ransom, I'm hoping there will be some appetite for a case study in an academic journal."

"You don't have all the information you need from the FBI?" There's a touch of incredulity in his tone, and I can't say I blame him. My research probably looks a tad nonsensical.

"Well, I was really hoping for insights into Larry Reyes."

"Larry." He tugs on his chin and continues walking. "We're right this way."

"I know the two of you were good friends."

"That's true." He sucks on the corner of his lip and slowly nods. His stride is so slow it requires effort to not sail past him. "He worked for me for a long time."

"You must have been very upset when he was murdered." I watch Wayne the way one watches a dramatic scene on a television show. I don't want to see the pain or hurt, but I can't not look. Only, that's not what I see.

Whatever thoughts cross through his mind, he blinks and shakes them off.

"The captain is right up here. There's over a thousand boats in this marina. Did you know that?"

He pushes forward with a quick pace. We turn onto a narrower section of dock, and he points. At the end of the dock, there's an enormous white boat churning water. The boat he's pointing at is so large a small boat is attached on the end, and there's a deck with a curved sofa and black glass on the back and all along the sides.

"She's gorgeous."

"She's my pride and joy. At the wife's insistence, I named her *El Capitan*."

The sliding door opens on the boat, and a man in shorts and a short-sleeved shirt steps out onto the deck. He waves to Wayne and heads to the front of the boat, where he bends and pulls in a white cushion that had been hanging down, presumably protecting the boat from rubbing against the dock.

"You have staff?" I ask.

Wayne chuckles. "Sure do. A boat this big, you gotta. Welcome aboard."

He holds out a hand for me, and I step from the dock, across the water gap, onto the yacht, because she's not just a boat, this is a yacht.

"Can I get you something to drink?"

"No, thanks."

"You sure?"

"Maybe later."

"Well, let's sit. It's gonna take a bit for Juan to get us set to depart." He sits on the white leather and crosses one ankle over a knee. I sit on the opposite end and rest my tote on the cushion beside me. "What's with the criminal profile on Larry? You don't think he just got involved with some group who found a good ransom prospect?"

"No, that doesn't fit. It never has. They were too slow to demand ransom." It's one piece of the puzzle that has always bothered me. You could conclude the refusal to engage in negotiation was due to inexperience or a dominant psychology, but waiting until we involved the FBI and went full-frontal to engage are curious elements of this case. I could share the current theories that it's all related to an illegal gun transaction gone bad, but sharing that with a Sullivan Arms executive would be the height of poor judgement. If the FBI or the ATF wants Wayne to know, they'll meet with him and share their theories.

Wayne's fingers top the back of the sofa leather. His sunglasses shield his eyes, but he's frowning.

"Do you go fishing?"

"What?" He lowers his glasses on the bridge of his nose. The noise from the engines might be making it difficult to hear me.

"Is this boat for fishing?" I don't see any fishing gear, but a boat this enormous has plenty of storage space.

"Nah. She's a cruiser. She can cross the Atlantic. Or the Pacific. Whatever you wish." He scratches his face. He's continually touching his face, now that I think about it. My dad once changed aftershave brands and couldn't stop scratching his jaw. Drove me nuts until I figured it out.

"Well, I appreciate you taking me out. It's a nice day for it."

"Oh, yeah. Least I could do. Jack's pretty worried about you, but you know, he's not feeling like he can get away to check on you himself."

"So you offered to do it?" Wayne really does do a lot for Jack. I hope Jack appreciates him.

"Eh, well, had to get my boat. You called." Again, he scratches his jaw and covers his mouth with his hand afterward. It's brief, but repeated. And now I'm rubbing my throat as I study him.

"Has Jack mentioned how Sophia is doing?" Since he seems to have talked to Jack more than I have, I'm curious what he's learned.

"Says she's doing good. Can't remember much of anything. I think that might help her, ya know?"

I understand his point. Lack of memory could be a blessing. "Do you talk to Jack regularly?"

"About as much as I can, you know, given his focus is on his daughter. And that'll be the case for quite a while. At least a year, I'd say."

Juan crosses to the far side of the boat without addressing either of us.

"A year? Are the therapists thinking she'll need that long?" She'll be so behind in school.

"Not sure about all that. But, you know, he took about a year off after Cassandra. Got her good and settled. When he's working, he's all work. It's hard for him to balance being present at home and work." He nods and slips his nail between his teeth.

Cassandra blamed an obsession with the company as the reason their marriage had come apart.

"You know, Cassandra said the same thing. That when Jacks works, he's all work."

"It's true," he says with a deep nod. "It's no wonder their marriage fell apart."

The thing is, those two may have grown apart, but at her funeral, no one doubted Jack's love for her. Her death broke him. To my knowledge, she never dated after their divorce either. She claimed her freedom, but she never seemed ready to truly move on. But I also didn't know about the affair. She never opened up to me. Maybe it was due to our age difference. Maybe we weren't as close as I wanted to believe.

"Are you thinking all of this," he waves his hand around, "has something to do with Cassie?"

I hesitate, uncertain how much to share. Curious what Wayne knows. But it's not my business, and that's not why I'm here.

A relatively short man wearing a white tank, black shorts, and black sandals waves from the far end of the dock. He gives Wayne a thumbs-up signal but remains positioned at the end of the dock.

"Santiago lives at this marina. Guy is always here," Wayne says.

My phone vibrates, and Wayne stares at me in a way that compels me to explain, "It's my TA."

"Alex. Hey. You're not going to believe this," Timothy says.

"What?"

"Someone broke into the building again last night. Your office is trashed."

"Only mine?" I ask, leaning forward on the seat and holding a hand over my other ear to help with hearing him.

"No, no. Like the whole floor. It's like crazy kids went tearing through searching for copies of exams or grades. Police tape is back up."

"You're kidding. They think it was students? Did they take exams?" Honestly, it wouldn't matter to me if someone did steal my exams. I plan to make new ones each year. "Why would someone tear through multiple offices for copies of exams?"

"To sell them. Who knows? But I wanted to let you know. No reason to stop by the office today. They aren't letting us up. It's like *Groundhog Day*."

The engines on the boat churn a greater amount of water, and a plume of dark smoke shoots out the back of the boat.

"I've got to go," I tell Timothy. "Thanks for letting me know."

"You ready?" Wayne asks.

"Let me make a phone call real quick. My office was broken into."

"Well, that's a shame."

My gaze falls to my phone as I pull up my contact list. The sun glares down on the glass, and I tilt it away so I can better read the screen. A shadow falls over the phone.

The barrel of a handgun points at me. Time freezes. I blink. Process.

"Get any funny ideas, and this bullet rips through your spine. Hand me your phone."

Across the dock, tied into the slip on the opposing side, there's another yacht with a deep, wide deck. I hurl the phone. It clatters across the deck of the boat.

Wayne has a choice. He can leave a traceable phone to my last location, or he can leave me with a chance to run.

"Think you're smart," he growls.

The hair on my arms rises. Wayne's affable tone has transformed into deep and savage. It's a complete personality transformation.

Think. Survive.

"Security cameras are out here." I raise an arm, pointing to one of the light poles. "They're going to figure out it's you."

The gun remains trained on my chest.

Reason. Buy time.

"If you do this, you will go to jail. Think about it. A street camera had to have seen you approaching the marina." Talking this through, it's clear. He will get caught. This doesn't bode well for him. Unless he has someone who can hack into Santa Barbara's street cameras.

"There will be no charges. I'm not getting caught."

Keep him talking. My father's deep voice calms me enough to think.

"Why come after me? This doesn't make any sense."

"I didn't come after you. Cassie loved you. I would've never come after you. A dumbass came to your office." He sits beside me on the white sofa, placing one arm casually behind my back. The gun is low in his lap. To anyone glancing at us, it might look like he's my lover, sitting as close to me as possible. "See, that's the problem with hiring these days. Goddamn millennials. Think they know best. Always. But I will say, he was smart enough to snap a photo of your whiteboard for me. And I saw you figured it out."

What did I figure out?

"Jack never did. Cassie and I saw each other behind his back for years. You know, he wanted a second chance? And she left me. She was going to give him one."

Holy shit. Cassie had an affair with Wayne.

"Did you kill her?"

The butt of his gun presses into my ribs.

"Cassie's death devastated me. At her funeral, everyone cared about Jack. They'd been divorced for years, and he was still the center of everyone's attention. More so than her daughter. I loved her. Her death nearly killed me."

"And yet you stepped in and covered for Jack at the office." I scan the marina, searching. Someone else has to be out here.

"No choice. It's not like I could tell him I mourned his ex-wife more than he did. Couldn't tell him that she was mine. Not his. The board asked me to step in. I kept things going while he played house. Did a better job than he could."

"But they still let him return to CEO."

"Family company. Nepotism runs strong."

"And your wife? She never suspected?"

"My so-called wife never gave a damn. I invoked her name as cover within the company. How did you figure it out? That's why you're here, right? You figured it out, but you're snooping for evidence?" He's leaning so close into me that his hot breath moistens my earlobe. "What. Did. You. Find?"

"Old email files."

"Cassie's?" I'm not about to mention Sophia's Remarkable files. She can't become a target again if he gets away with this.

The marina gate clicks.

"We're not alone. I can scream."

"If I go down, so will you."

My spine curves sideways, away from the intense pressure on my rib.

Keep him talking.

"The problem with your threat is that if I scream, I die. If I don't scream, I die. There's not a winning scenario for me." He's in sales. He should understand negotiation. "What about Sophia? Are you planning on eliminating Sophia?"

"Sophia won't be hurt. If you're a good girl, you won't get hurt either."

The sliding door on the deck to *El Capitan* opens. A man in a red t-shirt stands in the doorway, assessing the situation. Water churns below the yacht's engines. Exhaust poisons the air.

"You injected Sophia with heroin. And you expect me to believe you won't hurt her?"

"I told you. It was a personnel problem. That's why I'm taking care of this personally."

"Personnel," I repeat.

The man in the red shirt steps forward. There's a holster on his waist.

"Are you selling guns to the cartels?"

"Move." He jabs the gun into my side. "Into the cabin."

"So, Larry worked for you? You killed him so he couldn't tell?"

"Get her up. Get her inside." He stands, his back to the dock, his gun pointed at me. "Juan, let's go." The boat rocks and lurches forward. The other man comes to stand directly behind me.

"I don't get it, Wayne. Why risk everything? You're successful. Rich. You have it all."

"Do I?" His latency and pitch suggest extreme anger. He's speaking through gritted teeth. "You got that wrong. I *do* it all. But I don't *have* it all. Not by a longshot. Now. Inside."

It's late afternoon. We're the only occupied boat in this section of the marina. The parking lot is behind me, far off in the distance. I could lunge into him, but there's a good chance he'd accidentally pull the trigger.

Keep the assailant talking.

"The security agent who dropped me off knows I'm meeting you. Did you see him? He was the one driving the sedan I got out of."

"You think I didn't know about him?" The man behind me grabs a fist full of my hair and pulls me up. "You think I don't know about the security cameras out here?" The hard press of the red shirt man's gun presses into my back. "You think any of the men out here right now don't work for me?"

The moorings, one by one, pass by as the boat chugs out of the slip.

They'll have to shoot me to keep me on this boat. They plan on shooting me anyway. I lunge forward, eyes on the dock and the murky water.

CHAPTER 29

Ryan

"How's Germany treating you?" My question to Trevor has him chuckling.

"Let's just say I'm ready to get the hell home."

"When's your flight?"

"Scheduled three days out. Flying back with Karsyn. We've got two employees Stella is working to reassign back in Syria."

"CIA finally pulled their officer?"

"Yep. Not sure what was dragging those wheels."

"And we'll never know." I've never understood the CIA. Never will. In my career as a SEAL, we didn't come into close contact with them, but at times we did rely on their intel. Shaky, unreliable intel at times.

My phone buzzes. It's Patel from the front desk.

"Glad you're coming home. I gotta run. Patel's calling." She's not one to call. She handles business matters with email.

I click over.

"We've got a problem. Shift change at Haley Street." She pauses. That's Alex's house. A chill crosses my skin. My vision sharpens.

"Say it."

"Lucca's dead." *Fuck.* "Someone shot him. Looks like a walk-by. Had to have used a silencer. He had the windows rolled—"

"Where's Alex?"

"I tracked her phone. She's at the Santa Barbara Marina."

I jump up and tuck the phone between my ear and shoulder as I strap on my holster.

"Get Erik. Code Red. Have him access marina security cams and put everyone we have on surveillance."

My feet clamber down the stairs. I push open the stairwell door, and it slams against the back wall. Patel startles. A phone is pressed to her ear.

"Tell Jordan to get to the marina," I yell as I run full throttle out the door. "Send as many guys as possible."

Our office is two blocks from the ocean and marina.

My phone vibrates. I hold it out in front as I weave through sidewalk pedestrians. I dig my EarPods out as I break into a full run, and answer as I round a corner.

"Patel."

"Checked the police scanner. All calm."

"Almost there."

"Erik says it'll take him a few to hack into the cameras. And he says to remind you he can only do so if they loop back to a server or are online."

"Where was the car?"

"What?"

"Lucca's car. On the street?"

"In her driveway."

Damnit. Why the fuck would he do that? Her neighbor's fence provided cover.

I round the corner, and the marina comes into view. Nothing is amiss. Tourists ramble along the boardwalk in front of the marina. The Santa Barbara Harbor holds over a thousand boats. A man in a police uniform strolls casually along on the far end.

My phone vibrates.

"Row twelve," Erik says into my ear.

A neatly painted six marks the piling I passed. I reverse course, running back down the boardwalk in the opposite direction, scanning for the white painted number twelve. If she's out in the ocean — *Don't go there.*

"She boarded a boat with a man who looks a lot like Wayne Killington. Couldn't see his face. Only his back."

I skid to a halt at the end of the row. There's an empty slip.

"Patel said her phone is here." I press her name on my phone and scan the boats. Nothing.

"Listen for a beep," Erik tells me.

"Why?"

"I have everyone's phone in our system so I can locate it. It's the find-my-phone beep. Just listen for it."

Beep.

I spin, searching for the sound.

Beep.

It's louder. And then I see it. A dark green rectangle on the deck of the adjacent boat.

"Fuck. She must've thrown her phone. How do we track her?" I shout into the air at Erik, knowing he'll find a way.

"There's a camera at the entrance to the marina. Let me see if I can get the name of the boat she's on."

"What did it look like?"

I scan the marina. I don't want a big boat. I want a fast boat.

"Large. White. Black glass windows. Two stories."

"Like how many feet?"

"How the hell would I know that? I'm not a boat guy. It was a giant boat. Had a small boat on the back."

"Okay. A yacht."

A red Siesta fishing boat rocks against the slip, tied too loose. If memory serves, the Siesta is fast. And she's here. One quick scan at the center console, and if my nerves weren't frayed, I'd laugh. Some dipshit left his keys, along with a floatable buoy, in the ignition. I don't even need to hotwire it.

"Radio the Coast Guard. What time did she board the boat?"

"Ahm... Hold on."

I crank the engine on the Siesta and rush to untie her.

"The boat's called *El Capitan.* Exited the harbor at two forty-six."

Shit. Ten minutes ago.

"Can you see which direction she turned?"

I gun the engine and catch irate glares in my direction. Fuck the no-wake zone.

"Looks like she headed straight out. Hey, I'm texting with Patel. She said Jordan entered the marina. He's going to follow you for backup."

Minutes later, I'm out in the ocean. The Siesta flies from crest to crest, sending gales of sea spray out to her sides. I scan the horizon. If she's as big of a boat as Erik says, she should be visible. I scan the horizon and see white.

"I think I see her."

"Wolf. I'm looking at this footage, and it looks like she went willingly. Maybe he's just taking her for a boat ride."

"And she threw her phone onto a neighboring boat? And Lucca is dead?"

"Good point."

Behind me, a small jet boat bounces over the waves. It's Jordan. I give him a thumbs-up.

This borrowed Siesta is one of the few boats that can outrun the Coast Guard. She's a fishing boat with speed. I'll overtake the *El Capitan*. It's only a matter of time.

"Any idea why Wayne would take her?"

The wind combines with the boat's engine. Fishing rods rock in holders. An unsecured cooler slides across the boat floor.

"Probably the same reason he'd kill Larry Reyes. Eliminating loose ends. Did he steal that boat he's on?"

"Doubt it. We knew he owned a boat. He's got a credit card solely for gas at marinas. Like ten-thousand-dollar purchases."

"You didn't think to mention that?"

"It's not a crime to own a boat. Shiloh said she mentioned it to someone within the FBI. They'd already looked into it, and Wayne and his wife like to vacation on their yacht. If he's on his boat, then it's owned by an LLC, but again, not a crime. Just smart tax strategy."

Boats are notorious vessels for gun and drug smuggling. Why the hell wasn't Ryland all over that?

As I gain on the yacht, details take shape. She's a beauty. I'd guess between one hundred eighty to two hundred feet. European build. American flag off the back.

Wayne Killington steps out on the back deck. Dark glass blocks all interior views.

Wayne raises an assault rifle.

The noise of the engine combined with the wind and slamming of the boat on waves mute any external sounds. As a precaution, I crouch.

Given the motion of the yacht, and the motion of my boat, the chances Killington's aim will hit are slim.

He lowers the barrel of the gun and goes inside the boat, behind darkened glass.

The bow of the Siesta careens closer to the yacht. I could launch myself onto the back of the boat. How many armed men are onboard? Where are they? What's their training? Too many unknowns.

Jordan's tiny boat falls farther behind with every second. If I can stop the yacht, Jordan will catch up quickly.

Off in the distance, orange and blue stripes on iron siding crash through the waves. *Hells yeah.* Coast Guard. Never has it been so good to see our fifth defense branch.

Lights flash on the bow of the Coast Guard ship. She must have been in the area. Few ships can outrun the Coast Guard. And the *El Capitan*, while a luxurious cruiser, is not one of those ships.

El Capitan slows. I pull up beside the boat. The dark glass blocks all view inside. I search the red Siesta for a buoy to tie up beside the streamlined white yacht, and the engines roar. The yacht takes off.

Fuck, no.

I get back to the wheel and gun the Siesta. Jumping on the boat isn't smart. But there's a Coast Guard ship headed our way. She's backup.

I position the boat along the port side and leap. My body sails onto the stern. The dark glass door slides, and I pull up onto my side, gun pointing, finger on the trigger.

A Hispanic man steps outside with a pistol aimed at me.

I rise to my feet, gun aimed and ready.

Classic standoff.

"Coast Guard is behind us. You'll never outrun them."

"You attacked us. Jumped our boat."

"You've got a woman on board. Where is she?"

He's wearing sunglasses. I zero in on his trigger finger. Flex my index finger. On the ready.

The tip of his gun lowers. He places it in his holster.

"You not holstering yours?" he asks.

"No." Too many unknowns. The sun's position on the horizon casts the glass to near black. I don't have handcuffs.

I flick the tip of my Glock at the corner of the back of the deck.

"Over there." Off in the distance, the borrowed red Siesta bounces off waves, unguided. The man's jaw clenches.

The dark glass slides. Another man pointing a handgun at me joins us.

"You're not going to get away," I repeat as the man glances slowly between me and the man with the holstered gun.

He gazes out over the ocean at the approaching Coast Guard ship. The man with the holstered gun steps forward.

"Give me your gun. We're making it to international waters."

"You think they won't follow you into international waters? You abducted an American citizen. The only way this ends remotely well for you is if you surrender."

The man pointing the gun at me tells his colleague, "Get his gun. Tie him up."

"Where is she?" I can't see his shaded eyes, but I'd bet they're drilling holes in me.

The other man approaches and foolishly reaches out, his gun still holstered. With one fluid movement, I lift his body and hurl him over the back of the boat. He screams.

Moments later, his head bobs up, arms flailing. The *El Capitan* continues forward, slicing the waves.

The sliding doors open. Wayne Killington holds a gun to Alex's temple. Every molecule in my body stills.

She's limp, her head slumped forward. Wayne is holding her up at her waist. Her legs are bent.

"What the—"

"Stay there," Wayne commands.

The end of a pistol meets my brow. I knock the gun skyward. Kick the man's legs. His head cracks against the boat.

I toss his pistol over the side.

"Freeze. One more move, and she's dead."

My attention falls on Wayne. I have a direct shot at his head. But the man's been around guns his whole life. I don't know how quick his trigger finger is.

"Wayne, there's no way this ends well. The best course of action is for you to put the gun down. Surrender."

His lips pucker. He shakes his head, denial strong. "You're going to radio the Coast Guard. Tell them there's a kidnapping situation. They either let us drive away, or she dies."

"You don't know much about how ransoms work, do you, Wayne?" His face is unreadable. "They might be willing to let you get away if they were guaranteed a desirable outcome. The desirable outcome being a live hostage. But without a guaranteed outcome, there is no ransom granted."

"You and Alex. Always gotta talk. I'll let you go. You have my word."

"Yeah, into the ocean two miles out without a life raft."

"You take the dinghy. Just call them off."

"Who's driving the boat?"

"Hand your gun to Juan. We'll go inside. You'll radio the Coast Guard."

Movement flickers from my side. I block a fist. Juan attempts to body punch me, but the boat hits a wave, throwing us all off balance. From the bent knees position, I loop one arm between Juan's legs and heave up. He pounds my back with his fists.

With one big inhale, I heave and throw him. Juan makes a bigger splash than his compadre.

Off in the distance, Jordan slows. He's picking up the first guy.

"Now it's just us, Wayne."

Wayne steps back. Alex's ankles follow.

"Is she alive Wayne?" If she's not, Wayne will eat every single one of my bullets.

"She's fine. Just napping."

"What'd you give her?"

"A sedative."

"Name?" I demand. When I get her to the hospital, it's best if I have a name.

Wayne's Adam's apple bobs. There's a sweaty sheen across his forehead. A sweat droplet running down the side of his face glistens in the sun.

"If you work with me, I'll pay you. More money than you could dream."

"Wrong incentive."

"I'm not going to prison." He's saying it as much to himself as to me. I inch toward him.

"Alex is not going to die." Since we're laying out ultimatums, I'll place mine down.

"No one was ever supposed to get hurt. It was a simple plan. But they fucked it up."

"Who?"

He lifts the gun away from Alex and points it below his chin. A much better place for him to aim.

He lets Alex go, and she slides down to the ground, unconscious. *Motherfucker*.

Glock still aimed at Wayne, I bend down and find Alex's wrist. There's a pulse. *Thank god.*

"Wayne. You don't want to do that, do you? You've got a wife at home who loves you."

His lips unfurl into a sick smile. "You ever met my wife?"

"Can't say I have." He's never even used her name.

We're headed out into the deep blue. The wrong direction to get Alex medical care. The sliding door remains open. I peer into the cabin. I don't see anyone else. It's a reasonable assumption we're the last folks on the boat. The boat's on autopilot.

"Everything went to hell." Wayne slouches, legs splayed out, gun still planted under his chin.

"What'd you give Alex?" I'm pretty positive he's not looking at me. "Wayne. What did you give Alex?"

His lower lip protrudes. He lost.

I won't waste more time on this guy. Alex needs medical treatment.

I step forward with caution, my Glock trained on Wayne.

With one fluid movement, I snatch his gun. Send it over the side of the boat. The whites of his eyes seemingly expand. He holds a palm up.

A thick winding pile of white rope hangs off a hook on the side.

In under a minute, his arms are strapped to his sides. Thirty seconds later, and his feet are tied. Gotta love boats.

Chances are good more weapons are stored somewhere. To the right, I see a bathroom. It's small. It'll work.

I push him in and shut the door. The chairs are bolted down. There's nothing to barricade him in. But he's restrained. That'll do.

I kneel to Alex and lift her gently off the deck. I lower her onto a sofa inside the cabin. A thin line of blood trickles along her hairline. There's swelling on her right temple. She's cold to the touch. Her heartrate is too slow.

I move to the CB and radio in. "Medical assistance needed. Repeat. Emergency medical assistance needed. *El Capitan* returning to Santa Barbara Harbor. Ambulance needed. Emergency assistance needed."

CHAPTER 30

ALEX

"Heartrate stable. Blood pressure ninety over sixty."

"Is she going to be okay?" It's Ryan. He's here.

My eyelids are thick and heavy. Cotton fills my mouth. It's hard to breathe. I gasp for air.

"Alex? Are you waking up? You're okay. You're going to be okay."

I manage to get one eyelid cracked. The light is bright, but the light calms.

"I'm not going anywhere."

Warmth covers my hands. He's here.

Bright light forces me to squint. There's an IV taped to the back of my hand. Ryan's arm lies heavily over my thighs, and his head rests beside my hip. He's asleep. I'm in a hospital bed.

Tenderly, I tousle Ryan's hair. His eyelids flicker open, and he lurches upward.

"You're up."

"Water," I croak.

He shakily pours water into a small plastic cup and holds it up to my lips. "How do you feel?"

"Groggy," I manage to say. My throat is scratchy, but other than that, I don't feel pain anywhere.

"Wayne drugged you with something. Do you know what?"

I remember running. Trying to jump off the boat. Being dragged back. My head slammed against the boat. A fist. The sting. Throbbing pain. A needle in my arm. Struggling. Crying. But then it gets fuzzy.

"No." I remembered to ask. But if Wayne ever told me, I don't remember the answer.

"We don't have bloodwork back yet, but our best guess is Telazol. It's a tranquilizer used in veterinary medicine. But he could have used something else. You're lucky. He could have easily injected enough to kill you." Ryan's light blue eyes are watery. His thumb strokes my cheek. "The doctor didn't give you anything. She thought the best course of action was to hydrate and monitor. Since we don't know. You also suffered a concussion."

"I hit my head on the boat. And he punched me."

Ryan's jaw muscles clench, and he grits his teeth. He closes his eyes, and when he opens them, concern overrides any other emotion.

"You're bruising along here." His finger lightly touches my cheekbone, and I flinch. "Sore?"

I nod. That side of my face throbs.

"Your dad and I have been in touch. He knows you're here. I promised I'd call and give him an update." My thumb combs over his unruly eyebrow. He places his lips in the center of my palm. "I could have lost you."

"But you didn't."

He rests his head on my belly. The gesture is so unlike the force of a soldier that emotion chokes in my throat.

"Timothy. Sabrina. They've been in touch too. They're all waiting to hear from you. But I told them the doctors said you should be fine."

My fingers drag through his dark hair.

"When I found you on that boat..." His voice cracks. "Unconscious. I've never..."

I don't remember him on the boat.

"Wayne?"

"Police have him." He presses his lips to my knuckles. "I wanted to kill him."

"But you didn't," I whisper. Ryan is a good man. A truly good man. "And the others?"

"Ricky Morales and Juan Garcia. Both in custody."

"Wayne had an affair with Cassandra." Surprise flickers, but he keeps my palm pressed to his cheek.

"Did you know that?" he asks.

"No. But he thought I did because I wrote the word 'affair' beneath his photo on my whiteboard. It was all chance. If he hadn't assumed I knew, he would've gotten away with it. Honestly, even if I'd known, I don't know that would have made me think he'd..." If he truly loved Cassie, he would have never done that to her daughter.

Ryan's fingers tangle with my hair. "We assumed he did it to reclaim the position of CEO."

"He was angry. Angry that Cassandra chose Jack over him. Angry he didn't get to keep the CEO position after Jack stepped down." Anger fell short as a descriptor. He'd become irrational.

"And here I thought it was all about greed."

Greed is a likely motivator. Often, when one performs evil, the mind weaves multiple motives into justification.

I think about Cassandra. What on Earth was she thinking, having an affair with Wayne? When she and Jack drifted apart, was Wayne the one she turned to? Unless we uncover something she wrote about it, we'll never know her reasons.

"How's Sophia?"

"Jack says she's doing better. He has her home."

"Poor Sophia." I want to see her. "How long do I have to stay here?"

"As long as they say you need to."

"How long have I been here?"

His gaze drifts to the clock on the wall.

"Fifteen hours. You've drifted in and out. This is the longest you've stayed up. What do you remember?"

"Voices. Your voice."

"Do you remember me telling you that I love you?"

I shake my head slowly.

"You might not remember this time either. That's okay. I'll keep telling you." He lifts his head, and I'm completely taken in by his watery eyes. I cup his jaw. His bristly facial growth has softened with length. His hand covers mine.

"I love you, too, you know." A soft smile spreads. "Have I been telling you that?"

"First time." His lips press into my palm. "God, do you realize—"

"Hey. I'm okay."

He blinks, and his lips contort. He breathes in heavily, and some of that big, strong man surfaces.

"And Trace?" I ask, understanding that he needs to lighten the moment. A small smile returns.

"Stella has him. They surprised Trevor with a new puppy, so Trace has been keeping Astra, the older dog, company. Astra's apparently bent out of shape over the puppy."

"Oh, I love puppies. What kind?"

He pulls out his phone and shows me a photo of an adorable husky puppy with blue eyes similar to Ryan's.

"He has your Wolf eyes," I say, smiling at the adorable puppy photo, because that's what one does with adorable puppy photos, no matter how much one's face might throb.

"Actually, that's a common misbelief."

"Really?"

"In the wild, wolves eyes are gray or brown or even yellow. The light blue eyes are bred, something you only see in domesticated wolves."

"I didn't know there was such a thing. I guess people prefer blue over the other colors?" I certainly have developed a love for light blue.

"Friendlier, I suppose." He scrunches his nose, and his lips contort into a comical grin.

I laugh. But as I gaze up into those light blue eyes, I no longer see ice. Only adoration. And love.

"True story." He presses his lips against my forehead and squeezes my fingers. "Let me go find the doctor. Let's see when we can get you home."

EPILOGUE

Ryan

One month later

Island tunes waft through the salt-tinged breeze. The sun glitters across the ocean surface hours before sunset. Alex and Sophia returned from a long walk on the beach and are now sitting in the sand near the water's edge.

Alex and I arrived in San Diego this morning and plan to stay through the weekend so Alex can spend time with Sophia. It's our second weekend visiting since Sophia returned home. Alex's little dog Trace is somewhere in the house, probably napping with Sasha. The two dogs are now the best of buds.

Jack and I are camped out on the deck with a bird's-eye view of Jack's back yard, the beach, and the ocean. One Arrow security officer sits in a beach chair, beneath an umbrella. He's wearing shorts, an SPF shirt, and running shoes. There's an earpiece in his ear that would easily be mistaken for an EarPod. A second officer roams the grounds and oversees camera surveillance.

Earlier in the month, Jack converted a downstairs room in the basement into a control room for the security team. Arrow manages round-the-clock security for all of Jack's properties. He's also become a silent partner in Arrow.

At the moment, his priorities are Sophia and rooting out all those involved in Sophia's abduction and illegal gun sales, but he's made it clear at a future date he'd like to step away from Sullivan Arms and take a more active role in Arrow. Given his expertise in weapons, there are many ways he could contribute. He's a solid partner. And we'll never have to worry about finances.

"It's good to see Sophia talking to Alex." Jack's talking to me, but his focus hasn't strayed from his daughter since we claimed the shaded deck chairs.

"Is she still not talking to her friends?"

"They've been calling. Texting. But she gave her phone to me. Asked that I let them all know she's okay, but she needs time. I set her phone in my office, charging. She hasn't touched it." Plenty of men coming back from tours of duty desire solitude. One could argue the trauma level that Sophia endured matches battle.

"What's the therapist say?"

"We've gone through five therapists. She doesn't like anyone." He glances at his wrist. "I've got another one coming by shortly."

"To your home?"

"Don't worry." He side-eyes me. "Your security team knows she's coming." The thought didn't cross my mind, but I choose to remain silent and wait. I'm learning with Jack that if you wait it out, he'll keep talking. "My uncle is sending someone. A supposed expert in both addiction and trauma."

"You close to him?"

"Uncle Mark?" I give a quick confirming nod. "He and my dad

were super close. When Dad died, he told me he promised my dad he'd look out for us." He juts his lower lip out contemplatively. "He's held his end of the bargain. He's not around a lot, but believe me, he's present."

Jack and I knock back the rest of our beers while taking in the stellar view. Jack returned to work after everything went down with Wayne Killington and Larry Reyes. Prosecutors are still building the case against Wayne. He's being held without bond under tight security until his hearing. We don't believe Wayne was working for anyone, but in case he does have information that a powerful someone wants to remain hidden, he's in protective custody.

The case they are building against him includes kidnapping and abduction, as well as illegally trafficking guns. He blames the people he hired for Sophia's treatment, but I blame him for trusting her welfare to criminals in the first place. He may have thought he had the perfect resource in his gun trafficking buddies, but they work with a moral code the Texan just didn't grasp. Or maybe he did. The man killed to prevent getting caught. The FBI is still working on tracking down his hired guns.

In a lot of ways, the worst is over. Jack has his daughter back. But looking at the sour expression on Jack's face, you wouldn't think that. Other than he's getting sleep now, there's not much difference in the Jack sitting with me now and the Jack from a month earlier.

"What's wrong? You look pissed." Maybe there's something going on with him and his Uncle Mark. I've overheard him argue with him more than once, always about work related matters. Or maybe Alex has changed me into someone way too in touch with emotions. Before I met her, I'd never ask a guy what's wrong.

"It's...this." Jack gestures to the beach. "I hate this. I hate Sophia is still going through this. I hate she can't be comfortable with her friends. I hate it's not over." Alex and Sophia wade knee-deep into the ocean. "I can't get over Sophia knew Cassandra cheated. She was too young to have to deal with that. And now..."

"Did she know it was Wayne?" I haven't pushed Jack for information. I'm not working the case, and I'm pretty certain the FBI asks all the questions.

"She did. I always thought it was odd that Sophia refused to remain in the room when Wayne came over. She'd slip away the moment he walked through the door. But she says she found out long after it was over. Wayne wanted Cassie back, and she overheard them. When she approached Cassie about it, she says her mom swore it was over. And she died a few days after that. She said she never said anything to me because after Cassandra died, she didn't think it was worth mentioning."

"Do you think Wayne had anything to do with Cassandra's death?"

"Police investigated that wreck. Didn't find anything. But, given what he did do, I'll go to my grave wondering." He swallows his beer again. Like me, his focus is on the water's edge. "I'll go to my grave wondering how the hell I fucked it up so badly."

"What do you mean?"

"When you marry, you think, you believe, it's going to last. And...yet—"

"Hey, you're not the one who cheated."

"That's a copout. It's my fault. I dove into work. Left her alone. When things got tough, I walled off. I've always been like that. It's on me."

"Have you tried talking to a therapist?"

Jack looks at me like I've lost my mind. "I don't need a therapist."

"It might not hurt to talk to someone."

"When are you going to ask Alex to marry you?" His abrupt

change in conversation has me lowering my beer. He stares straight ahead, and I take a long, contemplative swallow. As the cold liquid glides down my throat, it hits me his question isn't a bad one. Deflective move on his part, but the question doesn't bother me.

"I've been doing my best to get her to officially move in with me. For all practical purposes, she already has. But it's not official."

"Why not pop the question?" The man is not laying off his target.

"Timing. We've been together all of two months."

"I knew Cassandra was it for me after one weekend."

"Yeah?" He nods. "But when did you ask her?"

"I waited a little too late on that one. Not until she was pregnant. I don't recommend that course of action. I had a hard time convincing her that I'd marry her anyway. My family didn't exactly help with that."

"That's right. You told me your dad was livid. No pre-nup. Have to agree with your dad. That wasn't the smartest move."

"Maybe." His gaze remains on the beach. An errant wave rises out of nowhere and nearly drags Sophia down. She tumbles backward, soaked and laughing.

"The two of you remind me of how Cassie and I used to be." His thumb circles the glass rim of his beer bottle as he stares out over the shore. "Word of advice. Hold on to her. When it gets hard, and it will, keep your priorities straight."

The doorbell rings. The chime is some classical music melody. I'd bet money he hasn't bothered to change the doorbell chime from the prior owner. He glances at his wrist.

"That your therapist?"

"If it is, she's forty-five minutes early."

"Better than forty-five minutes late."

He grunts as he pushes up off his lounge chair. Fisher, the

Arrow employee on rounds, ushers a woman through the front door.

"You want me to bring her out here?" I offer.

"Nah. Let's go greet her at the front door. If I don't like her, I won't bother introducing her to Sophia. If she seems okay, I'll have you send Sophia up from the beach."

I follow Jack through the house. We're both wearing board shorts and flip-flops. Fisher lurks over an attractive woman in the foyer. I'd estimate she's average height and in her thirties. A thick mass of dark bangs falls down to her eyebrows and almost overpowers her pale, angular face. She's wearing a black long-sleeve turtleneck and a straight black skirt with black military boots. One hand spins the stacked silver rings on her other hand, and her eyes dart about, no doubt taking in the grandeur of Jack's home. Can't say I blame her. The guy's got a glass elevator shaft with a view to the Pacific.

"This is Ava Amara. She has an appointment," Fisher announces to both of us. He's not a butler, and he shuffles on his feet, clearly uncertain what else he's supposed to do.

"Thanks, Fisher." He heads back outside, resuming his review of the property. Through the glass front door, I watch as he circles the ancient Subaru parked near the fountain.

"Hi." The softspoken greeting brings my focus back into the room. Black eyeliner and thick eyelashes augment unusually large eyes.

She glances nervously between me and Jack. Jack appears frozen. My guess is he's seriously questioning his uncle's recommendation. She's got a Goth vibe, and I can see how my conservative friend might be disconcerted.

"Hi," I say, because Jack's silence is awkward. "I'm Ryan Wolfgang. A friend in town for the weekend."

"Wolfgang." She pushes some hair behind one ear, revealing a shit ton of earrings. "Do you have a sister, by chance?"

"I do." I glance to Jack. I haven't mentioned my sister to Jack. If this therapist specializes in addiction, I have an idea how she knows Indigo.

"Indie?" she asks.

"Yeah. That's her."

"She may be coming to stay with us."

"Us?" My sister is doing better, but to my knowledge she's not ready to transition. I haven't authorized any other treatment facility.

"Well, I met with her yesterday," she says with a soft smile. "She mentioned she needed to talk to her family." She tilts her head up to look me in the eye. "You. Her brother."

Right. Because there's no one else.

"Do you have apartments?" Jack remains frozen, so I might as well learn what I can.

"We have a small community of apartments and townhomes. Mark Sullivan," she looks to Jack, "your uncle has been incredible. We wouldn't have been able to build our center without his help."

"Nueva Vida," Jack says. I give him a once-over, looking for signs he's had too much to drink. His pupils are abnormally large, but I suppose we did just come inside after staring at the sun.

"Right. He's our number one donor."

"What's Nueva Vida?" I ask.

"Well, it's designed to be a secure and safe place for recovering addicts to adjust to real life. We help with job-training skills and placement. We strive to provide a clean, safe environment because transitioning back to life is hard enough without worrying about your next meal or living in a dangerous place." Alex and I planned to visit Indie tomorrow. I wonder if she plans to tell us then. "We subsidize rent payments until each person can afford the full rent.

We let them live with us until they're ready, financially and emotionally, to fully re-enter the world. Rushing to return to normal can be a trigger for relapse."

"How do you know my uncle?" Jack's squinted eyes lend him a vicious expression that has me doing another double take.

"He's...Patrick," she begins. Jack's eyebrows practically join in the middle, and he crosses his arms in a bouncer pose. "Patrick is an incredibly close friend. He's like family to me."

"And Patrick is...?" Jacks asks her.

Her eyelashes flutter and surprise registers, but she pulls it together. She mirrors Jack by crossing her arms over her stomach. "He's a close friend of Mark's...your uncle. I've known your uncle for a long time."

Jack's head tilts, and he studies her for what feels like far too long. "My uncle said you're the best."

"I don't know about that." A light color seeps through her pale skin. "I don't force any one methodology. I support as much as I can. Ultimately, it's the individual who has to choose recovery." She tilts her head, once again mirroring Jack. "If you don't want me here..."

"I'll go check on Alex," I say, stepping back. I'd rather not witness Jack kick this woman to the curb.

Jack exhales. "Ask Sophia to come up."

"Nice to meet you, Ava." The center she described sounds perfect for Indigo, so I hope Jack doesn't screw anything up for my sister by being a complete jerk. I'm not sure what's up with him. Maybe he treats anyone who might come into contact with Sophia aggressively. If so, it might be a good thing her friends haven't been coming around.

I can't blame Jack for being suspicious. His right-hand man backstabbed him. For that matter, so did his wife.

So far, no other employees from Sullivan Arms have been

exposed for involvement with the scam. According to Ricky, he began working with Killington and Reyes on a plan using high-end yachts to smuggle guns into Mexico. They'd been working together for years when Wayne approached him about assisting with Sophia's abduction. Ricky claims Wayne instructed them to both drug and rape her, but not kill her. He wanted to ensure she would need her father to take a leave of absence. Of course, there is no documentation of Wayne's instructions or the agreement between the men.

Wayne's lawyer has indicated he'll strive to prove innocence, so I assume his story will differ greatly from Ricky's.

Alex has her back to me as I approach her on the beach. Sophia kicks her feet through the water, sending salt spray splattering. Alex glances over her shoulder at me and smiles. When I reach her, I loop an arm around her waist.

"Here's my woman." Sophia smiles over at us. She's standing about ten feet away with the water lapping her ankles.

Alex loops an arm around my waist and grins. "My woman? Are you for real?"

I shrug. "Want a different title?"

I smack a kiss on her temple. She lifts her chin, and I place another on her lips for good measure.

"I can't believe you." She shakes her head, pretending to be offended. She plants a palm against my chest and gives a soft push, but I place my hand over hers, trapping it against me.

Sophia steps closer. She's smiling, and if I saw her on the beach, I'd categorize her as a happy teenage girl. But her smile doesn't reach her eyes.

"Sophia, your dad has someone he wants you to meet."

Her gaze floats down her swim cover-up, soaked from about waist down.

"I'm wet." She states the obvious.

"Won't matter."

"Oh, god," she groans. "It's another shrink. Right?"

She stomps off before I can answer. The Arrow agent sitting against the back wall of the Sullivan property gets up to follow her.

"How's she doing?" It's a question I ask Alex too often. But my vocabulary for these situations is limited.

"Other than being sunburnt?" I did notice the skin below her eyes was a smidge red. "She refused sunblock, and with her blonde hair and pale skin, she should wear it, but...I think she's tired of being coddled. I think she's progressing from profound sadness into anger."

"Stages of grief. At least she's progressing."

"I wish I could undo it for her. Just make it all go away."

"We all do." I remember what the therapist back at the house said. "But Sophia ultimately has to navigate her recovery. You can't do it for her."

"I know."

The gate clicks, and Sophia's blonde hair disappears down the side path.

"Want to go for a walk? We can give them some privacy."

"Sure. Probably best Sophia doesn't feel like I'm trying to wiggle my way into meeting her new therapist."

"Judging by Jack's reception of the woman, I don't think she's going to be her new therapist."

"Bad?"

"You could say that. He was kind of an ass." I've never seen Jack act so cold. I kick off my flip-flops and toss them near the chair at the back wall.

"That's unfortunate," Alex comments. I agree but don't want to talk about it. I want to get back to enjoying a lazy afternoon at the beach.

Hand in hand, Alex and I stroll along the water's edge, barefoot. The summer sun warms our backs.

"What were the two of you talking about?" Alex asks.

"Marriage." I'm getting better about being upfront with Alex.

"Really?" I'm well aware she's checking me out. Searching to see if my hand is touching my mouth or my ears. She's probably annoyed she can't examine my pupils since I'm wearing sunglasses. I'm learning all the tricks of her trade. They actually aren't too different from some of the things the military teaches. Interpreting body language is an important skill.

"Yeah," I answer, stoic. I place effort in looking straight ahead and keeping my jaw muscles relaxed. She tries to pull her hand away from mine, but I don't let that happen.

"Jack was saying he knew Cassie was the one after his first weekend with her."

"Yeah?" She grins widely. Our arms swing in pace with our stride. "I call bullshit on that. They had ups and downs. I was there during their whirlwind courtship."

"Interesting. Maybe you'll have to call him out."

"Maybe I will. I'm good at reading people, you know." She's teasing me.

"Are you?"

"I am." She thrusts her chin out, but she's still smiling.

"Let me quiz you, then. At what point did I know you were the one?"

"I'm..." She stops walking, and since I'm not letting her hand go, I also stop. "The one?"

"Yeah, you." Wisps of her hair blow past her cheeks. I've surprised her. I can tell the way her lips open ever so slightly and how she's mindlessly using one hand to wrangle those fly-aways.

"Well, I mean, I know you want me to live with you."

"Forever." My heart pounds in my chest. It's early on. But I know I want to spend the rest of my life with her, so I charge ahead. "Alexandria, I don't want to ever wake up without you. I never thought I'd feel like this. But I do. And every day, that feeling grows stronger."

"Likewise." It's when her posh accent comes out that I know I have most definitely thrown her for a loop.

I chuckle. It's more of a full-on laugh.

"What?"

"You know, here in the States, we usually say 'ditto.'"

"I'll try to remember that."

"You do that." We resume our stroll, carefully stepping over broken shell fragments. "Alex?"

"Hmmm?"

"You said you can read people. Tell me when I realized I wanted to spend the rest of my life with you."

"Oh, well, I don't know if—"

"Take your best guess."

"I didn't know it until just now."

"Fair enough. But now you know it. Looking back, take your best guess."

"Maybe when you thought I'd died?"

"No. That's not it." A paddleboarder paddles by. Alex waves at the person. She's beginning to recognize some of the regular beachgoers. "Let's see. My first thought when I saw you was that Jack was a lucky SOB, because I thought you were his. And then when I realized he wasn't yours, you got under my skin. But I didn't do relationships, and you looked like a relationship kind of woman. Obviously, I broke my relationship rule for you. I mean, after our first time, I knew it wouldn't be a one-time thing. But I think I fell for you the moment you visited my sister and you showed me your compassion. And I think when I knew I wanted you in my life forever—"

"When I wanted to turn the tables on the kidnappers?" She loves figuring things out, but she's wrong on this point.

"When you turned the tables on me. You turned my world upside down."

"When?"

"When we found Sophia, and I couldn't stay away."

We slow to a stop, and she loops her arms around my neck. This time my back is to the sun, and the wind blows her hair behind her. She smiles the most beautiful smile.

"I remember. I remember how surprised I was that you kept coming around. I'd thought for sure I'd hear from you, but not for a couple of days."

I drop to one knee, and her hands fly to her mouth.

"Alex, I don't have a ring—yet. If I were a romantic man, I would have planned this out. Something spectacular. But I'm not a particularly romantic man. That's not my strength. But I'll love, honor, and protect you until the end of time. Will you marry me? If you say yes, we'll go ring shopping first thing in the morning."

"I don't need a ring." She drops down to the sand, on her knees, so she's once again close to my height, and lifts my sunglasses off my face. "I don't need a wedding." I lift her sunglasses, uncertain where she's going with this. "But I'll take one of those. One day." My chest eases. "For now, I'll take you... always. This heart," her palm flattens over my sternum, "is my heart. My Wolf."

FROM THE AUTHOR... AKA IZZY

Thank you so much for reading *Better to See You*!

If you enjoyed the story, I hope you'll take a moment to leave a review. Five-star reviews truly do sell books, bringing me closer to the day when I might be able to do this full time. So I'm deeply grateful for them.

Better to See You is technically the first in the Arrow Series, but it's a spin-off from the Twisted Vines series.

Erik's story kicks off the Twisted Vines series, and it's available here: Crushed.

Jack's story is up next in *Better to Hear You*. It should, if everything goes according to plan, release in 1Q, 2023.

ALSO BY ISABEL JOLIE

The Twisted Vines Series

Crushed (Erik and Vivi)

Breathe (Kairi and David)

Savor (Trevor and Stella)

Haven Island Series

Rogue Wave (Tate and Luna)

Adrift (Gabe and Poppy)

First Light (Logan and Cali)

The West Side Series

When the Stars Align (Jackson and Anna)

Trust Me (Sam and Olivia)

Walk the Dog (Delilah and Mason)

Lost on the Way (Jason and Maggie)

Chasing Frost (Chase and Sadie)

Misplaced Mistletoe (Ashton aka Dr. Bobby and Nora)

Coming this Holiday Season 2022...

How to Survive a Holiday Fling (Oliver and Kate)

ABOUT THE AUTHOR

Isabel Jolie, aka Izzy, lives on a lake, loves dogs of all stripes, and if she's not working, she can be found reading, often with a glass of wine. In prior lives, Izzy worked in marketing and advertising, in a variety of industries, such as financial services, entertainment, and technology. In this life, she loves daydreaming and writing contemporary romances with real, flawed characters and inner strength.

Sign-up for Izzy's newsletter to keep up-to-date on new releases, promotions and giveaways. Or stalk her on your favorite platform. And no, she's not on TikTok. Her teen daughters tell her to *Stay Away...*

CPSIA information can be obtained
at www.ICGtesting.com
Printed in the USA
LVHW041521150723
752290LV00004B/745